James Patterson is one of the best-known and biggest-selling writers of all time. He is the author of some of the most popular series of the past decade: the Women's Murder Club, the Alex Cross novels and Maximum Ride, and he has written many other number one bestsellers including romance novels and stand-alone thrillers. He has won an Edgar Award, the mystery world's highest honour. He lives in Florida with his wife and son.

Praise for James Patterson's novels:

'I can't believe how good Patterson is – he's always on the mark. I have never begun a Patterson book and been able to put it down' Larry King, *USA Today*

'Patterson knows where our deepest fears are buried . . . there's no stopping his imagination' *New York Times*

'Makes Kay Scarpetta's lot look positively fairytale' *Mirror*

'Patterson boils a scene down to the single, telling element that defines a character or moves the plot along. It's what fires off the movie projector in the reader's mind' Michael Connelly

'Brilliantly terrifying . . . so exciting I had to stay up all night to finish it' *Daily Mail*

'Skilfully put together' *Cosmopolitan*

'Patterson's action-packed story keeps the pages flicking by' *The Sunday Times*

'A fast-moving thriller . . . a good time is had by all' *Telegraph*

'Keeps the pedal down on the action and suspense' *Washington Times*

'This author knows precisely how to manipulate his readers' *Independent*

'Patterson is a phenomenon' *Observer*

'Another brilliant tour de force' *Books Magazine*

By James Patterson and available from Headline

When the Wind Blows
Cradle and All
Miracle on the 17th Green (*and Peter de Jonge*)
Suzanne's Diary for Nicholas
The Beach House (*and Peter de Jonge*)
The Jester (*and Andrew Gross*)
The Lake House
Sam's Letters to Jennifer
SantaKid
Honeymoon (*and Howard Roughan*)
Lifeguard (*and Andrew Gross*)
Beach Road (*and Peter de Jonge*)
Judge and Jury (*and Andrew Gross*)
Step on a Crack (*and Michael Ledwidge*)
The Quickie (*and Michael Ledwidge*)
You've Been Warned (*and Howard Roughan*)

Alex Cross novels
Cat and Mouse
Pop Goes the Weasel
Roses are Red
Violets are Blue
Four Blind Mice
The Big Bad Wolf
London Bridges
Mary, Mary
Cross
Double Cross

The Women's Murder Club series
1st to Die
2nd Chance (*and Andrew Gross*)
3rd Degree (*and Andrew Gross*)
4th of July (*and Maxine Paetro*)
The 5th Horseman (*and Maxine Paetro*)
The 6th Target (*and Maxine Paetro*)

Maximum Ride series
Maximum Ride: The Angel Experiment
Maximum Ride: School's Out Forever
Maximum Ride: Saving the World and Other Extreme Sports

THE 5TH HORSEMAN

JAMES PATTERSON

AND MAXINE PAETRO

headline

First published in Great Britain in 2006
by HEADLINE PUBLISHING GROUP

This edition published in 2009
by HEADLINE PUBLISHING GROUP

10

Cataloguing in Publication Data is available from the British Library

ISBN 978 0 7553 4930 2

Typeset in Palatino Light by Palimpsest Book Production Limited,
Grangemouth, Stirlingshire

Printed and bound in Great Britain by
Clays Ltd, Elcograf S.p.A.

Headline's policy is to use papers that are natural, renewable and recyclable products
and made from wood grown in sustainable forests. The logging and manufacturing
processes are expected to conform to the environmental regulations of the country of
origin.

HEADLINE PUBLISHING GROUP
An Hachette UK Company
338 Euston Road
London NW1 3BH

www.headline.co.uk
www.hachette.co.uk

Our gratitude and thanks to Dr Humphrey Germaniuk, ME, Trumbell County, Ohio, for bringing the art and science of forensic pathology to life; to top cop, Captain Richard Conklin, Bureau of Investigations, Stamford, Connecticut PD; and to our medical expert, Allen Ross, MD of Montague, Massachusetts.

We also wish to thank attorneys Philip R. Hoffman, Kathy Emmett and Marty White for sharing with us their legal expertise.

And special thanks to our excellent researchers, Lynn Colomello, Ellie Shurtleff, Yukie Kito and the irreplaceable Mary Jordan.

PROLOGUE

The Midnight Hour

Chapter One

R ain was drumming hard against the windows when the midnight-to-8:00 a.m. rounds began at San Francisco Municipal Hospital. Inside the ICU, thirty-year-old Jessie Falk was asleep in her hospital bed, floating on a Percocet lake of cool light.

Jessie was having the most beautiful dream she'd had in years.

She and the light of her life, three-year-old Claudia, were in Grandma's backyard swimming pool. Claudie was in her birthday suit and bright-pink water wings, slapping the water, sunlight glinting off her blond curls.

'Simon says, kiss like a butterfly, Claudie.'

'Like this, Mommy?'

Then the mother and daughter were shouting and laughing, twirling and falling down, singing out, 'Wheeeeeee,' when without warning a sharp pain pierced Jessie's chest.

She awoke with a scream – bolted upright – and clapped both of her hands to her breast.

What was happening? What was that pain?

Then Jessie realized that she was in a hospital – and that she was feeling sick again. She remembered coming here, the ambulance ride, a doctor telling her that she was going to be fine, not to worry.

Falling, nearly fainting back to the mattress, Jessie fumbled for the call button at her side. Then the device slipped from her grasp and fell. It banged against the side of the bed with a muted clang.

Oh, God, I can't breathe. What's happening? I can't get my breath. It's horrible. I'm not fine.

Tossing her head from side to side, Jessie swept the darkened hospital room with her eyes. Then she seized on a figure at the far edge of her vision.

She knew the face.

'Oh, th-thank God,' she gasped. 'Help me, please. It's my heart.'

She stretched out her hands, clutched feebly at the air, but the figure stayed in the shadows.

'Please,' Jessie pleaded.

The figure wouldn't come forward, wouldn't help. What was going on? This was a hospital. The person in the shadows worked here.

Tiny black specks gathered in front of Jessie's eyes as a crushing pain squeezed the air from her chest. Suddenly her vision tunneled to a pinprick of white light.

'Please help me. I think I'm—'

'Yes,' said the figure in the shadows, 'you are dying, Jessie. It's beautiful to watch you cross over.'

Chapter Two

J essie's hands fluttered like a tiny bird's wings beating against the sheets. Then they were very still. Jessie was gone.

The Night Walker came forward and bent low over the hospital bed. The young woman's skin was mottled and bluish, clammy to the touch, her pupils fixed. She had no pulse. No vital signs. Where was she now? Heaven, hell, nowhere at all?

The silhouetted figure retrieved the fallen call device, then tugged the blankets into place, straightened the young woman's blond hair and the collar of her gown, and blotted the spittle from her lips with a tissue.

Nimble fingers lifted the framed photo beside the phone on the bedside table. She'd been so pretty, this young mother holding her baby. Claudia. That was the daughter's name, wasn't it?

The Night Walker put the picture down, closed the patient's

eyes, and placed what looked to be small brass coins, smaller than dimes, on each of Jessie Falk's eyelids.

The small disks were embossed with a caduceus – two serpents entwined around a winged staff, the symbol of the medical profession.

A whispered good-bye blended with the sibilance of tires speeding over the wet pavement five stories below on Pine Street.

'Good night, princess.'

PART ONE

Malice Aforethought

Chapter Three

I was at my desk sifting through a mound of case files –
eighteen open homicides, to be exact – when Yuki Castellano,
attorney-at-law, called on my private line.

'My mom wants to take us to lunch at the Armani Café,'
said the newest member of the Women's Murder Club. 'You've
gotta meet her, Lindsay. She can charm the skin off a snake,
and I mean that in the nicest possible way.'

Let me see; what should I choose? Cold coffee and tuna
salad in my office? Or a tasty Mediterranean luncheon, say,
carpaccio over arugula with thin shavings of Parmesan and a
glass of Merlot, with Yuki and her snake-charming mom?

I neatened the stack of folders, told our squad assistant, Brenda,
that I'd be back in a couple of hours, and left the Hall of Justice
with no need to be back until the staff meeting at 3:00.

The bright September day had broken a rainy streak in the

weather and was one of the last glory days before the dank autumn chill would close in on San Francisco.

It was a joy to be outside.

I met Yuki and her mother, Keiko, in front of Saks in the upscale Union Square shopping district out by the Golden Gate Panhandle. Soon we were chattering away as the three of us headed up Maiden Lane toward Grant Avenue.

'You girls, too modern,' Keiko said. She was as cute as a bird, tiny, perfectly dressed and coiffed, shopping bags dangling from the crooks of her arms. 'No man want woman who too independent,' she told us.

'Mommm,' Yuki wailed. 'Give it a rest, willya? This is the twenty-first century. This is America.'

'Look at you, Lindsay,' Keiko said, ignoring Yuki, poking me under the arm. 'You're packing!'

Yuki and I both whooped, our shouts of laughter nearly drowning out Keiko's protestation that, 'No man want a woman with a gun.'

I wiped my eyes with the back of my hand as we stopped and waited for the light to change.

'I *do* have a boyfriend,' I said.

'Doesn't she though,' Yuki said, nearly bursting into a song about my beau. 'Joe is a very handsome Italian guy. Like Dad. And he's got a big-deal government job. Homeland Security.'

'He make you laugh?' Keiko asked, pointedly ignoring Joe's credentials.

'Uh-huh. Sometimes we laugh ourselves into fits.'

'He treat you nice?'

'He treats me sooooo nice,' I said with a grin.

Keiko nodded approvingly. 'I know that smile,' she said. 'You find a man with a slow hands.'

Again Yuki and I burst into hoots of laughter, and from the sparkle in Keiko's eyes, I could tell that she was enjoying her role as Mama Interrogator.

'When you get a ring from this Joe?'

That's when I blushed. Keiko had nailed it with a well-manicured finger. Joe lived in Washington, DC. I didn't. Couldn't. I didn't know where our relationship was going.

'We're not at the ring stage yet,' I told her.

'You love this Joe?'

'Big time,' I confessed.

'He love you?'

Yuki's mom was looking up at me with amusement, when her features froze as if she'd turned to stone. Her lively eyes glazed over, rolled back, and her knees gave way.

I reached out to grab her, but I was too late.

Keiko dropped to the pavement with a moan that made my heart buck. I couldn't believe what had happened, and I couldn't understand it. Had Keiko suffered a stroke?

Yuki screamed, then crouched beside her mother, slapping her cheeks, crying out, 'Mommy, Mommy, wake up.'

'Yuki, let me in there for a second. *Keiko.* Keiko, can you hear me?'

My heart was thudding hard as I placed my fingers to Keiko's carotid artery, tracked her pulse against the second hand of my watch.

She was breathing, but her pulse was so weak, I could barely feel it.

I grabbed at the Nextel at my waist and called Dispatch.

'Lieutenant Boxer, badge number twenty-seven twenty-one,' I barked into the phone. 'Get an EMS unit to Maiden Lane and Grant. *Make it now!*'

Chapter Four

S an Francisco Municipal Hospital is huge – like a city in itself. Once a public hospital, it had been privatized a few years back, but it still took more than its share of indigents and overflow from other hospitals, treating in excess of a hundred thousand patients a year.

At that moment, Keiko Castellano was inside one of the curtained stalls that ring the perimeter of the vast, frantic emergency room.

As I sat beside Yuki in the waiting room, I could feel her terror and fear for her mother's life.

And I flashed on the last time I'd been inside an emergency room. I remembered the doctors' ghostlike hands touching my body, the loud throbbing of my heart, and wondering if I was going to get out alive.

I'd been off duty that night but went on a stakeout anyway,

not thinking that one minute it would be a routine job, and the next minute I'd be down. The same was true for my friend and former partner, Inspector Warren Jacobi. We'd both taken two slugs in that desolate alley. He was unconscious and I was bleeding out on the street when somehow I found the strength to return fire.

My aim had been good, maybe even too good.

It's a sad sign of the times that public sympathy favors civilians who've been shot by police over police who've been shot by civilians. I was sued by the family of the so-called victims, and I could have lost everything.

I hardly knew Yuki then.

But Yuki Castellano was the smart, passionate, and supertalented young lawyer who came through for me when I really needed her. I would always be grateful.

I turned to Yuki now as she spoke, her voice choppy with agitation, her face corrugated with worry.

'This makes no sense, Lindsay. You saw her. She's only fifty-five, for God's sake. She's a freaking life force. What's going on? Why don't they tell me something? Or at least let me see her?'

I had no answer, but like Yuki, my patience had run out.

Where the hell was the doctor?

This was unconscionable. Not acceptable in any way.

What was taking so long?

I was gathering myself to walk into the ER and demand some answers, when a doctor finally strode into the waiting room. He looked around, then called Yuki's name.

Chapter Five

The name tag over the pocket of his white coat read 'Dennis Garza, MD, Dir. Emergency Services.'

I couldn't help noticing that Garza was a handsome man – mid-forties, six foot one, 180 pounds or so, broad-shouldered, and in good shape. His Spanish lineage showed in his black eyes and the thick black hair that fell across his forehead.

But what struck me most was the tension in the doctor's body, his rigid stance and the way he repeatedly, impatiently, snapped the wristband of his Rolex, as if to say, *I'm a busy man. An important, busy man. Let's get on with it.* I don't know why, but I didn't like him.

'I'm Dr Garza,' he said to Yuki. 'Your mother probably had a neurological insult, either what we call a TIA, a transient ischemic attack, or a mini-stroke. In plain English, it's a loss of circulation and oxygen to the brain and she may have had some angina – that's pain caused by a narrowing of the coronary arteries.'

'Is that serious? Is she in pain now? When will I be able to see her?'

Yuki fired questions at Dr Garza until he put up a hand to stop the onslaught.

'She's still incoherent. Most people recover within a half hour. Others, maybe your mother, take as long as twenty-four hours. Her condition is guarded. And visitors are off-limits right now. Let's see how she does tonight, shall we?'

'She is going to be all right though, right? Right?' Yuki asked the doctor.

'Miss Castellano. Take a deep breath,' Garza said. 'I'll let you know when we know.'

The door to the ER swung closed behind the unpleasant doctor, and Yuki sat down hard into a plastic chair, slumped forward, lowered her face into her hands, and began to sob. I'd never seen Yuki cry before, and it killed me that I couldn't fix what was hurting her.

I did all that I could do.

I put my arm around Yuki's shoulders, saying, 'It's okay, honey. She's in good hands here. I know your mom will be better really soon.'

Then I rubbed Yuki's back as she cried and cried. She seemed so tiny and afraid, almost like a little girl.

Chapter Six

There were no windows in the waiting room. The hands of the clock above the coffee machine inched around the dial, cycling the afternoon into night and midnight into morning. Dr Garza never returned, and he never sent us any word.

During those eighteen long hours, Yuki and I took turns pacing, getting coffee, and going to the ladies' room. We ate vending-machine sandwiches for dinner, traded magazines, and, in the eerie fluorescent silence, listened to each other's shallow breathing.

At just after 3:00 a.m., Yuki fell sound asleep against my shoulder – waking with a start twenty minutes later.

'Has anything happened?'

'No, sweetie. Go back to sleep.'

But she couldn't do it.

We sat shoulder to shoulder inside that synthetically bright, inhospitable place as the faces around us changed: the couple with linked hands staring into the middle distance, the families with young children in their arms, an elderly man sitting alone.

Every time the swinging door to the ER opened, eyes would snap toward it.

Sometimes a doctor would step out.

Sometimes shrieks and cries would follow.

It was almost 6:00 in the morning when a young female intern with weary eyes and a blood-smeared lab coat came out of the ER and mangled Yuki's name.

'How is she?' Yuki asked, bounding to her feet.

'She's conscious now, so she's doing better,' said the intern. 'We're going to keep her for a few days and do some tests, but you can visit as soon as we settle her into her room.'

Yuki thanked the doctor and turned to me with a smile that was far more radiant than was reasonable, given what the doctor had just told her.

'Oh-my-God, Linds; my mom's going to be okay! I can't say how much it means to me that you stayed with me all night,' Yuki said.

She grabbed both of my hands, tears filling her eyes. 'I don't know how I could have done this if you hadn't been here. You saved me, Lindsay.'

I hugged her, folded her in.

'Yuki, we're friends. Anything you need, you don't even have to ask. You know that, right? Anything.

'Don't forget to call,' I said.

'The worst is over,' said Yuki. 'Don't worry about us now, Lindsay. Thank you. Thank you so much.'

I turned to look behind me as I exited the hospital through the automatic sliding doors.

Yuki was still standing there, watching me, smiling and waving good-bye.

Chapter Seven

A cab was idling in front of the hospital. Lucky me. I slid in and slumped into the back seat, feeling like total crap, only much worse. Pulling all-nighters is for college kids, not big girls like me.

The driver was mercifully silent as we made our way across town to Potrero Hill at dawn.

A few minutes later, I slipped my key into the front door of 232 Missouri, the pretty, blue two-story Victorian town house I share with two other tenants, and climbed the groaning staircase to the second floor, two steps at a time.

Sweet Martha, my Border collie, greeted me at the door as if I'd been gone for a year. I knew her sitter had fed and walked her – Karen's bill was on the kitchen table – but Martha had missed me and I'd missed her, too.

'Yuki's mom is in the hospital,' I told my doggy. Corny me.

I wrapped my arms around her, and she gave me sloppy kisses, then followed me back to my bedroom.

I wanted to fall into the downy folds of bedding for seven or eight hours, but instead I changed into a wrinkled Santa Clara U tracksuit and took Her Sweetness for a run as the glowing morning fog hovered over the Bay.

At 8:00 a.m. on the nose, I was at my desk looking through the glass walls of my cubicle out to the squad room as the morning tour sauntered in.

The stack of files on my desk had grown since I'd seen it last, and the message light on my phone was blinking in angry red bursts. I was about to address these irritations, when a shadow fell across my desk and my unopened container of coffee.

A large, balding man stood in my doorway. I knew his pug-ugly face almost as well as I knew my own.

My former partner wore the time-rumpled look of a career police officer who had rounded the corner on fifty. Inspector Warren Jacobi's hair was turning white, and his deep, hooded eyes were harder than they'd been before he'd taken those slugs on Larkin Street.

'You look like you slept on a park bench last night, Boxer.'

'Thanks, dear.'

'I hope you had fun.'

'Tons. What's up, Jacobi?'

'A DOA was called in twenty minutes ago,' he said. 'A female, formerly very attractive, I'm told. Found dead inside a Cadillac in the Opera Plaza Garage.'

Chapter Eight

The Opera Plaza Garage is a cavernous indoor lot adjacent to a huge mixed-use commercial building that houses movie theaters, offices, and shops in the middle of a densely populated business district.

Now, on a workday morning, Jacobi nosed our car up to the curb beside the line of patrol cars strategically parked to block access to the garage entrance on Golden Gate Avenue.

No cars were coming in or going out, and a shifting crowd had gathered, prompting Jacobi to mutter, 'The citizens are squawking. They know a hot case when they see one.'

I excused our way through the throng as strident voices called out to me. 'Are you in charge here?' 'Hey, I've got to get my car. I've got a meeting in like five minutes!'

I ducked under the tape and took up a position on the entry ramp, making good use of my five-foot-ten frame. I said my name and apologized for the inconvenience to one and all.

'Please bear with us. Sorry to say, this garage is a crime scene. I hope as much as you do that we'll be out of here soon. We'll do our best.'

I fielded some unanswerable questions, then turned as I heard my name and the sound of footsteps coming from behind me. Jacobi's new partner, Inspector Rich Conklin, was heading down the ramp to meet us.

I'd liked Conklin from the moment I'd met him a few years back, when he was a smart and dogged uniformed officer. Bravery in the line of duty and an impressive number of collars earned him his recent promotion to Homicide at the ripe young age of twenty-nine.

Conklin had also attracted a lot of attention from the women working in the Hall once he'd traded in his uniform for a gold shield.

At just over six foot one, Conklin was buffed to a T, with brown eyes, light-brown hair, and the wholesome good looks of a college baseball player crossed with a Navy Seal.

Not that I'd noticed any of this.

'What have we got?' I asked Conklin.

He hit me with his clear brown eyes. Very serious, but respectful. 'The vic is a Caucasian female, Lieutenant, approximately twenty-one or twenty-two. Looks to me like a ligature mark around her neck.'

'Any witnesses so far?'

'Nope, we're not that lucky. The guy over there,' Conklin said, hooking a thumb toward the scraggly, long-haired ticket-taker in the booth, 'name of Angel Cortez, was on duty all night, didn't see anything unusual, of course. He was on the phone with his girlfriend when a customer came screaming down the ramp. The customer's name is . . .' Conklin flipped open his notebook . . . 'Angela Spinogatti. Her car was parked overnight, and she saw the body inside the Caddy this morning. That's about all she had for us.'

'You ID'd the Caddy's plates?' Jacobi asked.

Conklin nodded his head once, turned a page in his notebook. 'The car belongs to a Lawrence P. Guttman, DDS. No sheet, no warrants. We've got calls in to him now.'

I thanked Conklin and asked him to collect the parking garage tickets and the surveillance tapes.

Then Jacobi and I headed up the ramp.

I'd had way too little sleep, but a thin, steady flow of adrenaline was entering my bloodstream. I was imagining the scene before I saw it, thinking about how a young white female came to be strangled inside a parking garage.

Footsteps echoed overhead. Lots and lots of them. My people.

I counted a dozen members of the SFPD strung around the upward-coiling concrete-ribbon parking area. Officers were going through the trash, taking down plate numbers, looking for anything that would help us before the crime scene was returned to the public domain.

Jacobi and I rounded the bend that took us to the fourth floor and saw the Caddy in question – a black, late-model Seville, sleek, unscratched. Its nose was pointing over the railing toward the Civic Center Garage on McAllister.

'Zero to sixty in under five seconds,' Warren muttered, then did a fair imitation of the Cadillac musical sting from their TV commercials.

'Down, boy,' I said.

Charlie Clapper, head of CSU, was wearing his usual non-smile and a gray herringbone jacket that casually matched his salt-and-pepper hair.

He put his camera down on the hood of an adjacent Subaru Outback and said, 'Mornin', Lou, Jacobi. Meet Jane Doe.'

I tugged on latex gloves and followed him around the car. The trunk was closed because the victim wasn't in there.

She was sitting in the passenger seat, hands folded in her lap, her pale, wide-open eyes staring out through the windshield expectantly.

As if she were waiting for someone to come.

'Aw, shit,' Jacobi said with disgust. 'Beautiful young girl like this. All dressed up and no place to go. Forever.'

Chapter Nine

'I don't see a handbag anywhere,' Clapper was telling me. 'I left her clothing intact for the ME. Nice duds,' he said. 'Looks like a rich girl. You think?'

I felt a shock of sadness and anger as I looked into the victim's dreamy face.

She was fair-skinned, a light dusting of powder across her face, a hint of blush on the apples of her cheeks. Her hair was cut in a Meg Ryan-style mop of tousled blond lights, and her nails had been recently manicured.

Everything about this woman spoke of privilege and opportunity, and money. It was as if she'd been just about to step down the runway of life when some psycho had ripped it all away from her.

I pressed the victim's cheek with the back of my hand. Her

skin was tepid to the touch, telling me that she'd been alive last night.

'Larry, Moe, and Curly didn't whack this little lady,' Jacobi commented.

I nodded my agreement.

When I first got into Homicide, I learned that crime scenes generally come in two types. The kind where the evidence is disorganized: blood spatter, broken objects, shell casings scattered around, bodies sprawled where they fell.

And then there were the scenes like this one.

Organized. Planned out.

Plenty of malice aforethought.

The victim's clothes were neat, no bunching, no button-holes missed. She was even wearing a seat belt, which was drawn snug across her lap and shoulder.

Had the killer cared about her?

Or was this tidy scene some kind of message for whoever found her?

'The passenger-side door was opened with a slim jim,' Clapper told us. 'The surfaces have all been wiped clean. No prints to be found inside or out. And look over here.'

Clapper pointed up toward the camera mounted on a concrete pylon. It faced down the ramp, *away* from the Caddy.

He lifted his chin toward another camera that was pointed *up* the ramp toward the fifth level.

'I don't think you're going to catch this bird doing the vic on tape,' Clapper said. 'This car is in a perfect blind spot.'

I like this about Charlie. He knows what he's doing, shows you what he sees, but the guy doesn't try to take over the scene. He lets you do your job, too.

I directed my flashlight beam into the interior of the car, checking off the relevant details in my mind.

The victim looked healthy, weighed about 110 pounds, stood maybe five foot or five one.

No wedding band or engagement ring.

She was wearing a crystal bead necklace, which hung below a ligature mark.

The mark itself was shallow and ropy, as if it had been made with something soft.

I saw no defensive cuts or bruises on her arms and, except for the ligature mark, no signs of violence.

I didn't know how or why this girl had been killed, but my eyes and my gut told me that she hadn't died in this car.

She had to have been moved here, then posed in a tableau that somebody was meant to admire.

I doubted that someone had gone to all of this trouble for me.

I hoped not.

Chapter Ten

'Have you got your pictures?' I asked Clapper.

There wasn't much room to work, and I wanted to get in close for a better look at the victim.

'I've got more than enough for my collection,' he said. 'The camera loves this girl.'

He stowed his digital Olympus in his case, snapped the lid closed.

I reached into the car and gingerly fished out the labels from the back of the victim's pale-pink coat and then her slim black party dress.

'The coat is Narciso Rodriguez,' I called out to Jacobi. 'And the dress is a little Carolina Herrera number. We're looking at about six grand in threads here. And that's not counting the shoes.'

Since *Sex and the City*, when it came to shoes, Manolo

Blahnik was the man. I recognized a pair of his trademark sling-backs on the victim's feet.

'She even smells like money,' said Jacobi.

'You've got a good nose, buddy.'

The fragrance the victim wore had a musky undertone calling up ballrooms and orchids, and maybe moonlit trysts under mossy trees. I was pretty sure I'd never smelled it before, though. Maybe some kind of pricey private label.

I was leaning in for another sniff, when Conklin escorted a short, fortyish white man up the steep ramp. He had a ruff of frizzy hair and small, darting eyes, almost black dots.

'I'm Doctor Lawrence Guttman,' the man huffed indignantly to Jacobi. 'And yes, thanks for asking. That *is* my car. What are you doing to it?'

Jacobi showed Guttman his badge, said, 'Let's walk down to *my* car, Doctor Guttman, take a ride to the station. Inspector Conklin and I have some questions for you, but I'm sure we can clear this all up, PDQ.'

It was then that Guttman saw the dead woman in the passenger seat of his Seville. He snapped his eyes back to Jacobi.

'My God! Who is that woman? She's dead! W-what are you thinking?' he sputtered. 'That I killed someone and left her in my car? You can't think . . . Are you crazy? I want my lawyer.'

Guttman's voice was squelched by the roar and echo of a

large engine coming toward us. Wheels squealed as a black Chevy van wound up and around the helix of the parking-garage ramp.

It stopped twenty feet away from where we stood, and the side doors slid open.

A woman stepped out of the driver's seat.

Black, just over forty, substantial in every way imaginable, Claire Washburn carried herself with the dignity of her office and the confidence of a well-loved woman.

The ME had arrived.

Chapter Eleven

C laire is San Francisco's chief medical examiner, a superb pathologist, a master of intuition, a pretty fair cellist, happily married for almost twenty years, the mother of two boys, and, quite simply, my best friend in the universe.

We'd met fourteen years ago over a dead body, and since then had spent as much time together as some married couples.

We got along better, too.

We hugged now, right there in the garage, drawing on the love we feel for each other. When we broke from our hug, Claire put her hands on her ample hips and took in the scene.

'So, Lindsay,' she said, 'who died on us today?'

'Right now, she goes by the name of Jane Doe. Looks like she was killed by some kind of freako perfectionist, Claire. There's not a hair out of place. You tell us, though.'

'Well, let's see what we can see.'

Claire walked to the car with her kit and in short order took her own photos, documenting the victim from every angle, then taped paper bags over the young woman's hands and feet.

'Lindsay,' she finally called for me, 'come have a look here.'

I wedged into the narrow angle between Claire and the car door as Claire rolled up the girl's upper lip, then rolled down the lower one, showing me the bruising by the beam of her penlight.

'See all this here, sugar? Was this young lady intubated?' Claire asked me.

'Nope. The EMTs never touched her. We waited for you.'

'So this is trauma artifact. Look at her tongue. Appears to be a laceration.'

Claire flicked her light over the furrow at the girl's neckline.

'Unusual ligature mark,' she told me.

'I thought so, too. Don't see any petechial hemorrhaging in the eyes,' I said, talking the talk. 'Odd, isn't it? If she was strangled?'

'All of it's odd, girlfriend,' said Claire. 'Her clothes are immaculate. Don't see that too much with a body dump. If ever.'

'Cause of death? Time of death?'

'I'd say she went down somewhere around midnight. She's just going into rigor. Other than that, all I know is that this girl is dead. I'll have more for you after I examine young Jane under some decent light back at the shop.'

Claire stood and spoke to her assistant.

'Okay, Bobby. Let's get this poor girl out of the car. Gently, please.'

I walked to the edge of the fourth floor and looked out over the tops of buildings and the creeping traffic down on Golden Gate Avenue. When I felt a little more collected, I called Jacobi on my cell.

'I turned Guttman loose,' he told me. 'He'd just gotten off a flight from New York, had left his car at the garage while he was out of town.'

'Alibi?'

'His alibi checks out. Someone else parked that girl in his Caddy. How's it going over there?'

I turned, saw Claire and Bobby wrapping the victim tamale-style in the second of two sheets before inserting her into a body bag. The chalk-on-board sound of that six-foot-long zipper closing, the finality of encasing the victim in an airproof sack, feels like a gut-punch no matter how many times you've witnessed it.

My voice sounded sad to my own ears as I said to Jacobi, 'We're wrapping things up now.'

Chapter Twelve

It was almost half past six that night, ten hours after we'd found Caddy Girl's body.

The sheaf of paper in the center of my desk was a list of the 762 cars that had gone through the Opera Plaza Garage last night.

Since morning, we'd run the plates and registrations of those cars through the database, and no red flags had popped up, nothing even remotely promising.

We'd also struck out on Caddy Girl's prints. She'd never been arrested, or taught school, or joined the military, or worked for any government agency.

A half hour ago, we'd gotten a digital picture of her likeness out to the press, and depending on what else was happening in the world, she'd be in all the newspapers tomorrow.

I pulled the rubber band out of my hair, shook out my ponytail, threw a breathy sigh that riffled the papers in front of me.

Then I called Claire, who was still downstairs in the morgue. I asked her if she was hungry.

'Meet me downstairs in ten,' she said.

I greeted Claire at her private parking spot on McAllister. She unlocked the car, and I opened the passenger-side door of her Pathfinder. Claire's scene kit was on the seat, along with a pair of hip waders, a hard hat, a map of California, and her ancient 35mm Minolta.

I transferred the tools of her trade from the front into the back and wearily slid into the passenger seat. Claire gave me an appraising look, then burst out laughing.

'What's the joke, Butterfly?'

'You've got that third-degree look on your puss,' she told me. 'And you don't have to work me over, baby girl. I've got what you want right here.'

Claire waved some papers at me, then shoved them into her cowhide handbag.

Some people think Claire's nickname is 'Butterfly' because, like Muhammad Ali, she 'floats like a butterfly, stings like a bee.'

Not so.

Claire Washburn has a bright golden Monarch butterfly tattooed on her left hip. Now I pinned her with my eyes.

'I'm sooooo ready to hear your verdict,' I said.

Claire gave it up at last.

'It's a homicide, definitely,' she told me. 'Lividity was incon-sistent with a sitting position, so she was moved. And I found faint bruising across the tops of her arms, chest, and on her rib cage.'

'So the manner and cause of death?'

'I'm gonna say she was burked,' Claire told me.

I was familiar with the term.

In the 1820s, a couple of sweethearts named Burke and Hare were in the cadaver procurement business. For a while, they dug up bodies for sale to Edinburgh's medical schools – until they realized how easy it was to produce fresh corpses by grabbing live victims and sitting on their chests until they died.

Burking was still in good standing today. Postpartum mommies do it to their kids more often than you'd ever want to know. Slip the child between the mattress and box spring, sit on the bed.

If you can't expand your chest, you can't breathe.

And the victim's body shows little or no signs of trauma.

I buckled up as Claire backed the car out and headed to Susie's.

'It was a horror show for this girl, Lindsay,' Claire told me. 'What I'm thinking is, while one perp sat on her chest, another freak slipped a plastic bag over her head and smothered her. Rolled up the edge of the bag good and tight. That's where the ligature mark came from. Maybe he pressed his hand to her nose and mouth at the same time.'

'She had two killers?'

'If you ask me, Lindsay, that's the *only* way it could have been done.'

Chapter Thirteen

San Francisco's Business District slipped by as Claire piloted the Pathfinder through evening rush-hour traffic. We were silent for a few minutes, the eeriness of that young woman's death filling the space around us.

Images shifted in my mind as I tried to put it together one grisly piece at a time.

'Two killers,' I finally said to Claire, 'working as a team. Posing the victim inside a car after the fact. What's the point of that? What's the message?'

'It's cold, for one thing,' Claire said.

'And sick, for another. The rape kit?'

'Is at the lab,' said Claire, 'along with that pricey outfit Caddy Girl was wearing. By the way, the lab found a semen stain on the hem of her dress.'

'Was she raped?'

'I didn't see the kind of vaginal tearing or bruising you'd expect from a rape,' Claire mused. 'We'll have to wait to decide about that.'

Claire braked the car at the Muni rail crossing, and together we watched the train rattle by. Night was closing in over the city of San Francisco, and the commuters were all going home.

Questions were still flooding my little mind. Lots of them. About who Caddy Girl was. Who had killed her. How she and her killers might have crossed paths.

Had the killing been personal?

Or was Caddy Girl a victim of opportunity?

If it was the latter, we could be looking for a ritualistic killer, someone who liked to kill and was equally excited by patterns.

Someone who might like to do it again.

Claire made a left across a break in the oncoming traffic. A moment later, she executed a careful parallel-park maneuver between two cars on Bryant, right outside Susie's.

She switched off the engine, turned to face me. 'There's more,' she said.

'Don't make me beg, Butterfly.'

Claire laughed at me, meaning it took even longer for her to get it together and tell me what I was dying to know.

'The shoes,' she said. 'They're a size eight.'

'Couldn't be. That little girl?'

'Could be and are. But you're right that it's crazy, Linds.

Caddy Girl probably wore a size five. Those shoes weren't hers. And the soles have never touched pavement.'

'Huh,' I said. 'If they're not her shoes, maybe those aren't her clothes, either.'

'That's what I'm thinking, Lindsay. I don't know what it means, but those clothes are brand new. No sweat stains, no body soil of any kind. Somebody carefully, I want to say *artfully*, dressed that poor girl after she was dead.'

Chapter Fourteen

It was still early in the evening when Claire and I crossed the threshold to Susie's, the boisterous, sometimes rowdy Caribbean-style eatery where a group of my friends meet for dinner every week or so.

The reggae band hadn't yet arrived – which was fine, because when Cindy waved to us from 'our' booth, I could see from her expression that she had something big on her mind.

And words were her thing.

Cindy is the hot-shit crime reporter at the *San Francisco Chronicle* these days. We met four years ago while I was working on a particularly grisly case involving honeymoon murders, and she talked her way right into my crime scene. Her audacity and tenacity ticked me off enormously, but I came to respect those same qualities when her reporting helped me nail a vicious killer and send him to death row.

By the time Cindy crashed my next crime scene, we'd bonded and become trusting friends. I'd do anything for her now. Well, almost anything – she is a reporter, after all.

Claire and I wriggled into the booth opposite Cindy, who looked both boyish and girly with her fluffy blond hair, man-tailored black suit jacket over a mauve sweater, and jeans. Her front two teeth overlap minutely, which only makes her face look even prettier. Her smile, when it comes, lights you up inside.

I flagged down Loretta, ordered a pitcher of margaritas, turned off my cell phone, then said to Cindy, 'You look like you're hatching something.'

'You're *good*. And you're *right*,' she said with a grin. She licked salt off her upper lip and set down her glass.

'I've got a lead on a story that's going to be a bombshell,' Cindy said. 'And I think I've got it to myself – at least for a while.'

'Do tell,' said Claire. 'You've got the talking stick, girlfriend.'

Cindy laughed and launched into her story.

'I overheard a couple of lawyers talking in an elevator. They arrr-oused my interest,' Cindy said with a funny, leonine growl, 'and I followed up.'

'Don't you just love blabbermouths?' I said, pouring margaritas for Claire and myself, then topping off Cindy's glass.

'Some of my favorite people,' Cindy said, leaning in toward the center of the table.

'So here's the prepublication scoop. There's a malpractice suit starting against a huge hospital right here in Metropolis,' she told us. 'Last couple of years, a number of patients who were admitted through the emergency room, recovered fully. Then, a few days later, according to what I overheard between the lobby and fourth floor of the Civic Center Courthouse, those patients died. *Because they got the wrong medication.*'

I eyed Cindy over the rim of my glass. A feeling was starting to grow in the center of my chest, a feeling I hoped would disappear as she continued her story.

'This hotshot lawyer named Maureen O'Mara is going after the hospital, representing a bunch of the patients' families,' Cindy was saying.

'Which hospital?' I asked. 'Can you tell me?'

'Well, sure, Linds. San Francisco Municipal.'

I heard Claire say, 'Oh, no,' as the feeling in my gut mushroomed.

'I just spent the night at Municipal holding Yuki's hand,' I said. 'We brought her mom into the emergency room yesterday afternoon.'

'Let's not go crazy, here,' Cindy said quietly. 'It's a humongous hospital. There's one doctor in particular in the crosshairs, a guy named Garza. Apparently, most of the deceased in question were admitted on his watch.'

'Oh my God,' I said, my blood pressure spiking so I felt heat through the top of my head. 'He's the *one. I met him.* That's the doctor who admitted Yuki's mother!'

Just then, the air moved at the back of my neck, and silky hair brushed the side of my face as someone bent down to kiss my cheek.

'Did you just mention my name?' Yuki asked. She slipped into the empty seat beside Cindy. 'What'd I miss?'

'Cindy is working on a story.'

'It's something I think you should know,' said Claire.

Chapter Fifteen

Yuki's eyes were beaming question marks, but suddenly Cindy seemed reluctant to talk.

'You can trust me,' Yuki said earnestly. 'I understand what "off the record" means.'

'It's nothing like that,' Cindy said.

Loretta came by, greeted Yuki, and unloaded a tray of jerk chicken and spare ribs dripping sauce. After a few halting starts and a few sips of her margarita, Cindy repeated to Yuki what she'd just told us about Maureen O'Mara's pending case against Municipal Hospital.

'Actually, I know a lot about this,' Yuki said when Cindy was finished. 'O'Mara's been putting this case together for about a year.'

'Really? Come onnnn,' Cindy said. 'How do you know?'

'I have a friend, an associate at Friedman, Bannion and

O'Mara,' Yuki said. 'She told me 'cause she's thrown a ton of man-hours into this case. Tremendous amount of research involved. A lot of medical technicalities to plow through. It should be a hell of a trial,' Yuki continued. 'O'Mara never loses. But this time, she's shooting the moon.'

'Everyone loses sometimes,' Claire offered.

'I know, but Maureen O'Mara carefully picks cases she knows she can win,' Yuki said.

Maybe Yuki was missing the point, so I had to say it. 'Yuki, doesn't it worry you that your mom is at Municipal?'

'Nah. Just because Maureen O'Mara is taking on the case doesn't mean the hospital is *guilty*. Lawyer's credo: anyone can sue anyone for anything. Really, you guys,' Yuki said, her words going her usual rat-a-tat, sixty-five miles an hour. 'I had my appendix taken out there a couple of years ago. Had an excellent doctor. And first-class care throughout my stay at the hospital.'

'So how *is* your mom?' Claire asked.

'She's in fine form,' said Yuki. Then she laughed. 'You know how I know? She tried to fix me up with her cardiologist. Bald guy in his forties with tiny hands and dog breath.'

We all laughed as Yuki's animated reenactment lit up the table. She did her mom so well, I could see Keiko as if she were right there.

'I said, "Mom, he's not for me." So she said, "Yuki-eh. Looks mean *nothing*. Doctor Pierce honest man. He *good* man. Looks for mag-azines."I said,"Mom, Daddy looked like Frank Sinatra. What are you talking about?"'

'So are you going out with him?' Cindy asked, sending us into new rounds of laughter.

Yuki shook her head. 'You mean, if he asks me? You mean, if my mom grabs his cell phone and dials my number for him?'

We were having so much fun the band had to dial up the music a notch to be heard over our good time. Twenty minutes later, Yuki left the table before the coffee and chocolate mud pie, saying she wanted to see Keiko again before visiting hours were over.

Despite her rapid-fire talk, and our good-time chatter, there were worry lines between Yuki's beautiful brown eyes when she told us all good night.

Chapter Sixteen

Maureen O'Mara felt her pulse beating in her temples. Was that possible? Well, that's how pumped she was. She pulled open one of the massive steel-and-glass doors to the Civic Center Courthouse and entered the cool gray interior.

Goddamn.

Today was the day. She owned this place.

She handed her briefcase to the security guard, who put it on the X-ray machine and checked it as she cleared the metal detectors. He nodded good morning and returned her seven-hundred-dollar 'lucky' Louis Vuitton case with a smile.

'Best a' luck today, Miss O'Mara.'

'Thanks, Kevin.'

O'Mara showed the guard her crossed fingers; then she cut

through the milling crowd in the lobby and headed toward the elevator bank.

She was thinking as she walked – about how her stuffy, know-it-all partners had told her that she was *insane* to take on the huge, well-defended hospital, to try to weave twenty individual claims into one gigantic malpractice case.

But she couldn't have turned it down. This one was too good.

The first patients had found her – then she'd seen the pattern. The momentum had built rapidly, then snowballed, and soon she'd become the go-to lawyer for patients with serious grievances against Municipal.

Putting this case together had been like corralling wild horses while standing on the seat of a motorbike and juggling bowling balls. But she'd done it.

Over the last fourteen months, she'd slogged through the discovery process, the endless depositions, lined up her seventy-six witnesses – medical experts, past and present employees of the hospital, and her clients, the families of the twenty deceased who were all finally in accord.

She had a personal reason for her total, unwavering commitment, but no one needed to know *why* this case was a labor of love.

She definitely felt her clients' pain – that was reason enough.

Now she had to convince a jury of their peers.

If she could do that, the hospital would feel the pain, too, in the only way it could – by kicking out a gigantic payout, the many, *many* millions her clients richly deserved.

Chapter Seventeen

Maureen O'Mara made a rush for one of the courthouse elevators, stepping in, then starting as a man in a charcoal-gray suit joined her just as the doors were closing.

Lawrence Kramer gave her a brilliant smile, leaned forward, and pressed number four.

'Morning, Counselor,' he said. 'How are ya doing so far today?'

'Never better,' she chirped. 'And you?'

'Perfecto. I had about three pounds of raw meat with my eggs this morning,' Kramer said. 'Breakfast of Champions.'

'Sounds kind of bad for your heart,' Maureen said, giving the hospital's lead attorney a sidelong look. 'You do *have* a heart, don't you, Larry?'

The big man threw his head back and laughed as the elevator lurched upward toward the courtroom.

God, he has a lot of teeth, and they've been whitened.

'Sure I do. I'm going to get my cardio workout in court, Maureen. Thanks to you.'

At forty-two, Lawrence Kramer was a gifted defense attorney – smart, good-looking, and in his prime. All that and he was rapidly gaining national media presence as well.

O'Mara had seen him interviewed a few times on Chris Matthews' *Hardball* about one of his clients, a football star accused of rape. Kramer had held his own against Matthews' verbal machine-gun attack. It hadn't surprised Maureen, though. Hardball was Kramer's game of choice.

And now Lawrence Kramer was defending San Francisco Municipal Hospital in an action that could throw the hospital into receivership, even possibly shut it down. But more important was that Kramer was defending the hospital against *her*.

The elevator stopped on the second floor of the courthouse, and three more passengers crowded into the small mahogany-lined box, forcing Maureen closer to Kramer's side. It was a little too much contact with the man who was going to try to flatten her and run her clients into the dust.

O'Mara had a moment of doubt, felt a frisson of fear. Could she pull this off? She'd never taken on a case so complex – she didn't know anyone who had. This was definitely the Big One, even for Larry Kramer.

The elevator jolted to a stop on four, and she stepped out

just ahead of Kramer. She could almost feel her opponent's presence behind her, as if a high-voltage charge was coming off his body.

Eyes straight ahead, the two attorneys marched along together, the clacking of their shoes on the marble floor echoing in the wide corridor.

Maureen went inside her head.

Even though Kramer had ten years on her, she was his equal, or could be. She, too, was Harvard Law. She, too, thrived on a hard and bloody fight. And she had something that Kramer didn't have. She had right on her side.

Right is might. Right is might.

The affirmation was like cool water, soothing her and at the same time bracing her for the biggest trial of her career. This one might get *her* on *Hardball.*

She reached the open door to the courtroom seconds before her opponent and saw that the oak-paneled room was just about filled with spectators.

Down the aisle at the plaintiffs' table on her right, Bobby Perlstein, her associate and second chair, was going over his notes. Her assistant, Karen Palmer, was setting out the exhibits and documents. Both turned to her, flashing eager smiles.

Maureen grinned back. As she approached her associates, she passed her many clients, acknowledging them with a smile, a wink, a wave of her hand. Their grateful eyes warmed her.

Right is might.

Maureen couldn't wait for the trial to start.

She was ready. And today was her day.

Chapter Eighteen

Yuki was filing a motion on the ground floor of the Civic Center Courthouse at 400 McAllister that Monday morning, when she remembered that Maureen O'Mara's case against San Francisco Municipal was starting right about now.

This was something the lawyer in her wanted to see.

She glanced at her watch, bypassed the mob at the elevator bank, and took to the stairs. Slightly out of breath, she slipped into the wood-paneled courtroom at the end of the fourth-floor hallway.

Yuki saw that Judge Bevins was on the bench.

Bevins was in his seventies, wore his white hair in a pony-tail, and was considered fair but quirky, impossible to second-guess.

As Yuki settled into a seat near the door, she noticed a

dark-haired man across the aisle wearing khakis and a blazer over his pink button-down shirt and club tie. He was plucking at the wristband of his watch.

It took a second for the handsome face to click with a name; then, with a shock of recognition, Yuki realized that she knew him: it was Dennis Garza, the doctor who'd admitted her mother to the emergency room.

Of course. He's a witness in this trial, Yuki thought.

Her attention was pulled away from Garza by a rustling and buzzing in the crowded courtroom as Maureen O'Mara stood and took the floor.

O'Mara was tall, a solid size twelve, Yuki guessed, dressed in a fitted gray Armani pantsuit and low-heeled black shoes. She had strong features and truly remarkable hair, a dark-red mane that hung to her shoulders, swinging when O'Mara turned her head – as she did now.

The attractive attorney faced the court, said good morning to the jury, introduced herself, then began her opening statement by lifting a large and awkward cardboard-mounted photograph from a stack of photos on the table in front of her.

'Please, take a good, long look. This lovely young woman is Amanda Clemmons,' O'Mara said, holding up the picture of a freckled blonde who looked to be about thirty-five years old.

'Last May, Amanda Clemmons was in her driveway playing basketball with her three young boys,' O'Mara said. 'Simon Clemmons, her husband, the boys' father, had been killed in an automobile accident only six months before.

'Amanda wasn't much of a ballplayer,' O'Mara continued, 'but this young widow knew she had to be both a mother and a father to Adam, John, and Chris. And she was as up to the task as anyone could be.

'Imagine this plucky woman if you can. Picture her in your mind,' Maureen said, calling up the scene.

'She's wearing white shorts and a blue-and-gold Warrior T-shirt, dribbling circles around her little kids in the driveway, getting ready to make a shot through the hoop hanging from the garage door.

'John Clemmons told me that his mom was laughing and ragging them, just before she snagged her shoe on a crack in the asphalt and went down.

'Half an hour later, an ambulance came and took Amanda to the hospital, where she was X-rayed and diagnosed in emergency with a broken left leg.

'That injury shouldn't have been more than a temporary setback for Amanda Clemmons,' O'Mara continued. 'She was young; she was strong and resilient. She was a real warrior, that woman. A homegrown American hero.

But she had been admitted to San Francisco Municipal Hospital.

'And that was the beginning of the end of her life. Please, take a good, long look at this picture of Amanda Clemmons. This is the one the family used at her funeral.'

Chapter Nineteen

Maureen felt her anger rising exponentially as she told Amanda's story. Although Maureen had never met Amanda Clemmons, the young mother was as real to her as an honest-to-God friend, and since Maureen worked so hard, she didn't have that many friends.

Maureen felt that way about every one of her deceased clients, about every one of the *victims*, she reminded herself. She knew their backgrounds and their families, the names of their children and spouses.

And she knew precisely how they had died at Municipal Hospital.

She handed the picture of Amanda Clemmons to her assistant, and turned back to the jury, seeing in their eyes that she had their interest. They couldn't wait for her to go on.

'The afternoon Amanda Clemmons broke her leg,' Maureen said, 'she was taken to Municipal's emergency room, where the bone was X-rayed and set. This was a simple procedure. Then she was moved to another room, where she was to spend the night.

'Sometime after midnight and before the sun came up, Amanda was given a deadly dose of Cytoxan, a chemotherapy drug, instead of Vicodin, a painkiller that would have given her a good night's sleep.

'That terrible night, Amanda died an excruciating and senseless death, ladies and gentlemen, and we have to ask *why* this happened. Why this woman's life was ripped away from her long before her time.

'Over the course of this trial, I'll tell you about Amanda and about the nineteen other people who died from similar drug-related, lethal disasters. But I'll tell you right now *why* they died.

'It was because of San Francisco Municipal's rampant, irrefutable greed.

'People died because again and again, Municipal Hospital put cost efficiency above patient care.

'I'm going to tell you a lot of things about Municipal that you'll wish you didn't know,' O'Mara said, sweeping the jury box with her eyes.

'You'll learn that procedures have repeatedly been violated, and poorly trained people have been hired on the cheap and made to work mind-numbing hours. All in the interest of protecting the bottom line, all in the interest of keeping profits among the highest of all San Francisco's hospitals.

'And I can assure you, the twenty deceased patients I represent are just the beginning of this horrible scandal—'

Kramer leaped to his feet.

'Argumentative, Your Honor! I've been patient, but Counsel's remarks are inflammatory, and actually libelous—'

'Sustained. Don't test me, Counselor,' said Judge Bevins to Maureen O'Mara. He shook his head. 'Next time you cross the line, I'm slapping you with a fine. It will get much more serious after that.'

'I'm sorry, Your Honor,' O'Mara said. 'I'll be more careful.'

But Maureen was delighted. She'd said what she needed to, and Kramer wouldn't be able to unring that bell. Surely the jury got the message.

Municipal Hospital is a dangerous place, obscenely dangerous.

'I'm here for my clients,' O'Mara said, standing rock-still before the jury box, hands clasped together in front of her, 'the deceased and their families. All were victims of malpractice as a result of Municipal Hospital's greed and negligence.' Then Maureen O'Mara turned to face the courtroom. 'Please,' she said, 'please raise your hand if you have lost someone at Municipal Hospital.'

Dozens of hands went up around the courtroom. Others in the courtroom gasped.

'We need your help to make sure that these deadly so-called accidents never happen again.'

Chapter Twenty

As order was restored by Judge Bevins, Yuki slowly dragged her eyes away from Maureen O'Mara and looked across the aisle to Dr Garza's face. She was hoping to see anger, rage that his hospital had been falsely accused. But she couldn't find it. Rather, something like a smirk played over Garza's lips, and his entire expression was as cold as a winter landscape.

Fear constricted Yuki's chest, and for a long moment she couldn't move.

She'd made a horrible mistake!

Please, don't let it be too late.

Yuki stood up from her seat, pushed open the swinging courtroom door, and turned on her cell phone as soon as her feet hit the hallway. She pressed the phone's small keys, connecting her to the hospital's recorded telephonic menu.

She listened to the options, her anxiety rising as she stabbed at the number keys.

Was Keiko in room 421 or 431? She couldn't remember! She was blanking on the room number.

Yuki pressed the zero key, and a watery rendition of 'The Girl from Ipanema' plinked in her ear as she waited for a live operator.

She had to speak with her mom.

She had to hear Keiko's voice right now.

'Let me speak with Keiko Castellano,' she said to the operator finally. 'She's a patient. Please ring her room. It's 421 or 431.'

The ringing stopped abruptly as Keiko answered, her cheery voice crackling over the wireless transmission.

Yuki clapped her hand over one ear, pressed her cell phone to the other. The corridor was filling now as the court recessed. Yuki and Keiko continued to talk, to argue, actually. Then the two of them made up, as they always did.

'I'm doing fine, Yuki. Don't worry so much all the time,' Keiko finally said.

'Okay, Mommy, okay. I'll call you later.'

As she pressed End, she heard someone calling out her name.

Yuki looked around until she saw Cindy's excited face, the crowd parting as her reporter friend elbowed her way through.

'Yuki,' Cindy said breathlessly. 'Were you in there? Did you hear O'Mara's opening? What's your professional opinion?'

'Well,' Yuki told her, blood still pounding in her ears, 'lawyers like to say that you win or lose your case in your opening statement.'

'Hang on,' Cindy said, scribbling in her notebook. 'That's pretty good. The first line in my story. Go on . . .'

'Maureen O'Mara's opening was killer, actually,' Yuki said. 'She dropped a bomb on the hospital, and the jury isn't going to forget it. Uh-uh. Neither will I.

'Municipal hires cheap labor and patients die because of it. They're sloppy. They give out the wrong meds. Christ. O'Mara freaked *me* so far out, I called my mother and told her I wanted to move her to Saint Francis.'

'Are you doing that?'

'I tried, but she shot me down! Got really pissed at me,' Yuki said incredulously. '"Yuki-eh. You want to give me hot-attack? I like it here. I like my doctor. I like my room. Bring me my hot rollers. And pink nightgown with dragon."'

Yuki laughed and shook her head. 'I swear to God, she acts like she's at a spa. I wanted to say, "Ma, should I bring your tanning bed? Your cocoa butter?" You know, I didn't want to terrify her just because Maureen O'Mara's opening statement rocked. Jeez, when all those people raised their hands, I got a chill up my spine.'

'What if you went over there and checked her out of the hospital no matter what she wants?' Cindy asked.

'Sure, I thought about that, but what if I did that and I really did give her a hot-attack?'

Cindy nodded her understanding. 'When are they discharging her?'

'Thursday morning, according to Doctor Pierce. After her MRI. "Doctor Pierce good doctor. Doctor Pierce honest man!"'

'Doctor Pierce, your future husband,' Cindy cracked.

'That's the one.'

'You feel okay?'

'Yeah. I'll go see my mom later. Keep her company for a while.'

'So can you hang out here for the rest of the day?'

'I should get back to the office,' Yuki said, her resolve fading even as she spoke. 'But hell, I want to hear Larry Kramer's opening. How could I miss it?'

'Sit next to me,' Cindy said.

Chapter Twenty-One

Cindy watched with fascination as Larry Kramer unfolded his gray-suited six-foot-four breadth and length and took the center of the floor. His thick brown hair was combed back, accenting a jutting jawline and giving him the look of a sailor setting his face into the wind.

A man in perpetual forward motion, thought Cindy.

Kramer greeted the court, then turned an affable smile on the jury and thanked them for serving on this case.

'Ms O'Mara is right about one thing,' he said, putting his large hands on the jury-box railing. 'She's damned right this case is about greed. It's about the greed of her *clients.*

'I won't deny that it's tragic that through no fault of their own, people have died,' Kramer went on. 'But their families have come before this court with one thing in mind. They want to score big. They want to recoup from the deaths of their loved ones. They're here for the money.'

Kramer leaned into the jury box and looked into the faces of the jury members.

'To most people that might sound cynical or vengeful or mercenary. But it's not entirely the fault of the litigants.'

Kramer pushed off from the railing and moved out again into the center of the room, seeming to be lost in his own thoughts before turning to face the jury again.

'I understand grief. My father and my son both died in a hospital. My baby boy died only three days after he was born. He was a gift, a blessing that was ripped away from my wife and me. My father was my best friend, my mentor, captain of my cheering section. I miss them both every day.'

Kramer's scowl softened, and he began to pace slowly, hypnotically, in front of the jury box.

'I'm fairly sure every one of you has suffered the loss of a loved one, and you know it's perfectly natural to want to blame someone,' Kramer said.

'You suffer, you get mad, and, eventually, you turn anger into good by remembering the good times you shared with this person.

'You make peace with the fact that love doesn't conquer all, or that life can be unfair, or that God works in mysterious ways. And somehow you move on. *You move on.*

'You want to know *why* the plaintiffs aren't doing that?' Kramer asked. He put his hands back on the railing, giving the jury the full force of his attention.

'Because my opponent has led them down a path that is unworthy of them. Because of a law firm called Friedman, Bannion and O'Mara. Because of this woman, Maureen O'Mara.' He pointed his finger directly at his opponent. 'Because of her, these unfortunate people have come to see their personal tragedies as a financial opportunity. You've all heard the movie line – "show me the money." That's what this travesty of justice is really about. That's why those people raised their hands.'

Chapter Twenty-Two

Cindy actually clapped her hand over her mouth, stunned at Kramer's searing personal attack on O'Mara and her firm. Damn – and this was just the trial's first day.

O'Mara shot up from her seat.

'Objection,' she snapped. 'Your Honor, Counsel's statement is inflammatory and prejudicial and personally insulting. I move that it be stricken from the record.'

'Sustained. Ms Campbell,' the judge said to the court reporter, 'please strike Mr Kramer's last remark. Mr Kramer, what's good for the goose . . .'

'Your Honor?'

'*Tone down the rhetoric* and proceed, Mr Kramer. You could be fined, or worse.'

Kramer nodded. 'Yes, Your Honor,' and turned back to the jury with a strained smile.

'Ladies and gentlemen, during this trial you will hear abundant proof that San Francisco Municipal is a highly respected and responsible institution,' Kramer continued. 'That it has *above* industry-standard pharmaceutical safeguards and protocols, and that it follows them rigorously.

'That doesn't mean that the hospital is perfect. Human beings sometimes commit human error. But mistakes are one thing. Malpractice is something else *entirely*.'

Kramer paused to let his words sink in and used the long moment to look each juror in the eye again. He was talking to them, one at a time, making this personal.

'I'm afraid that this is going to be an emotional trial because people have died. But the judge will tell you that you can't let the plaintiffs' attorney obscure the facts by playing on your emotions.

'Weigh the facts as presented – that's the job you've accepted and it's your charge. The facts, ladies and gentlemen. The facts will convince you that my client is not negligent, and that my client performs an incredibly valuable service for our city of San Francisco.'

Cindy's mind leaped ahead as Kramer thanked the jury and took his seat. She saw the front-page headline in her mind – SAN FRANCISCO MUNICIPAL SUED FOR MALPRACTICE, the block of twenty victims' photos and the rest of her story carried over to page three.

This trial was the stuff of books and movies.

Twenty people had died.

And whether or not the hospital was guilty, the evidence would shock people. They would take it personally. And patients who were admitted to Municipal would be scared for their lives.

Hell, she was scared just listening at this trial.

Chapter Twenty-Three

It was mid-morning, four long days since we'd found Caddy Girl dead in the Opera Plaza Garage. I'd just come back from a meeting with Chief Tracchio, who told me that he was rotating some staff, moving some of my people out of Homicide to plug openings in other departments. Tracchio wasn't asking for my input, just informing me.

I hung my jacket behind the door, still seeing the chief in my mind, ticking off the reasons on his chubby fingers: *Budget cuts. Too much overtime. Gotta backfill here and there. It's just temporary, Boxer.*

It was infuriating, crippling, bureaucratic bs.

And now I had a pounding headache behind my right eye.

'Tell me something good,' I said to Jacobi as he walked into my office, parked his large butt on my credenza. Conklin followed him in, moving with the grace of a lynx, crossing his arms as he leaned against my doorway. Hard not to stare.

'Keep your expectations low,' Jacobi growled.

'Okay, Warren. They're subterranean. Give it to me.'

'We sent a text message over the NCIC system to all regional law enforcement agencies with everything we had on Caddy Girl—' Jacobi interrupted himself with a bout of coughing, a lingering symptom of the still-healing gunshot wound he'd taken to his right lung.

'Height, weight, approximate age, manner of dress, color of her hair, eyes, the works,' he continued at last.

'Checked all the possibles that came out of that,' said Conklin, optimism lighting his eyes.

'And?' I asked.

'We got a few approximate matches, but in the end they didn't check out. One piece of good news. The lab found a print on one of her shoes.'

I perked up.

'It's a partial,' Jacobi said, 'but it's something. If we ever get anything or anyone to match it to. That's the problem so far. No links.'

'So, what's your next step?'

'Lou, I was thinking that's a trendy haircut on Caddy Girl,' Conklin said. 'The cut and the color probably cost around three hundred dollars.'

I nodded, said, 'Sounds about right.' How did he know about three-hundred-dollar haircuts?

'We're going to canvass the fancy beauty salons. Someone might recognize her. Is that okay with you?'

'Let me see the picture,' I said, sticking out my hand.

Conklin handed me the dead woman's photo. I stared at her angelic face, her tousled blond hair lying soft against the stainless-steel slab. A sheet was pulled up to her clavicle.

My God. Who was she? And why hadn't anyone reported her missing? And why, four days after the girl's death, were we absolutely clueless?

The two inspectors left my glass-walled cube, and I called out to Brenda, who settled into the side chair and flapped a notepad open on her lap.

I began to dictate a memo-to-staff about my meeting with Tracchio, but found it hard to focus.

I wanted to *do* something today, something that *mattered*. I wanted to be out on the street with Conklin and Jacobi, showing Caddy Girl's picture around 'fancy beauty salons' and prospecting good neighborhoods for clues.

I wanted to wear out my shoes on this case.

I wanted to work in a way that made me feel as if I was doing my job instead of dictating useless, worthless memos.

Chapter Twenty-Four

At about 7:30 that Tuesday evening, Claire called, saying, 'Lindsay, come on down. I have something to show you.'

I tossed the *Chronicle* with Cindy's front-page story about the Municipal trial into the file basket. Then I locked up for the night and jogged downstairs to the morgue, hoping for a breakthrough.

Hoping for something!

One of Claire's assistants, a smart cookie named Everlina Ferguson, was closing a drawer on a gunshot victim when I got there. *Ug-ly.*

Claire was getting cleaned up. 'Give me half a minute,' she said.

'Take the full minute,' I replied.

I poked around the place until I found Caddy Girl's photos

tacked to the wall. God, this case was bugging the hell out of me.

'What did you make of that perfume she was wearing?' I called out to Claire.

'Funny thing about that. It was only evident on her genitalia,' Claire called back. She turned off the faucets, dried her hands, then extracted two bottles of Perrier from the little fridge under her desk.

She opened them and handed one to me.

'Lots of girls these days like to perfume their gardens,' she went on. 'So normally I wouldn't even mention it in my report. But this girl, she didn't dab it anywhere else. Not on her cleavage or wrists or behind the ears.'

We clinked bottles, each took a long drink.

'Struck me as unusual, so I sent a swab of the perfume to the lab. They kicked it back,' Claire said a moment later. 'They can't ID it. Don't have the right equipment. Don't have the time.'

'No time to solve the crime,' I groused.

'It's always a three-legged sack race around here,' Claire said, pushing papers about on her desk. 'But I got back the labs on the sexual assault kit. Hang on. It's right here.'

Eyes glinting, she seized on a brown envelope, pulled out the sheet of paper, and pinned it to her desk with a forefinger, saying, 'The stain on her skirt was, in fact, semen, and it matched one of the two semen samples that showed up inside Caddy Girl.'

I followed Claire's finger down the results of the toxicology screen. She stabbed the letters ETOH with her index finger. 'This is what I wanted to show you. Her blood was positive for alcohol. Point one three.'

'So she was wasted,' I said.

'Uh-huh, but that's not all. Look here. She was also positive for benzodiazepine. It's unusual to have booze and Valium in your system, so I had tox run her bloods again, this time looking for zebras. They narrowed it down to Rohypnol.'

'Aw, no. The date-rape drug.'

'Yeah. She didn't know where she was, who she was, what was happening, even if it *was* happening.'

The ugly pieces were there, but I still couldn't make sense of the whole picture. Caddy Girl had been doped up, assaulted and murdered with mind-boggling care and precision.

Claire turned to the wall of photos. 'It's no wonder she didn't have vaginal bruising and defensive wounds, Lindsay. Caddy Girl couldn't fight back even if she wanted to. Poor child never had a chance.'

Chapter Twenty-Five

I drove my Explorer home in the dark, feeling *female*, not female *cop*. I had to see the world through Caddy Girl's eyes if I were to understand what had happened to her. But it was horrific to imagine being that vulnerable to the will of violent men. Two of them, two animals.

I grabbed my Nextel out of its clip on my belt and called Jacobi before more time passed. He answered on the first ring and I filled him in on what Claire had told me.

'So I'm guessing she found herself in a room with a couple of guys who had sex on their minds,' I said, braking for a light at the next street corner. 'They got pushy – and Caddy Girl resists, rebuffs them. So, one of the guys puts roofies into her Chardonnay.'

'Yeah,' Jacobi agreed. 'Now she's so stoned she can't move. Maybe she even blacks out. They take her clothes off, spray her with perfume, take turns having sex on her.'

'Maybe they're afraid she might remember the assault,' I said, my thoughts neatly in sync with those of my former partner. 'They're not totally stupid. Maybe they're very smart, actually. They want to kill her without leaving a lot of evidence. One guy burks her; the other makes sure she's dead by suffocating her with a plastic bag. A nice clean kill.'

'Yup, sounds right, Boxer. Maybe after she's dead, they reload and do her again,' Jacobi said. 'Figure a little necrophilia never hurt anyone. Then what? They dress her in five thousand bucks' worth of clothes and take her for a ride? Drop her off in Guttman's Seville?'

'That's the craziest part of it all,' I said. 'I don't get it about the clothes. The clothes thing throws everything off for me.'

'Claire didn't have the results on the DNA?'

'Not yet. You know, if Caddy Girl was the mayor's wife, we'd know something by now. But since nobody's even reported her missing . . .'

'Good-looking girl like that,' said Jacobi. I could hear a tinge of sadness in his voice. Some small revelation of loneliness. 'Someone should be missing her.'

Chapter Twenty-Six

I opened the front door to my apartment and exchanged sloppy hellos with Martha.

'Hey, Boo. Howzmygirl?'

I hugged her squirming body as she yapped her enthusiastic approval of my return from the wars.

As exhausted as I was, jogging with my girl was the greatest encouragement I had to keep fit.

I leashed her, and soon after, we were running across Missouri in the dark, around the rec center, down and back up the hill, endorphins lifting my mood and giving me a slightly more positive outlook on Caddy Girl's murder investigation.

The perp's DNA was cooking in the lab right at this moment.

Cops were canvassing with her picture in hand.

There was hope after all.

Someone had to be missing her by now and would make a call soon. Or a witness would step forward who'd seen her likeness in the *Chronicle* or on our website.

Once we had a name, we'd have a chance to solve her murder. We could all stop thinking of her as Caddy Girl.

A half hour later I was back at home. I slugged down a cold beer and ate a Swiss and Hellmann's on sourdough in front of the TV while catching up on the news of the world on CNN, CNBC, and FOX. Then I stripped down, turned on the shower, and waggled my hand in the water to test the temperature.

That's when the phone rang. *Figures. Now what – another murder? Better yet, a break in the case?*

The caller ID flashed his name.

'Hey,' I said, feigning nonchalance, heart going *boom, da-boom, da-boom.*

'God, you're gorgeous.'

'I don't have a picture phone, Joe.'

'I know what you look like, Lindsay.'

I laughed.

'That's a very naked laugh,' said my fella. He wasn't clair-voyant. He could hear the shower running. I turned off the water, put my robe on.

'You're amazingly perceptive,' I said. By now, I was picturing him naked, too.

'Listen, naked lady, rumor has it I'm going to be in your town this weekend. The whole weekend.'

'Good, 'cause I miss you,' I said, my voice dropping down a few notches, getting a little throaty.'We've got a lot of catching up to do.'

We flirted until my skin was damp and my breath was short. When we hung up a few minutes later, we had a plan for our upcoming good time.

I dropped my robe, stepped into the shower, and, as the hot spray beat on my skin, I began to belt out a pretty good rendition of 'My Guy,' loving the vibrato in my voice coming back at me in my little tiled sound studio.

Whooo! Let's hear it for Lindsay Boxer, pop star.

For the first time in a whole lot of days, I put the job out of my mind.

I felt great, at least for the moment.

I felt gorgeous.

And very soon, I was going to be with my love.

Chapter Twenty-Seven

C hief Tracchio was obviously surprised to see me when I knocked on the partially opened door to his office. There was a lot of dark wood paneling in there and a big photo mural of the Golden Gate Bridge that took up the whole wall facing his desk.

'Boxer,' the chief said now. Then he actually smiled. 'Come in.'

I'd thought about my speech all night, rehearsed it in my mind all morning, had the first line all teed up and ready to go.

'Chief, I have a problem.'

'Drag up a chair, Boxer. Let's hear it.'

I did as he said, but as I looked into his face, I forgot the careful phrasing, the curlicues and fripperies, and blurted out the whole deal at once.

'I don't like being a boss, boss. I want to go back to investigation full time.'

His smile was gone, long gone. 'What are you saying, Lieutenant? I don't get you.'

'I wake up in the morning feeling wrong, Chief. I don't like supervising a lot of other people. I don't like being Lieutenant Inside,' I explained. 'I like being on the street, and you know that's where my abilities lie, Tony. You know I'm right.'

For a second or two I wasn't sure Tracchio had even heard me, his face was that stony. Was he thinking of all the killers I'd helped put away? I sure hoped so. Then he slapped the desk with such force, I inadvertently pushed my chair back a couple of inches.

He exploded verbally, spit actually flying in my direction.

'I don't know what you've been smoking, Boxer, but you've got the job. You – *no! Don't say anything!* You know how many men got bumped when you were promoted? You know how many guys in the squad still resent you? You were promoted because you're a leader, Boxer. You're squad commander. Do your job. End of conversation.'

'Chief—'

'What? Make it quick. I'm busy.'

'I'm better on the ground. I close cases, and my record bears that out. I'm spinning my wheels in my office, and those guys who want to be Lieutenant – well, you should promote one of *them*, Chief. You need someone in my job who wants it.'

'Okay, now that you've started this, I've gotta couple of other things to say to you,' Tracchio said.

He opened a desk drawer, pulled out a cigar, chopped off the tip of it with a pocket guillotine gizmo, and puffed blue smoke into the air as he lit his stogie.

I waited breathlessly.

'You've got room to grow in this job, Boxer. When it comes to crime solution, the SFPD is dead last across the board. *In the whole country!* You need to learn to supervise better. Help other cops with your experience. You need to put out a positive image of the SFPD. Be a beacon of good. You gotta help us recruit and train. You're *nowhere* when it comes to that stuff, Boxer, and – *I'm not finished!*

'Not long ago you got shot and almost died. We almost lost you for good. You weren't even on duty that night, and you showed no self-control at all. Jacobi invites you on a stakeout, you say, "Let me at it."'

Tracchio stood, whirled around, put his hands on the back of his chair. His reddened face radiated exasperation. 'You know, I don't even understand what the hell you're beefing about. You've got it easy. How would you like *my* job?'

I stared at him dully as he began ticking off departments on his sausage fingers: 'I've got Homicide, Robbery, Narcotics, Anticrime, and Special Victims. I got the mayor and I got the

JAMES PATTERSON & MAXINE PAETRO

governor, and if you think that's like getting the red-carpet treatment on Oscar night . . .'

'I think you're making my point for me, Chief.'

'*Look*, why don't you do yourself and everyone else a big favor and suck it up, Lieutenant. Request denied. Now we're done.'

I felt like a little kid as I picked myself up and left Tracchio's office. I was humiliated and felt mad enough to quit – but I was too smart to do so. Everything the man said was right. But I was right, too.

Recruit and train?

Learn to supervise?

None of that had anything to do with why I'd become a cop.

I wanted to be back on the streets of San Francisco.

Chapter Twenty-Eight

Cindy Thomas sat on the back bench of courtroom 4A of the Civic Center Courthouse, squeezed between a reporter from the *Modesto Bee* and a stringer for the *LA Times*. She felt keyed-up, focused, and very, very possessive. This was her town, her story.

Her laptop was warm on her knees, and she tapped at the keyboard, making notes as Maureen O'Mara's first witness was sworn in.

'Good morning, Mr Friedlander,' O'Mara said. The lawyer's long auburn hair glowed against the flat blue wool of her suit. She wore a white blouse with a plain collar and a simple gold watch on the wrist of her ring-free left hand.

'I hope you don't mind my asking, but how old are you?' O'Mara asked her witness.

'I'm forty-four.'

Cindy was surprised. With his creased face and graying hair, she would have put Stephen Friedlander's age at closer to sixty.

'Can you tell the Court about the night of July twenty-fifth?' O'Mara asked.

'Yes,' Friedlander said. He cleared his throat. 'My son, Josh, had a grand mal seizure.'

'And how old was Josh?'

'He was seventeen. He would have been eighteen this month.'

'And when you got to the hospital, did you see your son?'

'Yes. He was still in the emergency room. Doctor Dennis Garza brought me to see him.'

'Was Josh conscious?'

Friedlander shook his head. 'No.'

This prompted O'Mara to ask him to speak up for the court reporter.

'No,' he said, much louder this time. 'But Doctor Garza had examined him. He told me that Josh would be back at school in a day or two, that he'd be as good as new.'

'Did you see Josh after that visit to the emergency room?' O'Mara asked.

'Yes, I saw him the next day,' Friedlander said, a smile flitting briefly across his face. 'He and his girlfriend were joking with the fellow in the other bed, and I was struck by that because there was kind of a party atmosphere in the room. The other boy's name was David Lewis.'

O'Mara smiled, too, then assumed a more sober expression when she spoke again.

'And how was Josh when you got to see him the next morning?'

'They let me see my son's *body* the next morning,' Friedlander said, his voice breaking. He reached forward, clasping the rail of the witness box with his hands, the chair legs scraping the floor.

He turned his hopelessly sad and questioning eyes to the jury, and then to the judge. Tears sheeted down his furrowed cheeks.

'He was gone just like that. His body was cold to my touch. My good boy was dead.'

O'Mara put her hand on her witness's arm to steady him. It was a moving gesture and seemed quite genuine.

'Do you need to take a moment?' she asked Friedlander, handing him a box of tissues.

'I'm all right,' he said. He cleared his throat again, dabbed at his eyes. Then he sipped from the water glass.

'I'm fine.'

O'Mara nodded, then asked him, 'Were you given an explanation for Josh's sudden death?'

'They said that his blood sugar bottomed out, and I wanted

to know why. Doctor Garza said that he was *mystified*,' the witness said, stiffening his lips around the word, trying to control the quiver in his voice.

'I was mystified, too,' Friedlander continued. 'Josh had been stabilized the day before. He'd eaten a couple of meals. Went to the bathroom without help. Then, overnight, right there in the hospital, he went into a coma and died! It makes no sense.'

'Did the hospital do an autopsy on Josh?' O'Mara asked.

'I *demanded* it,' Friedlander said. 'The whole thing was fishy—'

'Objection, Your Honor,' Kramer bellowed from his seat. 'We all sympathize with the witness, but please instruct him to simply answer the questions.'

The judge nodded, then addressed the witness. 'Mr Friedlander, just tell us what happened, please.'

'I'm sorry, Your Honor.'

O'Mara smiled encouragingly at her witness. 'Mr Friedlander, were you ever given the results of the autopsy?'

'Eventually, I was.'

'And what were you told?' Maureen asked.

Friedlander exploded, his face turning the brightest red. 'They said that Josh's blood was loaded with *insulin*! I was told that it was injected into his IV bag sometime during the night. That Josh got that insulin by mistake. And that's what killed him. A *mistake* by the hospital.'

O'Mara stole a look at the stricken faces of the jurors before saying, 'I'm sorry to have to ask, Mr Friedlander, but how did you feel when you learned about that mistake?'

'How did I *feel*?' Friedlander asked. 'I felt like my heart had been cut out of my chest with a *spoon* . . .'

'I understand. Thank you, Mr Friedlander.'

'Josh was our only child . . . We never expected to be in the world without him . . . The pain never stops . . .'

'Thank you, Mr Friedlander. I'm sorry to have put you through this. You did just fine. Your witness,' O'Mara said, and motioned to Kramer.

The witness snatched several tissues from the box in front of him. He held them up to his face as hoarse sobs racked his body.

Chapter Twenty-Nine

Lawrence Kramer stood and slowly buttoned his jacket, giving the witness a moment to pull himself together, thinking that the man's son was in the ground, for God's sake. Now all he had to do was neutralize his awful testimony – without antagonizing the jury – and, if possible, turn Stephen Friedlander into a witness for the defense.

Kramer walked to the witness box and greeted Mr Friedlander in a kindly manner, almost as if he knew the man, as if he were a friend of the family.

'Mr Friedlander,' Kramer said, 'let me first express my condolences on the tragic loss of your son.'

'Thank you.'

'I want to clear up a few things, but I promise to keep this as short as I possibly can. Now, you mentioned that you met David Lewis, the young man who was sharing your son's room when you visited Josh on July twenty-sixth.'

'Yes. I met him the one time. He was a very nice boy.'

'Did you know that David has diabetes?'

'I think I knew that. Yes.'

'Mr Friedlander, do you know the number of the bed your son occupied in his hospital room?'

Friedlander had been leaning forward in his chair, but now he sat back.

'Number? I don't know what you mean.'

'Well, the hospital refers to the bed closest to the window as "bed one," and the bed closest to the door as "bed two." Do you remember which bed Josh occupied?'

'Okay. He would have been in bed one. He was by the window.'

'Do you know why hospital beds are numbered?' Kramer asked.

'I don't have any idea,' said the witness, his tone edgy, getting irritated.

'The beds are numbered because the nurses dispense medication according to the room and bed number,' Kramer explained. He went on. 'By the way, do you recall if you ordered a special television package for Josh?'

'No, he was only supposed to be there for the one day. What's your point?'

'My point,' Kramer said, shrugging his shoulders apologetically, 'my point is that David Lewis checked out of the hospital after lunch on the day you saw him there. Your son, Josh, expired in bed number two that night. Josh was in David's bed when he died, Mr Friedlander.'

'What are you saying?' Friedlander asked, his eyebrows flying up, his mouth twisting with anger. 'What the hell are you trying to tell me?'

'Let me say this in a different way,' Kramer said, showing the jurors with his body language and his phrasing, *I'm doing my job. But, I mean this man no harm.*

'Do you know why your son was found in bed number *two*?'

'No idea.'

'Well, it was because of the TV. Josh got out of his bed by the window, pulled his mobile IV pole over to bed number two so he could watch the movie channels – let's see . . .' Kramer referred to his notes.

'He ordered a movie on *Showtime*.'

'I don't know anything about that.'

'I am aware of that,' Kramer said, his voice compassionate, even fatherly, thinking, *knowing*, that the witness wasn't getting it. He still didn't have a clue what had happened to his son and why he had died.

'Mr Friedlander, you have to understand. Josh *did* get David

Lewis's insulin by mistake. The paperwork on David Lewis's discharge hadn't yet caught up with the nurse's orders. That can happen in a hospital the size of Municipal. But let me ask you this. Wouldn't any fair-minded person understand how the nurse didn't catch this error?'

Kramer delivered the final blow in his gentlest voice: 'David and Josh were about the same age. The nurse brought insulin for the sleeping patient in bed number two and injected it into the IV bag beside that bed. If Josh had stayed in his own bed . . .'

Kramer turned as an anguished howl rose from the gallery. A middle-aged woman stood, dark clothing hanging from her frail body, wailing, 'Nooo!' as she clutched at her face.

Friedlander reached out a hand to her from the witness box: 'Eleanor! Eleanor, don't listen to this. He's lying! It wasn't Joshie's fault . . .'

Lawrence Kramer ignored the roar of voices in the court-room, the repeated crack of the gavel. He dipped his head respectfully.

'We're very sorry, Mr Friedlander,' he said. 'We're very sorry for your loss.'

Chapter Thirty

It was a little after 8:00 p.m. as I grunted my way up Potrero Hill on the return leg of my nightly run.

I obsessed as I ran, the long blur of the investigation repeating itself in my mind – seeing the cops in my office all day, running their cases, me advising, giving orders, treading paper, going after warrants, settling disputes, hating the stress of the whole sorry business.

On most nights, the rhythmic slapping of my rubber soles on pavement had a calming effect, but it wasn't happening tonight.

And for this I blamed Chief Tracchio.

His lecture, or whatever it was, had gotten to me.

As I pushed forward into a cold wall of wind, I second-guessed every decision I'd made so far on the Caddy Girl case, worried that I was letting everyone down, including myself.

Martha was oblivious to my problems. She loped blithely ahead of me, often doubling back to bark at my feet, which is what border collies are born to do.

I panted, 'Cut it out, Boo,' but I couldn't stop my dog from dogging me. I was a lagging lamb, and she was my shepherd.

Twenty minutes later, I was home sweet home, showered, and smelling of chamomile shampoo.

I stepped into my favorite blue flannel pj's, put the Reverend Al Green on the CD player, and cracked open a beer. I took a long, frosty slug from the amber bottle of Anchor Steam. Yum.

My favorite one-pot pasta meal was simmering on the stove, and I was starting to feel seminormal for the first time that day when the doorbell rang.

Damn.

I shouted, 'Whoo-izit?' into the intercom, and a friendly voice shouted back.

'Lindseeee, it's meeeeeee. May I please come up?'

I buzzed Yuki in, and as she made the climb, I set the table for two and took out glasses for the beer.

A minute later, Yuki blew into my apartment huffing and blowing like a small storm.

'Ooh, I like that,' I said, examining her platinum-streaked forelock. It had been magenta a few days ago.

'That's two yes votes,' she said, throwing herself into an armchair. 'My mom said, "That hair make you look like *air hostess.*"'Yuki laughed. 'Hey, that's her one unrealized dream. So, what smells so good, Lindsay?'

'It's pot-au-feu, Boxer-style,' I said. 'Don't argue. I've made plenty for two.'

'Argue? You obviously don't know how carefully I timed this impromptu drop-in.'

I laughed; we clinked glass mugs and said, 'Cheers, dears,' in unison. And then I dished up the meal. I almost told Yuki what had been bothering me, but I couldn't find a trace of funk to whine about.

Over Edy's heavenly chocolate-chip ice-cream and brewed decaf, Yuki brought me up to date on her mother's condition.

'Her doctors were concerned because she's really young to get a TIA,' Yuki told me. 'But now she's passed a whole battery of tests, and they've moved her out of the ICU into a private room!'

'So when are you bringing her home?'

'Thursday morning, according to her personal savior, Doctor Pierce. Then I'm going to take her for a weeklong cruise on this monster ship, the *Pacific Princess*.

'I know, I know, it sounds corny,' Yuki said, hands in constant motion as she talked, 'but a floating hotel with a casino and a spa is just what the doctor ordered. And frankly, I need the time off, too.'

'Gee, I'm jealous,' I said, putting down my spoon and beaming into Yuki's face.

I meant every word.

I imagined myself on a ship at sea. A pile of good books, a comfy deck chair, and the gentle roll of the waves putting me to sleep at night. Plus Joe, of course.

No meetings. No unsolved homicides. No stress.

'Lucky you,' I said. 'And your lucky mom.'

Chapter Thirty-One

Yuki was driving home from Lindsay's, on Eighteenth Street just merging into I-280, when her cell phone's fluting melody sang out from the depths of her handbag, which was lying in the passenger-side footwell.

'Shoot. Wouldn't you know it.'

She set an angled course toward the right lane of the highway, and while holding the wheel with her left hand, she fished below eye level for her handbag.

A large bronze SUV honked at her as she threw magazines, her makeup kit, and her wallet out of the voluminous bag onto the floor.

'Sorry, sorry,' she muttered; then she palmed her phone on the third ring.

'Mom?' she said.

'Ms Castellano?'

Yuki didn't recognize the man's voice. She held the steering wheel with her elbow, buzzed up the windows, and turned off the radio so that she could hear a little better.

'Yes, this is Yuki.'

'It's Andrew Pierce.'

Yuki's mind scrambled as she fitted the two names together. It was *Doctor* Pierce. Her stomach lurched. Dr Pierce had never called her before. Why was he calling now?

'Doctor Pierce. What's wrong?'

His voice was tinny on the cell phone, overwhelmed by the roar of the traffic surrounding her. Yuki pressed the phone even tighter to her ear.

'Your mom's in some trouble, Yuki. I'm on my way to the hospital now.'

'What do you mean? What happened to her? You said that she was okay!' Yuki's eyes were fixed on the road ahead, but she saw nothing.

'She's had a stroke,' Dr Pierce told her.

'A *stroke*? I don't understand.'

'She's hanging in,' Dr Pierce went on. 'Can you meet me at the hospital?'

'Yes, yes, of course. I'm less than ten minutes away.'

'Good. Your mother's in the ICU on three. She's a fighter, which is good news.'

Yuki tossed the phone onto the seat beside her. Images and words cascaded inside her head.

A stroke?

Her mother had been eating ice-cream four hours ago. She'd been chatty. Funny. Perfectly fine!

Yuki forced her focus back to the road, realizing too late that she'd passed her exit. 'Damn it!'

Frantically, desperately, she sped down I-280 to where it ended at Berry Street, then gunned through a yellow light as she took a sharp turn onto Third.

With her heart pounding, Yuki pointed her little Acura north toward Market Street. This was a slower route, more cars, more lights, more pedestrians crossing against them, but it was her only alternative now.

Yuki reviewed her brief conversation with Dr Pierce. Had she heard him right? *She's hanging in,* he'd said.

Tears gathered in Yuki's eyes. Her mother was strong. Always. Her mother was a fighter. Even if Keiko was paralyzed . . . Nothing could keep her down.

Yuki wiped tears away with the back of her hand.

Visualizing every cross street and stoplight between her car and San Francisco Municipal Hospital, Yuki floored the accelerator.

Hang on, Mommy. I'm coming.

Chapter Thirty-Two

Fighting down panic, Yuki exited the elevator on Municipal Hospital's third floor; she followed the arrows around turns and through doorways until she found the ICU waiting area and the nurses' station beside it.

'I'm here to see Doctor Pierce,' she said tersely to the nurse at the desk.

'And you are?'

Yuki gave her name and stood there until Pierce came out into the waiting room. His weathered face was buckled with concern as he led Yuki to a pair of small straight-backed chairs.

'I can't tell you much right now,' the doctor finally spoke. 'Most likely, plaque flaked off an arterial wall and formed a block to her brain. She's on an anticoagulant—'

'Just tell me. What are her chances?'

'We'll know soon,' Pierce told her. 'I know this is hard—'

'I have to see her, Doctor Pierce. Please,' Yuki said. She reached out and clamped her hand around the doctor's wrist. *Please.*

'Thirty seconds. That's all I can do for you.'

Yuki followed the doctor through the swinging doors to the curtained-off slot where Keiko was lying. Wires and IV lines were running from her body to machines that had been assembled around her bedside like concerned friends.

'She's unconscious,' Dr Pierce said. 'But she's not in any pain.'

How could you possibly know that? Yuki wanted to yell at the man.

'Can she hear me?' she asked instead.

'I doubt it, Yuki, but it's possible.'

Yuki bent close to her mother's ear, spoke urgently. 'Mommy. It's me. I'm here. Hold on, Mommy. I love you.'

She heard Dr Pierce speaking to her, as if from miles away. 'Will you be waiting outside? Yuki? If I can't find you out there, I'll call your cell—'

'I'm not going anywhere. I'll be right outside. I'm not leaving under any circumstances.'

Yuki walked blindly out of the ICU, took up a position on a hard-backed chair.

She sat, staring straight ahead, nerves screaming, all of her frightened thoughts fused into one.

There was only one way this could turn out.

Her mom was going to make it.

Chapter Thirty-Three

Keiko Castellano had never been more frightened in her life. She felt the prick of a needle in the back of her hand.

Then she heard a rhythmic beeping sound – then the whoosh of machines.

Voices mumbled around her, but they were not her concern.

She had a flash of understanding. *She was in the hospital.* She'd had a serious incident of some kind – there was a pressure in her head, jamming her thoughts.

She remembered being a young girl at the Dontaku Festival, the street full of people in bright-colored costumes playing samisen and beating drums.

Thousands of paper lanterns floated on the water. Kites with tails of red ribbons danced overhead, and fireworks burst open the sky.

Keiko felt more pressure building inside her head, a

thunderstorm. Dark and cold and terribly threatening. The noise of the storm was a loud rumble, drowning out all other sound.

Was she passing now?

She did not want to go!

Keiko was inside this darkness that was not sleep, when suddenly Yuki's voice, close but distant, broke through the numbness.

Yuki was speaking to her. Yuki was there.

'Mommy. It's me. I'm here. Hold on, Mommy. I love you.'

She tried to call out, *'Itsumademo ai shiteru, Yuki.'* I love you forever, my daughter. But a large tube filled her mouth, and she could not speak.

And then Keiko drifted farther into the darkness. But she came back – she was fighting the storm.

Someone was inside her room. Someone here to help?

She heard footsteps around her, felt a pull at the IV line in the back of her hand. Her heartbeat sped up!

This was not a dream. Something was wrong. This person hadn't come to help.

An explosion of pain bloomed inside Keiko's head.

She couldn't see. She couldn't hear. Keiko screamed out in fear, but nothing came out of her mouth.

She understood what was happening now – she was being murdered; then her thoughts melted as she slipped into the void.

Keiko never felt the cold, metallic touch of a coin, first on one eyelid, then on the other.

She didn't hear the whispered words in her ear.

'These coins are your transfers, Keiko. Good night, princess.'

PART TWO

Murder, Murder Everywhere

Chapter Thirty-Four

Yuki woke up in the dark, her heart racing in leaps and bounds. Everything came back to her immediately, and with unusual clarity. Dr Pierce mouthing condolences in the hospital waiting room. Lindsay driving her home from the hospital, putting her to bed, sitting with Yuki until she finally slept.

Still, it made no sense.

Yesterday, her mother had been well! Today, she was gone.

Yuki grabbed the clock – almost 6:15 a.m. She called Municipal Hospital, punched her way through the Audix menu. At last she got a live operator who connected her to the ICU.

'You can come anytime, Ms Castellano,' the ICU nurse said. 'But your mother isn't here. She's in the basement.'

Yuki's rage was instant and blinding. She sat upright in her bed.

'What do you *mean* she's in the basement?'

'I'm sorry. What I meant to say is that we can't keep deceased patients in the ICU—'

'You put my mother in the hospital morgue? You insensitive—'

Yuki slammed down the receiver, then picked it up again and dialed for a cab. She couldn't trust herself to drive right now. She dressed quickly in jeans, a cardigan, running shoes, and leather jacket, and dashed outside her apartment building to Jones Street.

She struggled during the seven-block cab ride to assimilate the frankly unbelievable.

Her mother was gone. There was no more Keiko in her life.

Inside the hospital, Yuki wove her way through the shuffling people in the lobby, sprinted up the stairs to the ICU. Eyes darting, she looked from one to the other of the nurses at their station. They were talking to one another, acting as if she didn't exist. She lifted a chart and banged it sharply down on the counter. That got their attention.

'I'm Yuki Castellano,' she said to the nurse, the one with the bran-muffin crumbs clinging to the front of her uniform. 'My mother was here last night. I need to know what happened to her.'

'Your mother's name?'

'Keiko Castellano. Doctor Pierce was her doctor.'

'May I see your medical power of attorney?' the nurse asked next.

'I'm sorry?'

'You know about HIPPA? We can only tell you about your mother if you have medical power of attorney.'

Anger blazed through her. 'What are you saying? Are you mad?' What did her question have to do with patients' rights? Her mother had just died. She had a right to know why that had happened.

Yuki fought for control of her voice. 'Is Doctor Garza here, please?'

'I'll call him, but Doctor Garza can't tell you anything either, Miss Castellano. He's bound by HIPPA, like we all are.'

'I'll take my chances,' said Yuki. 'I want to see Doctor Garza!'

'Take it easy, okay,' said the nurse, training her huge, expressionless eyes on Yuki, letting her know that she thought she was out of her flipping mind. 'I'll see if he's still here.'

Chapter Thirty-Five

D r Garza was inside his stark, windowless office when Yuki knocked on the open door. She almost hesitated as he looked up at her, his face hard, showing his instant resentment at her intrusion. *What a dick,* Yuki thought.

But she pushed on, taking the chair across the desk from him, coming right to the point.

'I don't understand why my mother died,' she said. 'What happened to her?'

Garza plucked at his watchband.

'I'm sure Doctor Pierce told you, Ms Castellano. Your mother had a stroke,' he said. 'You understand? A thrombus, a blood clot, went to her brain, preventing blood flow. We put her on anticoagulants, but we couldn't save her.'

The doctor flattened his hands on the desk in front of him, a gesture that signified 'That's it. End of story.'

'I understand what a stroke is, Doctor Garza. What I don't understand is why she was chirpy at dinner and dead by midnight! She was inside *a hospital*! And you people didn't save her. Something about that stinks, Doctor.'

'Please take your tone down a few notches, if you don't mind,' Garza said. 'Bodies aren't machines, Ms Castellano. And doctors aren't miracle workers. Believe me, we did our best.'

Garza reached out and covered Yuki's hands with his. 'It's a shock, I know. I'm sorry,' he said.

It was an oddly intimate gesture that startled Yuki, and repelled her. She jerked her hands away instinctively, and the doctor retracted his.

'By the way,' said Garza, turning cold again, 'you'll need to speak to Nurse Nuñez on your way out. Your mother has to be transferred to a funeral home within twenty-four hours. I'm afraid we can't keep her here longer than that.'

Yuki stood up abruptly, knocking over the chair as she got to her feet.

'This isn't over. I'm a lawyer,' Yuki said. 'I'm going to look into this thoroughly. I'm going to find out what actually happened to my mom. Don't move her until *I say so,* understand? And by the way, Doctor Garza, you have the bedside manner of an eel.'

Yuki turned toward the door, stumbling over the upturned chair, her feet catching the legs, pitching her forward.

She stopped her fall by grabbing at the wall, snapping off the light switch with the flat of her hand as she clumsily regained her balance, plunging Dr Garza's office into blackness.

She didn't stop to say a word, or even to turn the light back on.

Feeling wobbly, Yuki negotiated the doorway, the hallway, the stairwell. And from there, she ran out to the street.

The air outside was heavy and damp, and suddenly she felt faint. Yuki sat down on the sidewalk under a large sycamore tree and stared at the people going to work as if it were a normal day.

She thought about the last time she'd seen her funny, feisty mom. Keiko had been eating ice-cream in bed, dispensing her crazy old-world advice with the conviction of a judge.

And she remembered most how much they'd always laughed.

Now, all of that was over.

And it just shouldn't be.

'Mom,' Yuki said now. 'It wasn't a dignified exit, I know, but I left that bastard sitting in the dark.'

She laughed to herself, thinking how much her mother would have enjoyed that scene.

Yuki-eh, why you never act like lady?

Then the pain swamped her.

Yuki drew her legs up and hugged them to her chest. With the solid old tree against her back, she put her head on her knees and wept for her mother. She sobbed like a child, one who would never be the same again.

Chapter Thirty-Six

I t was too early for this kind of crap, just 7:00 in the morning when I pulled up to the curb in front of an old Tudor-style house on Chestnut Street. A large evergreen tree sent fingers of dark shade across the grass between the house and the garage. A handful of cops already dotted the front lawn.

I slammed the door shut on my three-year-old Explorer, buttoned my khaki blazer against the morning chill, and marched across the well-shorn grass.

Jacobi and Conklin were at the front doorstep interviewing a seventy-something couple wearing matching awning-striped bathrobes and slippers. With their stricken faces and spiky bed heads, the septuagenarians looked as shocked as if they'd just put their fingers into wall sockets.

The elderly gentleman screeched at Jacobi, 'How do you know we don't need police protection? You can see into the future?'

Jacobi turned his weary expression on me, and then introduced Mr and Mrs Robert Cronin.

'Hello,' I said, shaking their hands. 'This is a terrible ordeal, I know. We'll make it as easy on you as we possibly can.'

'CSU is on the way,' Conklin told me. 'I'm okay here to do the interview, Lieutenant.' He was asking permission, but letting me know he was more than ready.

'It's all yours, Inspector. Do your job.'

I excused myself and Jacobi, then we walked together toward the dark-blue Jaguar XK-E convertible parked with its top down in the driveway. A beautiful car, which only made things worse.

I'd known what to expect since getting Jacobi's call twenty minutes ago. Still, when I looked into the victim's face, my heart lurched.

Like Caddy Girl, this woman was white, probably eighteen to twenty-one, petite. Her blond hair fell to her shoulders in loose waves. The girl had lovely, lustrous hair. She was 'looking' out onto Chestnut Street with wide-open blue eyes. As with Caddy Girl, she'd been posed to look as though she were still alive.

'God, Jacobi,' I said. 'Another one. Has to be. Jag Girl.'

'It was in the low fifties last night,' he told me. 'She's cold to the touch. And here we go again with the high-ticket clothes.'

'Head to toe.'

The victim was wearing a blue scarf-type blouse and a subtle blue-and-gray plaid tulip skirt. Her boots were Jimmy Choo, the kind that zip up the back. It was an outfit that would cost about three months of a cop's salary.

One little discrepancy though. The dead girl's jewelry struck me as wrong. Her tennis bracelet and matching ear studs flashed with the prismatic light of fake diamonds. What was that all about?

I turned at the wail of sirens, and watched both the EMT and CSU vans roll up, park next to the lineup of squad cars.

Conklin crossed the lawn toward the EMTs. I heard him tell the driver, 'She's gone, buddy. Sorry you wasted the trip.'

As the ambulance shifted into reverse, Charlie Clapper stepped out of the scene-mobile with his kit and camera in hand. He walked over to where we were standing, said, 'Another day, another body,' and asked us to kindly stand aside.

Jacobi and I stood a few yards from the Jaguar as Clapper shot his pictures.

I was thinking that I knew what he was going to find: a ligature mark at the young woman's throat, no handbag, no ID – and that the car would otherwise be clean as a whistle.

'Smell that?' said Jacobi.

It was faint at this distance, but I'd smelled it before: a musky fragrance that made me think of orchids.

'Caddy Girl's eau de toilette,' I said to my former partner. 'You know, the first one you think, maybe it's personal. But again? Another girl? Similar physically. Another immaculate crime scene? They're getting off on the killings, Jacobi. They're doing it for fun.'

We watched Clapper's team dust the car for prints in silence. I knew that Jacobi and I were cycling the same unspoken questions.

Who were these two girls? And who was the kinky tag team that had murdered them?

What had triggered the killings?

What was the meaning of the odd dress-up tableaux?

'The balls on these guys,' said Jacobi, as the ME's van arrived. 'Putting the vics on display like this. They're not just having fun, Boxer. They're giving somebody the finger.'

Chapter Thirty-Seven

I grabbed the phone in my office on the first ring when I saw that it was Claire.

'I've got some preliminary findings on Jag Girl,' she told me.

'Want me to come down?'

'I'll be up in a few minutes,' she said. 'I'm ready for a change of scene.'

The smell of oregano and pepperoni preceded Claire, who ambled into my office with a pizza box and a couple of cans of Diet Coke, saying, 'Lunch is served, baby girl. Nature's most perfect food. *Pizza.*'

I moved files from the side chair, cleared the stuff on my desk onto the window ledge, put out my finest paper napkins and the plastic cutlery.

'I took the stairs,' Claire said, dropping into the chair, beginning to carve up the pie.

'Well, give them back. We're gonna need them later.'

'As I was saying before your awful joke,' she said, laughing at me, 'I *climbed* the stairs. Three steep flights. That's about a hundred calories, wouldn't you think?'

'Uh-huh, I'd say. Probably cancels out a quarter of a slice of nature's perfect food.'

'Never mind that.' She chuckled, flopping a steaming slice onto my paper plate. 'I don't believe in making war with food. Food is not the enemy.'

'A truce on pizza,' I said.

'To the truce,' Claire said, touching her cola can to mine.

'The whole truce,' said I. 'And three kinds of cheese.'

I joined in with Claire's long, rolling laugh, one of my favorite sounds in the world. Whenever work got particularly grisly, the two of us got giddy. Sometimes, it even helped. We polished off one of Pronto Pizza's best in about ten minutes as Claire brought me up to date on our latest Jane Doe.

'Taking into account her exposure to the low temperature last night, I'm calling Jag Girl's time of death somewhere round midnight,' she said, lobbing her empty can into the trash basket.

'The clothes were gorgeous,' she said, 'but a bad fit. Too small on top, too big across the hips, but this time her shoes fit.'

'And she never walked in them, right?'

'Clean soles. And just like with Caddy Girl, that funky perfume was only on her labia.'

'When are you starting the post?'

'Soon's I get back downstairs.'

'Want some company?'

I phoned Tracchio's office and blew off the staff meeting. Was I rebelling against authority? *Yep.* Then I went out to the squad room and invited Jacobi. I filled him in as we jogged down the stairs to the morgue.

Chapter Thirty-Eight

I always found the stark reality of the morgue, Claire's place, a shock to the nervous system – the unforgiving white light on the dead, the sheets hiding that their insides were out. The empty faces. The harsh scent of antiseptics.

Somehow, the circumstances didn't completely dim Jag Girl's material beauty. If anything, she looked younger, and more vulnerable, than she had dressed up in designer clothes.

The purple bruise circling her neck and the dusting of bluish bruising on her upper arms seemed like an insult to her flawless skin. After several hours in the morgue, she was starting to have a bad hair day, too.

I watched as my friend slipped into her gear – cap, gown, plastic apron, and gloves. 'It looks like another soft kill,' she said. 'No knives, no guns.'

She pulled up her mask, lowered her face shield, spoke into the mike as she made a layer-wise dissection of the strap musculature of Jag Girl's neck.

Claire positioned her scalpel to make the deep, Y-shaped incision that would run from shoulder to shoulder, meeting at Jag Girl's breastbone and extending down to her pubis.

She peeled back a flap of skin with her forceps. Showed me and Jacobi the brownish stain in the shape of a thumbprint.

'This young lady was asphyxiated by two complete nutjob assailants,' Claire said. 'Just like with Caddy Girl, there's no petechial hemorrhaging. So someone held her down and burked her. Pressed her neck right here with his thumb. This boy is strong.

'Someone else applied a ligature. Sort of crinkly-like. Looks like a patterned impression, consistent with the rolled edge of a plastic bag. Probably put his paw over her nose and mouth to seal the deal.'

I couldn't help but stare at the victim and imagine the freaking outrageous homicide.

'It's making me think that this is some kind of porn fantasy come to life,' I said. 'No peep-show booth, no magazine or computer screen. What fun. Real girls without any barriers. The perps can drug them, rape them, dress them up, do whatever the hell they want.'

'There's no sign this young lady fought back,' said Claire.

'So until I get the tox screen, I'm gonna go out on a limb and say she was probably drugged, too.'

Jacobi seethed, 'Fucking cowards.'

'Keep the faith, you guys,' said Claire. 'I'll call in a favor at the lab. See if I can put a rush on the DNA.'

I stepped closer to the table and looked into the victim's lifeless face again. Finally, I reached over and closed her clouded blue eyes.

'We will get these bastards,' I told her.

Chapter Thirty-Nine

Claire saw Lindsay and Jacobi to the door, saying that she wished she had given them more to work with, hoping for all of them that this poor dead girl would have a name unrelated to luxury cars very soon.

She made her call to DNA and got the usual, 'Of course, Doctor Washburn, we'll get right on it,' an assurance that came with an unspoken disclaimer, namely, 'Do you understand how long this procedure takes? Do you know how many cases are ahead of yours?'

'I mean it,' she said to the lab supervisor. 'This is urgent, rush, high priority.'

'Yes, ma'am. I got it.'

Claire was sliding Jag Girl into a drawer, when her cell phone rang. Yuki's number flashed on the caller ID.

'Yuki! Darlin', how are you holding up?' she asked. 'Do you

want me to pick you up or can you drive over by yourself? Edmund's really looking forward to meeting you, and he's cooking mushroom risotto tonight.'

'Claire, I'm sorry. I just can't – I can't be with people right now.'

Claire gave it a respectful beat; then she said, 'Of course, honey. I understand.'

'But I have to ask a favor,' Yuki said, then sighed loudly.

'Whatever you need.'

'I want you to do an autopsy on my mom.'

Claire listened intently as Yuki described her meeting with Garza, and said that she was completely unsatisfied with his explanation for her mother's death.

Claire wanted to sigh out loud, too, but she held it in. She didn't want to show any disrespect to Yuki.

'You're sure you want me to do this, baby? Can you handle whatever I find?'

'I swear I can. I have to know if her death was avoidable. I *absolutely* have to know what happened to my mom.'

'I understand. I'll arrange to have her brought here in the morning.'

'You're the best,' Yuki said, her voice cracking from the pressure of tears.

'Don't you worry, honey. She's family. Just leave your mom to me.'

Chapter Forty

The following afternoon, Friday, Yuki was in her mother's kitchen, standing over the sink. She stuffed a bite of toast into her mouth, hardly chewing. Everything about this still seemed so unreal.

She'd been up the whole night, phoning her mother's friends, going through albums and scrapbooks, losing herself in memories. Now she wrenched herself back to the present, wondering when Claire would call and what Claire would say.

When the phone finally rang, Yuki lunged for it.

Claire asked, 'How are you doing, honey?'

'I'm okay,' Yuki said, but that was a lie. She felt light-headed, her guts twisting as she waited for Claire to tell her about the end of her mother's life. Finally, she couldn't stand it another second.

'Did you find out anything?'

'I did, honey. For one thing, Garza was right when he told you that your mom had an embolism around her brain stem. What he didn't tell you was, it had to have been more than three hours before someone noticed that she was in trouble.

'The doctors should have given her an MRI to assess the damage,' Claire continued. 'But instead, they loaded her up with streptokinase, an anticoagulant.'

'He said something about an anticoagulant.'

'Uh-huh. Well, streptokinase isn't the newest drug on the market, but it's okay if used properly. Which it *wasn't*. Your mom was already hemorrhaging. There was no place for all that blood to go, and that's why she died, Yuki. I'm so, so sorry. I can't tell you how sorry I am.'

Yuki felt the news like a gut-punch.

My God, Keiko had been bleeding into her brain for hours – and no one even noticed?

What the hell was going on in that hospital?

Why had her mother had the stroke at all?

'Yuki? Yuki? Are you still there?'

'I'm okay . . .'

Yuki finished up with Claire; then she dropped the phone into its cradle. She went into the bathroom and threw up in the toilet. She took off her clothes and got into her mother's pink-and-green shower stall, stood for a long time sobbing, pressing her head against the wall as the hot water streamed down her body. She decided what she needed to do next.

A half hour later, wearing one of her mother's outfits – black pants with a stretch waistband and a red velour top – Yuki drove to the 800 block of Bryant Street. She parked in front of a bail bondsman's office across from the Hall of Justice.

Yuki entered the gray granite building, stopping at the security desk to give her name. She was on a mission now. She'd made up her mind; there was no turning back.

She took the elevator to the third floor and the Southern Division of the SFPD.

Lindsay was waiting when she got there. She put her arm around Yuki's shoulders and walked her back to her small glass-enclosed office.

Yuki took the desk chair across from Lindsay. Her face felt stiff, and her throat was tight. Lindsay was peering at her with concern. What a good friend she was, Yuki thought. I shouldn't do this to her. But I have to.

'I want to file charges against Municipal,' Yuki said. 'Someone at that damn hospital murdered my mother.'

Chapter Forty-One

Colma, California, is called the City of the Dead; located five miles south of San Francisco, it's our city's graveyard. With more than a million people buried in its neatly manicured cemeteries, it's the only place in America where the dead outnumber the living, upwards of twelve to one.

My mom was here at Cypress Lawn Cemetery, and now Yuki's mom would be here, too.

That Saturday, about seventy of us were grouped under a tent at Keiko's graveside, a breeze riffling the white canvas panels, twisting the thin plume of smoke coming from the incense pot next to the portrait of Yuki's parents, Bruno and Keiko Castellano.

Yuki stood with her arm around a small Japanese man in a dusty black suit. This was Keiko's twin brother, Jack. He choked out a few words in halting, broken English: 'My sister was precious woman. Thank you for . . . bringing honor to my family.'

Yuki hugged her uncle. A smile crossed her tired face as she began to speak about her mother.

'My mom liked to say that when she came to San Francisco she picked out the important landmarks right away. The Golden Gate Bridge, Saks, I. Magnin, Gump's, and Nordstrom. Not necessarily in that order.'

Warm laughter rose up as Yuki brought images of Keiko to life.

'I used to go shopping with her after school and race around the clothing racks. She would say, "Yuki-eh, you must learn to be a lady."

'I don't think I ever quite learned to do that.' Yuki laughed. 'I liked my music loud, my skirts short – I know, Mommy, even this one is too short! She wanted me to marry a lawyer – instead I became one.

'My life isn't what she dreamed for me, but she always gave me her love, her support . . . her everything.

'We were a team, Mom and me. Best friends, always. As I stand here with my uncle, I cannot imagine my world without her. Mommy, I will love you and miss you forever.'

Yuki lowered her head, her lips trembling. Then she and her uncle turned so that they faced Keiko's coffin.

Pressing a bracelet of stone beads between her palms, Yuki

held her hands in front of her face. She and her Uncle Jack chanted a Japanese prayer that swelled as the voices of Keiko's friends and family joined in.

Then Yuki bowed to her mother's coffin.

I gripped Claire's hand with my right hand, Cindy's hand with my left, feeling my own grief well up in me as tears rolled down Yuki's face.

'This is just the saddest damn day,' Claire said.

Chapter Forty-Two

I found my mother's grave by walking east and south for ten minutes with a map in my hand, stepping around carved lions and angels, and ornate mausoleums, until I found the simple granite stone that I carried around like a weight in my heart.

The carved letters had darkened with almost fifteen years' growth of lichen, but the legend was clear and indelible. *Helen Boxer, wife of Martin, devoted mother to Lindsay and Catherine. 1946–1989.*

A picture came to me of being a little kid, Mom making breakfast as she got ready for work, her yellow hair pinned up in a twist, pulling hot Pop-Tarts out of the toaster for me and Cat, burning her fingers and crying out, 'Oooh-oooh-ooooh,' to make us laugh.

On those days, workdays, I wouldn't see her again until dark.

I remembered how my little sister and I would come home from school to an empty house. Me, making the mac-and-cheese dinners. Waking up at night to our mom screaming at Dad to shut his trap and let the girls sleep.

And I remember what it was like after my father left us: my mother's beautiful, short-lived freedom from my father's iron fist over all of us. She cut her hair into a flingy bob. Took singing lessons with Marci Weinstein, who lived down the street. Had six or seven years of what she called 'breathing free' before runaway breast cancer knocked her down.

I had a dim memory of standing at this very spot when Mom was buried, not having a shred of the grace or eloquence Yuki had shown today. I was mute, torn up with anger, bent on keeping my face turned so that I didn't have to look at my father.

Now, sitting cross-legged beside my mother's grave, I stared out at the autumn-brown hills of South San Francisco as an Alaska Air jet liner crossed overhead. I wished that my mother could see that Cat and I were both okay, that Cat was strong, that her little girls were smart and fine, and that my sister and I were friends again.

I wished I could tell her that being a cop had given my life meaning. I hadn't always been sure of myself, but I think I had become the woman she would have wanted me to be.

I ran my hand over the curve of her headstone and said something that I didn't often admit to myself.

'I really miss you, Mom. I wish that you were here. I wish I'd been sweeter to you when you were alive.'

Chapter Forty-Three

My thoughts flitted between love and death as I drove back from Colma to San Francisco. Images kept coming to me of the people I'd loved deeply who had died.

Lights glinted on the Bay Bridge as I entered the city and threaded my way through the narrow, rising streets of Potrero Hill.

I parked the Explorer a few doors down from my front door, thinking ahead to my small chores and pleasures, ready to settle in for the night.

I had my keys in hand, about to open the front door, when I heard Martha's distinctive bark coming from outside the house!

It couldn't be, because it made no sense.

Was I crazy? Or had Martha somehow slipped out the door when I left this morning for the funeral?

I whipped my head around, listening intently, frantically sweeping the street with my eyes.

Then I saw my doggy leaning out of the passenger-side window of a black sedan that had pulled up to the curb and was parked behind my car.

I was overwhelmed with gratitude. A good Samaritan had found her and brought her home.

I peered in through the car's open window to thank the driver for bringing my girl back – and my heart almost stopped.

How could I have forgotten?

It was Joe.

Chapter Forty-Four

Joe's arms were full of grocery bags as he got out of the car, but I grabbed and hugged and kissed him anyway as Martha leaped at my legs.

'When did you get here?' I asked.

'At ten a.m. As planned.'

'Oh, no.'

'I had a nice day. Watched some football. Took a nap with Martha. Went shopping with her.'

'Oh, God, Joe.'

'You forgot that I was coming, didn't you?'

'Oh, man. I'm so sorry. I really blew it.'

'That's not good enough, sister. Not by half. Not even close.'

'I can explain.'

'Make it good,' he said, 'and don't even think of lawyering up.'

I laughed. Put my arm around his waist as we all clambered up the stairs.

'I'll make it up to you.'

'You bet you will,' he growled, then hugged me tight.

Inside the kitchen, Joe put the groceries on the counter, the ice cream into the freezer. Then he sat on a stool at the counter, crossed his arms, and gave me a look that said 'I'm waiting.'

'Yuki's mother,' I said. 'We buried her today. Out in Colma.'

'Aw. Jeez, Lindsay. I'm sorry.'

'Joe, it was so sudden. Yuki and her mom were going to go on a cruise together next week!'

Joe opened his arms to me, and I leaned into him. Then I talked for ten minutes straight about how close Yuki had been to her mom, how the hospital might have screwed up by giving Keiko the wrong meds.

My voice tightened in my throat as I told him about my own mom, about visiting her grave that afternoon.

'It's a rotten shame that I messed up, Joe. I wish you'd been with me today. I've really missed you.'

'How much?' he asked, the glint in his eyes showing me that I was out of the doghouse.

I stretched out my arms, making the universal symbol for 'this much.' Joe pulled me closer, giving me a full-body hug and a five-star kiss.

We clung together for a long moment, me with a hand in

Joe's thick hair, holding his cheek tightly against mine, feeling his strong arms wrapped around me. This was good, so good.

He walked me backward to the bedroom, his hands cupping my buttocks. He was hard against me and holding me so that there was no space between us.

He lowered me onto the bed, lay down next to me and moved my hair off my face.

So handsome, my Joe.

'I missed you more,' he said.

'No way.' I took his hand and put it over my heart. 'Feel that?'

'You know that I love you, Lindsay.'

'I love you, too.'

Joe unzipped my skirt, kissed me, undid the buttons of my blouse, unclipped the barrette from my hair, slowly tugged off my clothes, until I was bare and flushed and, well, panting.

I hugged pillows to my chest as Joe tossed my clothes and his onto the lap of the chair. Neither one of us was talking now.

When I couldn't stand to wait another minute, he flipped up the covers, took away my pillows, and got into bed beside me, his naked body hot against mine.

I hooked my arms around his neck, pressed my toes against the tops of his feet, fitted my mouth to his, dissolved into the smell and feel and taste of Joe.

He opened me with his hands and his mouth, and then he moved into me.

Oh my God.

It had been a long time since nothing mattered but this.

Chapter Forty-Five

Joe and I were leaning into the wind at the bow as the ferry chugged across the Bay on the return trip from Sausalito to San Francisco. Joe looked pensive, and I wondered why that was.

I reviewed our lazy roll out of bed at around 11:00 this morning, the brilliant blue sky as we held hands on the top deck of the outbound ferry. We'd had a cozy late lunch at Poggio, an outstanding restaurant overlooking the water.

It was as if we'd been transported to the coast of Italy, dining on pasta at the edge of the blue Mediterranean Sea. Yep, it was that good.

I squeezed Joe's arm.

It had been a spectacular six months for the two of us. We'd bridged the geographical distance between us with phone calls and e-mails. Then, once or twice a month, we'd have a magical weekend like this one.

And then it would be over, which seemed so cruel and wrong.

In a half hour, I'd be in my apartment, and Joe would be heading to Washington on an air force jet.

'Where are you, Joe? You look like you're very far away. *Already.*'

He put an arm around me, pulled me to him. I savored these last moments, the gulls calling and swooping alongside the ferry, the spray of water on my face, Joe's arms tight around me, the feel of his sweater against my cheek.

'I can't keep doing this,' he said. 'Making love eleven times in twenty-four hours. I'm forty-five, for Christ's sake.'

I threw back my head and laughed. 'Aerobics are always a good thing.'

'You think it's funny? You do, don't you? My manhood's at stake here.'

I hugged him hard, reached up and kissed his neck, then kissed it again.

'Don't start up with me, blondie. I'm out of steam.'

'Seriously, Joe. Is everything okay?'

'Seriously? There's a lot on my mind. I just haven't known when or how to get into it.'

'I guess you'd better start talking,' I said.

Joe turned his blue eyes on me as the ferry eased closer to the dock.

'I think we need to spend more time together, Linds. This weekend stuff is unbelievable but—'

'I know. The drama gets in the way of reality.'

He paused before saying, 'Would you ever move to DC?'

I know I must have looked shocked. I'd always figured that sometime we would discuss where our relationship was headed, but I hadn't expected it today.

How could I live in DC?

I saw my startled look register on his face.

'Okay, hang on. There's another way to look at this,' he said.

Joe began to tell me some of what I already knew: that the Port of Los Angeles is the entry point for all of the cargo containers coming by ship from Hong Kong, the largest container port in the world.

Then he told me the Homeland Security viewpoint.

'There's an honest-to-God fear that terrorists could smuggle a nuke – say from North Korea – by way of a container coming from Hong Kong into LA,' Joe said. 'And the chance that we'd detect such a device, at present, is practically nil.

'We don't yet have effective systems in place. I see an opportunity to help secure the port. I think I could do important work out here.'

The ferry engines ground into reverse with a roar, and the bulky wooden ship coasted into dock. Suddenly we were in the center of a shoving mob, moving us down the gangway.

Talking was impossible as our handhold was broken apart and strangers seeped between us.

Joe's Town Car was waiting beyond the docks, gleaming and black. He held open the door for me and asked the driver to take us to the lot where I'd parked my car.

'I know it's a lot to think about,' he said.

'Joe, I *want* to talk more about this. I hate that you're leaving. I really hate it, especially this time.'

'Me too, Linds. We'll find a way.'

The Town Car stopped in the parking lot, and we both got out. I leaned against the sun-heated flank of my old Explorer.

I felt tears coming into my eyes as we embraced, exchanged 'I love yous' and wishes for a safe trip home.

We hugged and kissed again.

It had been another beautiful day added to our scrapbook of special memories. I could still feel the pressure of his lips on mine, the sting of salt against my whisker-burned cheeks.

I could still feel him, as if he were right there beside me.

But Joe was gone.

PART THREE

In Search of Car Girls

Chapter Forty-Six

On Monday I came back to the squad room after lunch with Cindy, feeling several pairs of eyes tracking me as I made my way to my office. A week had passed since Caddy Girl's picture had been posted in the *Chronicle*, and now Jag Girl's photo would be running beside it.

It was infuriating that we were still hoping for tips from the public.

Where were the leads?

Why was there so little evidence?

What the hell were we overlooking? How were we messing up?

I waved Jacobi and Conklin into my glass cube and closed the door, hung my jacket up. Conklin sprawled in the chair, his long legs spanning the length of my desk, while Jacobi parked, as usual, on the edge of my credenza.

I told Jacobi and Conklin that I'd put the photo of Jag Girl out to the press and asked if they had anything new.

'My partner's got something for you, Boxer.' Jacobi isn't prone to smiling, but I thought I saw a spark of pride light up his stony eyes.

'Yeah, we've got sorta good news,' said Conklin as he sat up straight in the chair.

'Any kind of news is good news on this case.'

'We got the DNA back on Caddy Girl's rape kit.'

'Excellent. What do we know?'

'We got a cold hit, Lou,' Conklin said.

My rising hopes crashed. A cold hit is a little bit of not much to go on. In this case, there was a matching DNA profile in the database – but the donor's ID was unknown.

Conklin spread the computer printout on my desk, spun it so it faced me. Then he took me through it slowly, patiently, the way I took *my* bosses through detail they were too thick to get.

'This sample came from the sexual assault kit of a white female who was killed in LA two years ago,' Conklin said. 'She was in her early twenties – raped, strangled, and found in a field a few days after she was dumped there. No ID on the victim, and she was never identified. LAPD thinks she was a transient.'

'What was she wearing?' I asked him.

'No designer clothes. A polyester top pulled up to her neck.

It's no wonder we didn't get a hit before,' Conklin said. 'Completely different MO than the Car Girls. This victim wasn't dressed up or posed in a car, but for sure, the same guy who had sex with this victim two years ago, had sex with Caddy Girl.'

'Maybe the LA vic was our perp's first kill,' Jacobi added. 'And he's been polishing up his act ever since.'

'Or maybe he's got a partner now,' I said, trying on another theory. 'Maybe this new cat has a lot more imagination.'

Chapter Forty-Seven

L eo Harris was locking up the register in his Smoke and Joke shop when the bell jingled over the front door.

'I'm done for the night,' the black man said without turning around. 'Register's closed. Come back in the morning. Thank you.'

He heard footsteps shuffling toward the counter anyway, baggy pants whiffing around the customer's ankles.

'I said, we're *closed*.'

'I need some smokes,' the voice said, soft and slurry, a young man's voice asking, 'You got Camels?'

'Try the Searchlight Market,' Mr Harris said. 'You can see it from the door. Right on the corner of Hyde.'

The sixty-six-year-old man closed the cash drawer, turned his blank eyes toward the customer, seeing just his outline, waiting for the kid to leave his shop.

'Put the money on the counter, old man,' the voice said. 'Back up to the wall. Keep your hands up and maybe I won't hurt you.'

Harris was aware of every sound now – the deep breathing of the boy, the buzzing of the neon sign in the window, the dull *clang* of the trolley at the intersection of Union and Hyde.

He said, 'Okay, okay. We don't have a problem. Let me open the register. I got a hundred bucks under the drawer. Hell, take a carton of cigarettes and just get—'

'Get your hand away from that button!' the boy yelled.

'I'm just opening the register.'

Harris pressed the silent alarm under the counter and at the same time heard the jangle of Midnight's collar as she ran downstairs from his apartment, starting her nightly patrol of the store.

Harris thought, *Oh, no,* even as he heard the police dog's growl. Then the click of the gun, the kid's scared shout: 'Fucking get away from me, dog.'

There was an explosion, a gunshot; then Leo Harris called out, 'Midnight!' Then came another deafening explosion that seemed to rock the small room.

Harris clutched at his chest. He fell, grabbing at the toiletries and cigarette cartons, hearing the sound of the punk busting out the door, the door slamming, the tinkling bell . . .

Then he was thinking about his companion and friend of

twelve years, hearing poor Midnight's yelping and whining over the sounds of bottles falling, broken glass scattering on the floor.

'Someone help us, please! We've been shot.'

Chapter Forty-Eight

Leo Harris awoke lying on his side, face turned to the wall. He felt Midnight's muzzle against the back of his neck, her hot breath on his cheek. Then he heard a man's voice saying, 'You okay, Mr Harris? It's Larry. Officer Petroff. Can you hear me?'

'My dog. I think he shot Midnight.'

'Yes, sir, she's right here; looks like she took a shot to her hip. Dragged herself over to you. *Easy girl,* I'm not going to hurt you. Tell her it's okay, Mr Harris.'

'Be still. Thatsa girl.'

'I've got EMS coming for you, Mr Harris, and my partner and I, we're driving your dog to the animal hospital. She'll be fine, good as new.'

Leo Harris went out again. When he came to, he felt the bumps as the paramedics jostled him into the ambulance, heard someone call it in: 'Emergency room. Paramedic Colomello. We've got a male, approximately sixty-five years old, with a GSW to the right thorax. Blood pressure's one forty over one hundred. Pulse, one fifty. We've got decreased breath sounds on his right side. Heart sounds are good. No other obvious injuries. We're about to transport him. We've got normal saline running wide open.'

'Imagine. The little prick shooting a blind man,' Officer Larry Petroff said to his partner.

'*Legally blind,*' Leo Harris called out from inside the ambulance. 'Legally blind is not totally in the dark.'

'I stand corrected, Mr Harris. Now don't worry about anything. They've got good docs on board at Municipal. Traffic or not, you'll be there in three minutes. Midnight's going to be fine, too. You're both very lucky.'

'Yeah, today's my lucky day,' said Leo Harris.

Chapter Forty-Nine

N urse Noddie Wilkins was fuming. If she got into her car this minute, she'd still be a half hour late for her date with Rudolpho. This job sucked. It was sucking up her whole life! Plus, the damn hospital was cutting back on her benefits every chance it got. The cheap bastards.

She bumped open the door to room 228 with her hip, careful not to spill the tray. The only light in the room came from the TV. 'Hey, Mr Man,' she called out over the cheers of 49ers fans in an uproar about something stupid and ridiculous.

The nurse angled the tray onto the swinging arm of the bedside table, staying out of her patient's reach. Mr Harris was sixty-six and recovering from his gunshot wound; still, she had to move quickly or, legally blind or not, he'd grab her with his good arm. He was nice enough, though, a sweet older guy who sure loved his dog, Midnight.

'I got your dinner, Mr Harris, and your *two* ice creams, soon's I take your blood pressure.'

The nurse turned away from her patient, rolled the blood-pressure machine from the corner toward the bed, expecting to hear his 'Sweetheart, fluff my pillow. Thatsa girl.'

Noddie glanced over to the bed and her stomach dropped the equivalent of half a dozen stories.

Something was wrong.

'Mr Harris! Mr Harris!'

She shook the patient's arm, and his head lolled, coins slipping off his eyes onto the bedding. One of the coins dropped to the floor, rolling to the corner of the room, rattling before it fell flat to the linoleum.

Dear sweet Jesus, it had happened again!

Those horrible coins. On the eyes of Mr Harris this time.

Chapter Fifty

For the third morning in a row, Yuki pulled open the heavy glass-and-etched-steel door at the Civic Center Courthouse. This was now officially an obsession. The question – was she completely crazy?

She flashed her ID at the security guard and then took the elevator to courtroom 4A.

She was on leave from her job, and it was either come to court every day or go insane with heartbreak and fury. The *only* thing that got her out of bed in the morning was that she could watch Maureen O'Mara make her case against Municipal Hospital.

Court was already in session when Yuki entered the packed room. She saw one vacant place in the center of the gallery and wriggled past a dozen pairs of resistant knees before finally taking a seat. 'Sorry,' she whispered.

Yuki then sat riveted as men and women who'd lost family

members at Municipal took the stand, each witness telling in wrenching testimony how he or she lost a child, or a spouse, or a parent because of medical neglect and malpractice.

Yuki was still so raw it was all she could do to stop herself from weeping along with the witnesses. But she didn't cry. She forced herself to look at O'Mara's case the way a lawyer would.

It was exactly as Cindy had said at Susie's more than a week ago.

The patients had been admitted to the emergency room, they recovered in the ICU, then something happened and the patient died.

That was exactly what had happened to her mom.

If only she could go back in time and check her mother out of that hellhole.

If only she had done that.

Yuki heard Lawrence Kramer dismiss a tearful mother on the stand. 'I have no questions for this witness, thank you.'

As the poor woman choked back sobs, Yuki pressed a handkerchief hard against her own eyes with both hands.

She took deep, painful breaths as Maureen O'Mara called the next witness.

'Call Doctor Lee Chen.'

Chapter Fifty-One

Yuki leaned forward in her seat, scrutinizing the plaintiffs' witness, Dr Chen, who spoke with the controlled fervor of an intelligent person who didn't want to come off as sounding *too* smart. She knew all too well how that felt. Hell, it was practically her life's story.

Chen listed his credentials – an MD from Berkeley, followed by twelve years in the emergency room at San Francisco Municipal.

In response to O'Mara's questioning, the serious-looking doctor in black-framed glasses told the court about a night when he was the attending physician in the ER and a thirty-year-old woman named Jessica Falk was brought in by ambulance.

'Ms Falk had been swimming in her pool,' said Chen. 'She felt woozy and dialed nine-one-one. She was in ventricular fibrillation when she came into the ER. We defibbed her, got her heart back into normal sinus rhythm so she was stabilized. She was doing just fine,' Chen told the jury. 'Then she was transferred to the ICU.'

'Please go on, Doctor Chen,' said O'Mara.

'I knew Ms Falk pretty well – our daughters go to the same daycare center – so I stayed on top of her case. I looked in on Jessie about six hours later, when I was going off my shift. We talked for a while, and she was okay. She missed her little girl, was all. But when I checked her chart the next day, I learned that she'd had irregular heartbeats, probably the result of conductive disturbance – and she died.'

'Doctor, did you find that unusual?'

'I thought it was unusual for a woman of Jessica's age and physical condition.'

'And so what did you do?'

'I called for a postmortem and a board review.'

'And what were the findings of the autopsy?'

'Somehow Jessie Falk had received epinephrine. It was not prescribed.'

'And what would be the effect of epinephrine on *that type* of cardiac patient?'

'Epinephrine is a synthetic form of adrenaline, for God's sake. She should have gotten lidocaine, an anti-arrhythmic. That would have smoothed out her heart rate. Administering epinephrine was like giving her *cocaine*. It would be *lethal* for a cardiac patient.'

'So that's a pretty big mistake, isn't it, Doctor Chen? What happened when the hospital board reviewed Ms Falk's case?'

'Actually, no action was taken,' the doctor said, biting off his words.

'*No* action?'

'Well, nothing with respect to Jessie Falk, anyway. I was terminated two weeks later.'

'Because you blew the whistle?'

'Objection! Counsel is leading the witness,' Kramer said, coming to his feet.

'I'll rephrase, Your Honor. Doctor Chen, why was your employment terminated after twelve years?'

'I was told it was for *"budgetary reasons."'*

O'Mara dropped her head, letting the power of the doctor's words stand without embellishment. Then she lifted her face to the witness.

'I only have one more question, Doctor Chen. Who was the doctor who admitted Jessica Falk to the emergency room?'

'Doctor Dennis Garza.'

'To your knowledge, did he conduct a follow-up exam of Ms Falk when she was in the ICU?'

'His signature was on the chart.'

'Thank you. That's all I have for you, Doctor.'

Chapter Fifty-Two

As Kramer got up to cross-examine Dr Chen, Yuki swung her head, scanning the courtroom until she found Dr Garza three rows ahead on the aisle. *That scum.*

He was getting up from his seat, raking his black hair away from his forehead as he headed toward the door. Yuki's face burned.

Where is that bastard going? Get back here, Garza. You need to listen to this!

Yuki stood, too, excusing herself, working her way across the row of knees again, stepping on toes, banging the bench-back with her briefcase.

'Sorry, sorry, sorry.'

By the time she reached the hallway, Garza was out of sight.

Yuki saw elevator doors closing. She ran forward, pressed the button, reversing the doors. But the elevator car was empty.

She arrived at the lobby in time to see the back of Garza's navy-blue jacket, the man striding purposefully away from her and out of the courthouse.

Yuki followed him, her heels clacking loudly on the lobby floor. Now she was wondering what she was going to say or do when she caught up with him.

This was so unlike her, Yuki thought as she pushed open the heavy door, stumbling into the blinding light outside. She wasn't this impulsive.

She was organized, disciplined.

But right now, she couldn't stop herself. The obsession was taking over, as if she were in a wild Hitchcock movie.

Yuki searched the sidewalk, saw Garza heading along McAllister toward the Civic Center, head up, forging through the pedestrian traffic.

Yuki followed, running at times to catch up with him, then pacing herself behind him; finally, she called out his name. 'Garza!'

The doctor stopped, and he spun around to face her. He squinted his eyes against the sunlight.

Yuki drew closer, stopping just short of handshaking distance.

'I'm Yuki Castellano.'

'Yes, I know who you are. The question is – why are you stalking me?'

'I asked the medical examiner to autopsy my mother's body,' she said.

Garza struggled not to look surprised. 'I hope that made you feel a lot better. Did it?'

'I *do* feel better, Doctor, because I don't feel *crazy* anymore. But I am in a rage. My mother died because you screwed up. *Again.*'

Garza looked incredibly annoyed now. 'Me? Personally? You're sure of that?'

'Don't play games with me. I'm talking about my mother!'

'I'm sure the ME will send me her report. Maybe I'll even read it.' Then Dr Garza turned away and walked to a black Mercedes Roadster parked at the curb.

He opened the car door and stooped to get in, but then he stopped. He looked back at Yuki. 'Hey, why don't you sue me, bitch? What an original idea. Join the crowd.'

Chapter Fifty-Three

It was 6:15 on Wednesday night, and Claire and I were in our favorite booth at Susie's. The calypso band was tuning up with the Jimmy Buffett national anthem, and we'd ordered a pitcher of draft while we waited for Yuki and Cindy to show.

Claire and I clinked glasses, then continued unloading the small complaints that are like fleas on a dog – not life-threatening, but annoying as hell.

'You know Bob Watson?' Claire said.

'Your assistant, Bob?'

'Yes. My dear, strong, willing, smart, workaholic assistant, Bob. He's moving to Boston, and now I have to promote the mayor's twenty-two-year-old niece.'

'What? She's a courtesy hire?'

'Shoved right down my larynx. Child's called *Bunny*.' Claire moaned. 'Bunny can hardly lift her coffee cup, let alone a two-hundred-fifty-pound body. Keeps changing the CDs from Shostakovich to hip-hop. "Doctor Washburn, we need the right *music*." Sure thing, Bunny. No rush. Mr Doe here is resting comfortably.'

I laughed, snorting beer up my schnozz just about the time Cindy blew in and plopped into our booth.

'Greetings, girlfriends.'

'Back at you, girl reporter,' said Claire. 'Where's Yuki?'

'I just left her in front of the courthouse. She sends her regrets.'

'She's still really hurting?'

'Terribly,' Cindy said, 'but she's focused on the trial. She's even more obsessed than I am.'

Loretta dropped off the menus and a basket of plantain chips as Cindy told us about her past few days in court.

'Doctor Dennis Garza's name came up *again* today. A ten-year-old girl lost her mother because of an overdose of her prescribed medication. Garza checked her into the ER. Jamison Funeral Home checked her out.

'You listen to the stories in court, and you really want to nail someone for this shit,' Cindy continued, blowing the wrapper off a drinking straw. 'Don't *ever* go to a hospital if you can help it. More people die of accidents in the hospital than die from breast cancer, AIDS, or in car accidents.'

'Come on!'

'Lindsay, medical errors are among the top ten causes of death in America. And I've done some research on Garza. Statistically, he's holding up his end.'

'Do tell,' said Claire.

'Every place Garza worked,' Cindy said, 'Cleveland, Raleigh, Albany, and here. The body count climbs when he shows up at a new hospital.'

'What you're talking about, it's a national *scandal*,' Claire said, setting her glass down hard on the table. 'Dirty medical practitioners moving around the country and the hospitals don't turn them in 'cause they don't want to get sued.'

Cindy nodded her agreement. 'It's how so-called angels of death rack up dozens and sometimes hundreds of victims before they're caught – if they ever are.'

'It's no wonder Yuki's obsessed with Garza,' I said. 'She's sure he's responsible for killing her mother.'

'I can tell you this for a *fact*,' said Cindy. '*Someone* at that hospital is responsible for what happened to Keiko. She should be at home right now. Drinking tea. Telling Yuki what to wear and how to get married.'

Chapter Fifty-Four

S an Francisco's morning rush-hour snarl had eaten up fifteen precious minutes of drive time, and now Cindy was late. She pushed open the courtroom door, waved at Yuki, who was sitting behind the rail, then bumped everyone in the press row down a seat as she squeezed in.

A sidebar was in progress, a fairly heated one, Cindy thought. O'Mara and Kramer were arguing in lowered voices at the base of the judge's bench.

Judge Bevins had listened long enough. 'I don't see the problem, Mr Kramer.' Bevins flicked his ponytail, adjusted his bifocals. 'Both of you, step back. Let's get going.'

Kramer spun away from the bench, and Maureen O'Mara took the lectern. She tossed her mane of titian hair. A sign of victory? Then she called a witness to the stand.

There was a buzz in the courtroom as a striking fortyish

woman with short platinum-blond hair was sworn in. Her slim European designer suit in shades of olive green combined with her crisp, white man-tailored shirt spoke of uncommon style and confidence.

'What's going on?' Cindy whispered to the reporter beside her. This dude was like Clark Kent in the flesh – early thirties, dark-haired, bespectacled, remarkably cute in a nebbish sort of way.

'Hello. I'm Whit Ewing. *Chicago Tribune*,' he said.

'Sorry. I'm Cindy Thomas.'

'Of the *Chronicle*?'

'That's me.'

'I've been reading your reports. Not too bad.'

'Thanks, Whit. So, what's the beef?'

'O'Mara is calling a defense witness as part of her case-in-chief. It's a pretty clever tactic. Kramer can't cross-examine his own witness—'

'So she gets over on him until he puts the witness on himself.'

'Very good.'

'Thanks, bud. I owe you one.'

'I just may hold you to that,' he said, grinning.

The sharp crack of Judge Bevins's gavel brought the court to order.

'Please state your name,' said O'Mara.

'Doctor Sonja Engstrom.'

'Doctor Engstrom, what is your position at Municipal?'

'I'm director of pharmacy.'

'Here we go,' Whit Ewing said to Cindy. 'The windup for the pitch.'

Chapter Fifty-Five

Sonja Engstrom listed her credentials succinctly, said that she'd been at Municipal for seven years and was responsible for the systems and people who dispensed medication. She seemed suitably impressed with herself, too.

O'Mara asked, 'Could you tell the jury about those systems that you've put in place, Doctor?'

'Sure. We have an automated computer system linked to a dispensing mechanism.'

'What can you say about the accuracy of this system?'

'I'd say it's ninety-nine point nine percent bulletproof.'

'Could you please explain?'

Cindy got it all down on her laptop. A physician would take a patient's lab results and enter the diagnosis into the computer. The computer program would offer a menu of appropriate drugs, and the doctor would pick one. Then a nurse would pull up the patient's name on the computer and enter her code.

'It's a password, right? Everyone has their own code?' O'Mara asked.

'Exactly.'

'Please go on.'

'At the same moment the nurse enters her code, one of our pharmacists reviews and enters the order for that patient. This releases the brake on the machine that dispenses the drugs.'

'So it's a kind of digital vending machine.'

'Correct,' said the witness, seemingly pleased with herself and with O'Mara for getting it right. 'The nurse takes the patient's drug out of a pocket in the machine and administers it to the patient.'

'A "bulletproof" system?'

'Very close. The program can't be altered, and the security codes leave an auditory trail.'

'I see,' said O'Mara. She walked back to her table, consulted her notes, turned back to the witness.

'Could a technician load the wrong drugs into the machine's "pockets"?'

'I suppose it's possible . . .'

'Please answer yes or no.'

'Yes.'

'Could someone withhold a drug after removing it from the machine? Divert it, say, for personal use?'

'Yes.'

'If a physician makes a wrong diagnosis, wouldn't the wrong medication be dispensed to the patient?'

The witness was blinking her eyes rapidly. Flustered maybe, Cindy thought, but more than that, she looked pained. So much for 99.9 percent reliability.

'Yes, but—'

'Thank you,' O'Mara cut in. 'Now, isn't it true that the number of pharmaceutical-based fatalities has increased three-fold since Municipal was privatized three years ago?'

'Don't you think this worries me? I've turned over every stone,' Engstrom said, her voice rising, wavering for the first time since she'd taken the stand.

'Come on, Doctor Engstrom. Just answer the question. You're head of this department. You're on the hospital board. Have the number of pharmaceutical-based fatalities more than *tripled* in the last three years?'

'Yes, but . . . Well, yes.'

'Do you dispute that my clients' loved ones died because they received the wrong medication?'

'No, I can't dispute that,' Engstrom said in a barely audible voice.

'So whether these fatalities are the fault of your bulletproof vending machine or human error is irrelevant, right? I mean, either way,' O'Mara pushed on, 'isn't it true that these deaths are the result of negligence on your part and the part of the hospital?'

'Objection! Argumentative.' Kramer was up on his feet.

Cindy felt the little hairs on her arms lift. Beside her, Whit Ewing whistled softly.

'Sustained,' Bevins said.

'Withdrawn,' said Maureen O'Mara. Her eyes went to the jury and stayed there. 'Your Honor, the plaintiffs rest.'

Chapter Fifty-Six

I'd been told that it was a beautiful fall day, but I sure couldn't swear to it. I was having ham and Swiss on a roll in my office, with its dark-alley view, when Inspector Conklin knocked on the door.

'Come on in,' I told him.

Conklin was in his shirtsleeves, his brown eyes lit up with something. Whatever it was, I really wanted to know.

'Lou, we've got someone in the lunchroom you should meet. Like, right now if you can.'

'What's going on?'

Conklin started out of my office, saying, 'C'mon, Lieutenant,' taking long strides away from me and down the hall.

'Conklin?'

I tossed down the report I'd been editing and followed him

to the small, cluttered room that was home to our microwave and yellowing Kenmore fridge.

Jacobi was sitting at the battered table across from a pretty young woman in her early twenties wearing a blue Polarfleece shirt and stretch pants. Her long dark hair was in a braid down her back. She looked up at me with reddened, mascara-smudged eyes.

Clearly, she'd been crying.

Jacobi had his 'Uncle Warren' face on. It was short of a smile, but I could read happiness in his eyes.

'Lieutenant,' Jacobi said, 'this is Barbara Jane Ross. She was throwing out newspapers when she found this.'

He pushed the newsprint picture of Jag Girl into the center of the table, the pretty blonde girl we'd found displayed like a mannequin in the Jaguar convertible on Chestnut Street.

Innumerable dead-end tips had flooded our phone lines since Jag Girl's picture had run in the *Chronicle*. From the look on Jacobi's face, I knew this young woman had something valuable to say.

Barbara Jane Ross and I shook hands. Hers were cold as ice. 'May I see that?' I pointed to the photo she clutched in her left hand.

'Sure,' she said, handing me a snapshot of herself and Jag Girl on the beach. Both girls were wearing wide-brimmed hats and small bikinis; they had identical braids, and both were grinning broadly.

'She was my college roommate,' said Barbara Jane, her eyes scrunching up with tears. 'I can't believe this is happening. I can't believe that Sandy is dead.'

Chapter Fifty-Seven

I handed Barbara Jane a box of tissues, stared over her head, first at Jacobi then at Conklin, as she blew her nose. Holy shit. We'd finally gotten a break on Jag Girl.

'Barbara, what's your friend's last name?'

'It's Wegner. But Sandy goes by other names. I don't know them all.'

'She's an actress?'

'No, an escort.'

I was stunned. Sandy Wegner had been a party girl. So how had she kept her prints out of the system?

'Are you an escort, too?' Conklin asked.

'No *way*, I teach. Special ed, right here in the city.'

Jacobi put new grounds in the Mr Coffee as Barbara Jane Ross told us how she and Sandy had been roommates at the University of California, Santa Barbara.

'When we were in school, Sandy needed some extra cash, so she went on a few "dates" for an escort service. A lot of girls do it,' Barbara said. 'You never, *ever* have enough money in school.

'She didn't do it often, but when she did, she thought it was exciting and fun,' Barbara continued. 'Sandy loved having a secret life. She wasn't the only coed doing it, either.'

'Did she ever mention that one of her dates was giving her a hard time?' I asked. 'Maybe someone got possessive? Or violent?'

'Nothing like that,' Barbara said. 'She would have told me. We talked about everything, even her work.'

'Did Sandy have a boyfriend? Maybe someone who could have found out that she was doing this kind of thing on the side?'

'There was no one special in her life or she would have quit her night job,' Barbara told us. 'She wasn't a slut. I know how that sounds, but honest to God, she *wasn't* – oh, God! Her parents don't know. They live in Portland.'

'Do you know their names? Maybe you have their phone number?'

Barbara Jane dug into her Coach bag; she pulled out her PDA.

'Listen,' she said, 'I just remembered who she worked for. The escort service. I think it was called Top Hat.'

'Thanks. You've been a big help. Hang around, won't you, Barbara Jane? Inspector Conklin has some more questions for you.'

As I walked out of the door, Conklin took my chair. I saw Barbara Jane Ross look into his face and smile.

Chapter Fifty-Eight

The three-story beige-stucco apartment building was on California Street at the edge of the Financial District.

I badged the doorman, and he called up on the intercom. 'SFPD is here to see you, Ms Selzer.'

A female voice crackled over the speaker. 'I'm not home. I didn't see anything, don't know anyone. I'm a shut-in. And I mind my own business.'

'A comedienne,' Jacobi said to the doorman. 'We're going up.'

A tiny, small-boned woman was standing at her apartment door when we got there. She was definitely under five feet, glossy hair pinned up with a tortoiseshell comb, pale lipstick, wearing a black silk V-neck sweater and satin pants.

I put her at thirty-five, but the crow's-feet told me she was either older than she appeared or she'd had a rough-and-tumble life. Probably both.

'Officers, I run an *introduction* service. My license is totally in order,' she said by way of a greeting.

'You mind inviting us in?' Jacobi said, flashing his shield. 'There's a nasty draft out here in the hallway.'

The small woman sighed her exasperation, but she stepped back and let us in. A mirrored foyer led to a living room painted and upholstered in every shade of gray. Helmut Newton's black-and-white photos lined the walls.

We followed her to a red swivel chair and a black enameled worktable up against the front window.

'I'm Lieutenant Boxer. This is Inspector Jacobi. Homicide.'

I snapped the pictures of Sandy Wegner and Caddy Girl down on the table. Two pallid faces. Sheets drawn up to the ligature marks around their necks.

'Do you recognize these women?'

Selzer sucked in her breath, then put her finger on Wegner's image.

'This is Sandra Wegner. Calls herself Tanya. I don't know the other girl. You're saying she's *dead*?'

'What can you tell us about Sandy?'

'I only met her once. Talked to her on the phone after that. Great sense of humor, really nice body. I could've kept her busy every night, but she was strictly part-time. Look, you're not thinking I had anything to do with this?' she said, directing her question to me.

'Was Sandy working on the night of September fifteenth?' I asked.

Selzer dropped into the swivel chair and worked the computer keys, resting her chin in her cupped hands as squiggles of data scrolled up.

'Her date that night was a Mr Alex Logan. I remember now. He called from the Hotel Triton. Said he was in town for the evening and wanted a petite blonde to go with him to a show. *Henry the Fifth*. I don't know why I remembered that.'

'Is Logan a regular?'

'Nuh-uh. A first-timer.'

'You sent this girl out on a date with someone you didn't know?' Jacobi's voice was hard, the way it should be. Selzer instantly shrunk away from him.

'I ran his credit card. No problem. Checked his name and address on AnyWho.com. Called the hotel and he was registered. It was all kosher.'

'Have you heard from him since?' I asked.

'Nope. Nothing. But you don't usually get feedback from out-of-towners.'

'How much did Mr Logan pay for his date with Sandy?' I asked.

'Her usual. A thousand for the night. I took my cut, made a direct deposit into Sandy's account. Any tips, she got to keep.'

'Was anyone hassling her? Stalking her? Did she mention having any trouble from anyone?' Jacobi asked. 'Give us some help here.'

'No, and Sandy wasn't shy. She would've told me. *What?*' she said defensively. 'I called her the next day, and when I didn't hear back, I figured she quit. Ticked me off, believe me. I had to cancel her bookings. Look, I'm not a den mother, for Christ's sake! *She was a free agent.*'

Jacobi gave Selzer a scathing look. Her indignant expression crumpled. 'Selzer, you're pissing me off,' he said.

'Oh, man, I feel bad. I really do. You think I screwed up? I don't know what I could've done differently.'

The woman pulled the comb from her hair, shook her head so that her gleaming hair sprayed around her face, playing the sex card in an unconscious defense of her worried conscience.

The move didn't distract Jacobi, not even a little bit.

'You didn't just screw up,' he said. 'You sent this girl on a date with a killer.'

Selzer clapped her hands to her face.

'Give me the john's particulars,' said Jacobi.

Selzer wrote numbers on a Post-it note. Jacobi snatched it up and put his card in its place.

'If he calls you again, fix him up with a girl who doesn't exist and call me immediately. You got that? Any time, day or night. My cell phone's on the back of the card.'

Selzer called out as we reached her front door.

'*Officers.* I'm sorry about Sandy. You should know that. I hope you get whoever killed her.'

'Yeah,' Jacobi called back, 'we want to ease your guilt if we possibly can.'

Chapter Fifty-Nine

Conklin opened the door for us when we arrived at Sandy Wegner's apartment. I said hey to Charlie Clapper, who was coming out of the bathroom, bagging the victim's hairbrush and toothbrush, plus some medications.

'Doesn't look like a crime scene, Lieutenant,' Conklin told me. 'The door was double-locked. No signs of a struggle.'

'What else?'

'She had yogurt for dinner. She left some clothes on the bed, like maybe she'd tried on a few things before she went out. Towel rumpled on the towel bar. Her clothes are okay, but not superexpensive, by the way.

'The message light on her answering machine was blinking. Two calls. Her mother and the library saying she had a book overdue. I took the tape. Pressed redial. Her last call was to "time and weather." Probably called just before she went out that night.'

'Good work,' I said to Conklin. I asked a CSU tech, 'How's it coming?'

'We've got our pictures, Lieutenant.'

I looked around Sandy Wegner's place. It was dark, like my office, a view of the alley from every room.

Her style was Pottery Barn right down to the swirly iron wall-hanging over the couch. A vase of dead flowers was on the windowsill, and contemporary novels and historical biographies, along with textbooks – math, physics, art history – lined the bookshelves.

Sandy's bedroom was small, about eleven feet square, painted a pretty lilac-blue with white trim. Primitive watercolors of birds hung over her bed, her name signed in the corner of each one. The personal touches always kill me.

I opened her bifold closet doors, saw that Sandy took care of her clothes. Her Agnes B. T-shirts were on padded hangers; dresses, suits, and jeans in dry-cleaner's bags. Shoes lined up, polished, heels in good condition.

She had a tasteful wardrobe, but it was definitely off the rack. Nothing like the quality of what she was wearing when we found her body. Jacobi was going through the dresser drawers, shutting them noisily as he went.

He stopped, called me over when he found the drawer with her underthings. I took a look. Lace demi-bras, thongs, and transparent panties in Jell-O colors, a vibrator.

Could be tools of the trade.

Could be a girl with a sassy love life.

We searched all four of her rooms, not finding anything really, not even an address book or a diary or a drug more powerful than Tylenol PM.

Looked to me like Sandy Wegner's night job was a small part of how she lived.

I asked Conklin to go back to the Hall to run Alex Logan's name through every database. Then Jacobi and I sealed the apartment and went down to the street.

The sky was the color of dull steel at 6:45 p.m. The sun was going down early now, and it left a pall over the city. Or maybe I was just projecting.

'Our guys are pattern killers,' I said to Jacobi as he started the car. 'If Sandy's an escort, Caddy Girl is probably an escort, too. That means the DNA we got from her rape kit—'

'You're reading my mind,' said Jacobi, pulling out into the traffic on Columbus. 'Sperm lives inside the body for about seventy-two hours. It could have come from her killer, or a john, or a boyfriend.'

'Whatever,' I said. 'The DA's going to say it's not evidence of murder.'

Chapter Sixty

B ut maybe we were getting closer to the evidence.

The Hotel Triton was busy that night, but it always had a brisk turnover. Fronting Union Square, steps away from the trolley line, across the street from Chinatown, it had a frisky Cirque du Soleil decor and a midrange room rate.

Jacobi pushed to the front of the line at the reception desk; he badged the clerk and brusquely told him to find the night manager. 'Chop, chop. Move it before you lose it.'

A chunky man of forty stepped out of the back room. The name tag on his jacket read 'Jon Anderson, Mgr.' He nodded at us, asked if there was a problem.

'There's a big problem. We're investigating a homicide,' I told him. 'We need the sign-in records for September fifteenth and whatever you have on a guest named Alex Logan.'

Jacobi added, 'And we need the tapes from *that* camera,' he said, stabbing his forefinger toward the camera behind the desk. 'Also need the tape from the hall camera outside the room Logan used on that date, the fifteenth.'

The manager got huffy on us. 'I suppose you have a warrant?'

'Do we need one? 'Cause we can get one and close this place down while we do a complete search.'

He appeared to quickly think over the implications of a search, then said, 'The videotapes are on a forty-eight-hour loop. There won't be anything on them from September fifteenth.

'But everyone here,' he said, pointing to the line of five college kids manning the reception desk, 'all of them were on duty that night. I'll pull the records for you. See how co-operative I am?'

A thin, distracted desk clerk by the name of Gary Metz had checked Alex Logan into room 2021.

'I think I remember this Mr Logan,' Metz told us. He drummed his fingers on the desk, looked past my shoulder into the lobby, then focused on my eyes again. 'He was with another man.'

I think I may have stopped breathing for a moment; I was *that* hopeful that we'd run this lead to ground.

'If I've got him right, he was about my height, kind of regular size. Maybe he was Chinese,' said the clerk.

'Alex Logan? He looked Chinese?'

'I think so. Maybe part Chinese. The other guy was a bruiser. Six two, two thirty, and blond. He's the one that said he wanted a smoking room. Both of them looked straight, if you want my opinion.'

'And how do you figure that?' I asked.

'They wanted a room with a king-size bed, but they didn't dress well enough to be gay. The bigger guy's haircut looked like he did it himself.'

'Do you remember if they had any luggage?'

'The big guy had a large rolling bag. I noticed because it was leather. Maybe Tumi? Looked expensive.'

'Thanks, Mr Metz,' I said, doing my level best to keep the excitement out of my voice. 'We need to see the room.'

Chapter Sixty-One

Room 2021 was two doors down from the elevator, and it had the same whimsical decor as the lobby; a checkered-fabric headboard, three-legged chairs, a starred royal-blue carpet throughout. The current occupants had been hustled out at our behest, leaving their suitcases open on the bed and toiletries in the bathroom. There was an opened mini-bottle of Scotch on the night table.

I tried to imagine how the murder had gone down. The Chinese guy answering the door. Sandy Wegner saying hello. Throwing her coat down on the chair. The first guy spiking her drink with Rohypnol. The second guy, the bruiser, coming out of the bathroom for the kill.

I felt as if I could sense the murder happening around me. Sandy Wegner, helpless as she was raped, killed by two freaks.

The inexpressible horror grabbed me as I looked around for

anything that might jump out. But the room had been slept in and cleaned many times since Sandy's death.

'I hate hotel rooms,' I said to my former partner.

'The carpet probably has a million pubic hairs, none of them matching anything.'

'Thanks for putting that image in my head, Jacobi.'

The manager came to the door, said he was upgrading the current occupants and would keep 2021 free for as long as we needed. I thanked him, said we'd be leaving soon, but that CSU would be arriving shortly.

'CSU could find a print or, God willing, a hair with a skin tag,' I said to Jacobi.

'Doesn't hurt to hope,' he said with a shrug.

I said, 'Doesn't hurt to pray.'

Chapter Sixty-Two

Ducks hung by their necks in the front window of Wong Fat, a Chinese restaurant a five-minute walk from the Triton. 'I like this place already,' I said.

Inside, the eatery was bright, fluorescent light bouncing off the linoleum floors and Formica tables. The menu, written in Chinese letters on strips of red paper, hung against the walls.

It was good to be in out of the dark and the chill at least. The tea was hot. The hot-and-sour soup was excellent.

As we waited for our entrées, Jacobi laid down the printout of Alex Logan's charges at the Triton.

'Here's the phone call to Top Hat,' he said. 'Lasted four and a half minutes. Logan and his buddy also raided the honor bar. Champagne, nuts. Pringles, for Christ's sake. They ordered pay-per-view at nine. What do you think? Football or porn?'

'I think that these killers plan it all. They book the room, book the hooker, rape and kill her in a place that's a contaminated crime scene by definition.

'Then they wash her off in the shower, clean up any hairs and fibers on her body.'

'Don't forget the perfume.'

'Right, thank you,' I said. 'Then they spray her privates, dress her up, comb her hair, and make her up like a little doll.'

'They used the suitcase to bring in the clothes. Used it again to take out the body,' said Jacobi. 'That "bruiser" simply rolls it out to the car.'

'And then they plant her so we can find her.'

I was about to wonder out loud where they got the clothes, when my cell phone rang.

It was Conklin.

'I ran Alex Logan's name and credit card number, Lieutenant. Wait until you hear this. Alex Logan is a *woman*. I pulled up her license info – petite blonde, twenty-three years old. I think we found Caddy Girl.'

'What else have you got?'

'I went to her apartment building, Lieutenant. Nice place on Jones. According to her doorman, she hasn't been home in a while. I also called American Express, and her card is active, but there's only been one charge in the last ten days. *The Hotel Triton on September fifteenth.*'

'I'll call the DA. Get a search warrant for her apartment. Richie?'

'Yes, ma'am?'

'You're gonna be a star.'

I hung up and turned to Jacobi, who was watching me, his fork in the air.

'What is it, Boxer?'

'Conklin made her,' I said. 'The perps used her credit card to book Sandy Wegner and pay the hotel tab. Alex Logan is Caddy Girl.'

Chapter Sixty-Three

I looked out over the squad room the next morning, anticipating a giant leap forward in the Car Girl case.

The victims had names, and with that crucial bit of news, there was a decent chance that the lives of Alex Logan and Sandy Wegner would intersect in a big fat lead that would help us nail their killers.

I could see Jacobi and Conklin through the glass, working the phones, reaching out to the girls' parents, when a beam of sunshine sailed past Brenda's desk and came through the gate.

It was Claire with a young woman in tow. She rapped on my office wall, and I waved her in.

'Lindsay, this is Bunny Ellis.'

'Nice to meet you – and welcome.'

Claire's new assistant had gray eyes, slightly crossed, and a gap between the front teeth of her Crest-strip smile. The cosmetic flaws made her look touchingly appealing.

'Bunny was helping me get Misses Wegner and Logan ready to be released to their families,' Claire said. 'Tell the lieutenant what you told me, Bunny.'

'I've been sooooo fascinated by these murders, you know? Such young women and such brutal—'

'The short version, child.'

'I'm sorry. It's about their perfume, Lieutenant Boxer. I noticed it when they were brought in, but I didn't know it was important.'

'Please go on,' I said, thinking about that haunting scent the killers had sprayed on the young women's genitalia.

'My husband gave me that perfume for my birthday,' said Bunny. 'Black Pearl. It's made exclusively for Nordstrom.'

I looked at Claire, then back at Bunny. 'You can't get Black Pearl anywhere else?'

She shook her head emphatically. 'Only at Nordstrom.'

I felt a shot of adrenaline, a hit of hope. Someone had bought that exclusive perfume at Nordstrom, a purchase that could lead to a credit card number, a name, or a good visual ID.

'Bunny, see those two inspectors over there in the corner?'

'The gray-haired guy and Inspector Conklin?'

I tried not to roll my eyes. Bunny had been with Claire for

only a short time, and she could already pick Rich Conklin out of a lineup.

I nodded. 'Go introduce yourself. Tell them about Black Pearl. You're going to make their day.'

Chapter Sixty-Four

Jacobi and Conklin had just headed out to Nordstrom on the perfume detail when Brenda called me on the intercom.

'Lieutenant, there's a lady on the phone, says she needs protection. Won't talk to anyone but the head of Homicide.'

'What's her name?'

'Mrs Anita Haggerty. Calling from Municipal Hospital. She's a patient there, she says.'

The woman spoke in a low voice, just above a whisper.

'Lieutenant Baxter?'

'It's Boxer. How can I help you?'

'Have you ever been so scared you're throwing up? That's how scared I am.'

'Back up, Mrs Haggerty. Start from the beginning.'

'Okay, but I might have to suddenly hang up.'

I took down the woman's room number and encouraged her to get to the point.

'I was in a hospital in Raleigh with a concussion three, four years ago. My roommate was in for a bleeding ulcer. Dottie Coombs – that was her name. Dottie was ready to go home when she suddenly went into seizures and died. Right in front of me.'

'Go on, Mrs Haggerty.'

'She shouldn't have died. The nurses closed my curtains, but they were *very upset,* saying, "How could this happen?" And I heard her doctor say something to those nurses that I'll never forget as long as I live. It was burned into my brain.'

'I'm listening.'

'He said, "Sometimes a bad wind blows."'

'What did that mean to you?'

'It meant *Friday the Thirteenth.* It meant *Nightmare on Elm Street.* I don't know, Lieutenant Baxter, but my friend was dead, and her doctor's reaction was creepy and sick. And now he's *here.* He poked his head into my room, and I think maybe he remembers me. I've got surgery tomorrow for a hernia,' Haggerty continued breathlessly. 'Supposed to be a simple operation, but as God is my witness, I'm scared for my life.'

I was having the kind of premonition where you know what someone's going to say before they say it. Cold sweat trickled down the sides of my body.

I pressed the receiver hard to my ear.

'Do you remember the doctor's name?'

'I'll never, ever forget it,' Haggerty said. 'It was Garza. Doctor Dennis Garza.'

PART FOUR

Show Girl

Chapter Sixty-Five

Sometimes a bad wind blows.

It was an eerie phrase, and the fear in Mrs Haggerty's voice had given me chills. I heard Yuki's voice, too. *Someone at that damn hospital murdered my mother.*

I drove to the hospital alone, telling myself that I wasn't working a case. This was just an inquiry. A courtesy call, I guess you could say.

San Francisco Municipal Hospital is a humongous stone fortress of a place with a low wall and a smattering of shade trees between the entrance to the hospital and the sidewalk.

I parked in the lot and entered the gloom of the lobby. Crossed the granite-block floor to the elevator, got out on the third floor, and followed the arrows to room 311.

I was about to open the door to Haggerty's private room, when a nurse's aide came out with a load of sheets in her arms. I waited for her to clear out of the way; then I stepped inside room 311.

I had pictured Mrs Haggerty from the sound of her voice, imagined her as having a wiry frame and dark, hennaed hair.

I hadn't imagined for a second that her bed would be empty.

I stood blinking stupidly in the doorway, astonished by what I didn't see. Then I spun around, out into the hall.

The nurse's aide had already stuffed the sheets into a canvas trolley and was walking away from me.

'Wait,' I said, lunging out and grabbing for her arm.

Her face stretched with surprise. Kind of jumpy for hospital personnel.

'Take your hands off me. *Please.*'

'I'm sorry,' I said, showing her my badge. 'Lieutenant Boxer, SFPD. I came to see Mrs Haggerty in room 311.'

'Well, you're too late.'

'Too late? I just spoke with her on the phone. What happened?'

I envisioned the woman hunched over the phone, scared out of her mind.

I'd just spoken with her!

'She checked herself out without doctor's approval. I wheeled her out to the street myself. Helped her into a taxi. Yellow Cab, if that matters. You done with me now?'

I nodded, said thanks.

The nurse's aide continued down the hallway, leaving me in the corridor alone.

I was heading toward the exit when a nurse in blue scrubs beckoned to me from a room across the hallway. She was a light-skinned black woman, about twenty-five, rounded face, her reddish hair in twists. The ID tag hanging from the ball chain around her neck read 'Noddie Wilkins, RN.'

'You're with the police?' she asked, her voice low and urgent. 'I have to talk to you. I have to tell you what I know. The police should be involved with what's happening.'

Chapter Sixty-Six

We decided to talk somewhere outside the hospital. Noddie Wilkins and I sat together in my Explorer, sipping cafeteria coffee from paper cups.

'There's something weird going on around this hospital,' Noddie told me. 'Last week, when I found one of my patients dead, I totally freaked out. Mr Harris was frisky. He was getting ready to go home, not die. Cardiac arrest? Far as I know, there was nothing wrong with his heart.'

'You found that suspicious?'

'That – and the fact that when I found him dead, he had coins on his eyes.'

That threw me for a loop.

'Coins? What kind of coins?' I asked.

'Well, they look like coins, but they're really buttons, like from a jacket or a blazer. They have a raised pattern – what do you call that?'

'Embossed?'

'That's it. They were embossed with a medical symbol – snakes winding up a pole with wings at the top.'

'You're talking about a caduceus?'

'That's right. A caduceus.'

I felt like I'd dropped through an open manhole, and was still falling.

Markers had been placed on the eyes of a dead patient.

How could that be anything but the signature of a killer?

'This is bad, isn't it?' said Noddie, taking in the shock on my face. 'There's more.'

She homed in on me with her big oval eyes, as if she'd been pent up for a long while, and now she needed to talk.

'First time, maybe six months ago, I found these things on another dead patient's eyes,' she said, 'I thought, Coins to pay the ferryman, something creepy like that.

'But when I found Mr Harris, I honestly got the screaming-jeebies. And I got *mad*. I liked that old guy and he liked me – and those things on his eyes? Uh-uh. It stunk like old cheese. Something is not right here, Lieutenant.'

'Why didn't you call the police?' I asked the nurse, who was nice but didn't strike me as the sharpest blade in the shed.

'I reported it to my supervisor, and she said we would take it to Mr Whiteley. He's the CEO of the hospital.'

My heart was pounding, booming in my ears. How had the hospital kept something this bizarre, this sinister, under wraps for so long?

'I'd like you to swear out a complaint,' I said to Noddie, but the young woman pulled away from me, backed up against the car door.

'You've gotta keep me out of this,' she said. 'I can't swear out anything. Jeez. I need my job. I'm raising two small kids alone . . .'

'I hear you,' I said. 'I'll be as discreet as I can. Did you talk with the CEO?'

'Yeah. He was real stiff with me,' the young woman said, shaking her head at the memory. 'Said the coins were someone's idea of a joke, and that if I blabbed, it could cost the hospital plenty – and that would mean *cutbacks*. He was making a threat.

'So I dropped it,' she said. 'What else could I do? Now I hear talk, that other people have found these things and just go about their business. Months go by and nothing happens.

'Then bing, bing, bing. Dead patients one after another with coins on their eyes.'

'How *many* patients, Noddie? *How many?*'

'I don't know. See these goose bumps? I'm freaking out all over again,' the nurse said, holding out her arm for me to see. 'I mean, if it's just *a joke*, like Mr Whiteley said, what's the punch line? 'Cause I just don't get it.'

Chapter Sixty-Seven

I sat impatiently in a big upholstered chair, dense carpeting underfoot, *Fortune* magazine splayed out on the blond-wood coffee table – the hushed outer office of Carl Whiteley, Municipal Hospital's CEO.

Whiteley's assistant hung up a phone and told me that Mr Whiteley could see me now.

I entered a many-windowed office, where a gray-haired man with smooth pink cheeks and wire-rimmed glasses stood up from behind his desk. He looked like a Republican senator or Santa Claus with a really close shave.

I shook his hand and showed him my badge, thinking how I had no partner, no warrant, no case file, just Noddie Wilkins's fear and an unsettling image of Yuki's mom in my mind.

'I don't understand, Lieutenant,' Whiteley said as he sat

down and I took the seat across from him. The sun beat through the plate glass and jabbed me in the eyes. 'Someone made a complaint to the police? Who? Over what?'

'You're surprised? Now I'm the one who doesn't understand. Your hospital is being sued for malpractice.'

'That lawsuit is total crap. It's a travesty.' Whiteley laughed. 'This is a hospital, a very good one, but patients die. We're living in litigious times.'

'Even so, I have some questions for you.'

'Okay,' he said, linking his hands behind his head, leaning back in his cushy executive chair. 'Shoot.'

'What can you tell me about the coins your staff have found on the eyelids of deceased patients? How long has this been going on?'

'Coins,' he said, returning his chair to its original position. Whiteley gave me a condescending look. 'You mean *buttons*, don't you?'

'Coins. Buttons. What the hell difference does it make? In my business we call them *clues*.'

'Clues to what, Lieutenant? This place is crawling with doctors. We know every patient's cause of death, and none of them were homicides. Want my opinion? These buttons are a prank. A cruel prank.'

'And that's why you didn't inform the police about any of this?'

'There's nothing to report. Patients sometimes die. Where's the crime?'

Whiteley was incredibly smug, and I didn't like him. Not his smooth baby face or his jackass laugh. Or the way he was trying to put me down and fake me out.

'Covering up evidence is *illegal*, Mr Whiteley. Either tell me about those *buttons* or this pleasant chat of ours is over, and I'm going to arrest you for obstruction of justice and for interfering with a police investigation.'

'Arrest me? Hang on, Lieutenant. I'm calling my attorney.'

'Be my guest,' I said. 'And while you're at it, think about this. You've still got a pretty good reputation. How's it going to look when squad cars pull up with sirens blasting and I march you out to the curb in handcuffs?'

Whiteley reached for the receiver. He punched out a few numbers before angrily pounding the phone back into its cradle.

'Look, this is *ridiculous*,' he said, burning a couple of holes into me with his eyes. 'We've got nothing to hide.'

He opened a desk drawer, pulled out a cream-colored envelope with the hospital's logo in the upper left corner. He tossed it lightly onto his desk top.

'You can buy these buttons in any uniform supply store in the country, Lieutenant,' he said. 'I'm cooperating, okay? This idiocy can't go public. If you do anything to damage our reputation, I'm prepared to take legal action against the city for libel, and against you in particular.'

'If there's no causal relationship between the buttons and the patients' deaths, you've got nothing to worry about.'

I reached for the envelope, my pulse pounding as I opened the flap and peered inside.

Shiny brass circlets glinted up at me.

There were dozens of them, each button smaller than a dime, with a tiny shank on the back, a raised emblem of a caduceus on the front.

The buttons rattled inside the envelope as I shook it. Maybe Whiteley was right. They were common blazer-cuff buttons. Nothing special about them.

But we both knew that each pair represented a person who had died here at the hospital.

'I'll need a list of all of the patients found with these things on their eyes,' I told him.

'I can fax it to your office,' said Whiteley.

'Thanks,' I said, crossing my arms. 'Nice of you to offer, but I'd prefer to wait.'

Chapter Sixty-Eight

I drove back to the Hall through medium-heavy afternoon
traffic, still feeling the heat of my confrontation with Whiteley
and the chilling sight of those damn buttons.

What in God's name did it all mean?

Placing markers on the eyes of the dead was grim, and it
was freaky. Was someone playing a cruel prank as Whiteley
had said? Or was Municipal Hospital covering up a long history
of serial murders?

The list of the dead that Whiteley had given me rested on
the seat beside me.

I braked at the light at California and Montgomery, snapped
on my dome light, and opened the folder. A two-page spread-
sheet was inside – the names of thirty-two patients who'd
been found dead over the last three years with buttons on
their eyelids. For God's sake!

Across the top of the grid were the headings 'patient's name,' 'patient's physician,' 'date of death,' 'cause of death.'

I skimmed the data, then flipped to the second page.

Leo Harris was last on the list, and just above his name – *Keiko Castellano*.

My heart lurched as I stared at the name of Yuki's mom. I saw her sweet face in my mind, then her eyes covered with those vile brass markers.

Blaring car horns brought me out of my trance.

'Okay, okay!' I shouted, putting the Explorer in gear. The car jumped forward as I stepped on the gas.

I was thinking ahead as well.

Whiteley said he didn't want details of the buttons to get out – but a sleazy cover-up wasn't evidence of a murder.

We already had stacks of bona fide homicides to solve and too few inspectors to handle them. I needed more than a handful of buttons and a list of names before I went to Tracchio or the DA.

If I wanted some answers, I'd have to work around the edges of the system.

And I'd have to ask a big favor of a friend.

Chapter Sixty-Nine

Yuki settled into her seat in the courtroom as the lunch recess ended. Larry Kramer had begun to mount his case in defense of his client, Municipal Hospital. And she'd watched Maureen O'Mara attack his witnesses on cross.

It had been a spirited dance and good theater for the media, but these had been emotionally draining, grueling days for Yuki.

She tried to read the jurors' faces, and it seemed to her that they had been satisfied with Kramer's string of witnesses, nodding their heads as each doctor, each clever executive, explained away deaths that should never have happened.

Yuki opened her pad and looked over her notes on Carl Whiteley's testimony that morning. The hospital CEO had been fluent, even funny, under Kramer's soft-ball questioning.

Then O'Mara had drilled the CEO, asking him what she had asked the others: 'Isn't it true that pharmaceutical-based fatalities have increased *threefold* since Municipal was privatized three years ago?'

Whiteley had agreed – but unlike Sonja Engstrom, he hadn't flubbed his lines. He whitewashed the individual deaths and threw national statistics at O'Mara, enough data to numb the jurors' minds.

'Redirect, Mr Kramer?'

'Yes, Your Honor.'

Kramer stood, addressing his witness from the defense table. 'Those statistics you quoted, Mr Whiteley. Between fifty thousand and a hundred thousand patients die annually from medical errors in the United States. This is commonly accepted knowledge?'

'That's right,' said Whiteley. 'According to the ISMP, approximately seven thousand people die each year from medication errors alone.'

Yuki had scribbled in her notebook, getting it all down. The facts were shocking, but she didn't care about what Whiteley had to say. He was an apologist, a corporate suit, the warm-up act. She'd stolen a glance at the defense table during the last recess.

She'd seen the witness lineup.

For a week, she'd waited for the next witness to take the stand.

As soon as Kramer was done with Whiteley, he was going to call Dr Dennis Garza.

Chapter Seventy

K ramer shuffled papers as Dennis Garza was sworn in, thinking to himself, You don't always get the witnesses you want. You get the witnesses you get.

Kramer looked up to see the undeniably good-looking doctor straighten his Armani jacket as he took the witness seat. He shot the cuffs of his tailored shirt, crossed his legs, sat perfectly straight and completely at ease.

Garza looked more like a Hollywood actor than a guy who was up to his wrists in blood and guts sixty hours a week.

But even that wasn't the problem.

What worried Kramer was that Garza was as volatile as he was cocky. He'd resisted being prepped, saying that after twenty-two years of medical practice, he was fully capable of answering the charges against the hospital.

Kramer hoped to hell he was right.

Garza's testimony could tip the case. *This was it.* Kramer smiled tightly, and greeted his witness.

'Doctor Garza, you're aware of the plaintiffs' charges?'

'Yes. And I feel very sorry for the families.'

'I'm going to ask you specifically about the patients who were admitted to the emergency room while you were on duty.'

Kramer questioned Garza, beginning to feel better by the minute as the doctor explained away each of the patient fatalities in a reasoned, believable, authoritative voice. Garza was in a great groove.

'Do you see any pattern in these deaths, Doctor Garza? Anything at all?'

'I see the *absence* of a pattern,' Garza said, raking his thick hair away from his forehead. 'I see the random, regrettable errors that happen every day in every hospital in the country. In the world, for that matter.'

'Thank you, Doctor Garza. Your witness,' Kramer said to O'Mara.

Kramer watched Maureen O'Mara walk to the lectern, an expression on her face that cast a cold shadow over Kramer's newborn feeling of relief. He knew Maureen. Had gone against her a few times before. She was always prepared, always smart, and a strong interrogator.

But he saw something now in her face that alarmed him. She looked *eager*.

Chapter Seventy-One

Yuki leaned forward in her seat as Maureen addressed the witness. 'Doctor Garza, Jessica Falk was your patient,' O'Mara said. 'Do you remember her?'

'Yes. Of course I do.'

'Your Honor, it's been established that Jessie Falk was admitted to Municipal for cardiac arrhythmia. That her death was caused by the wrongful administration of epinephrine that caused her subsequent cardiac arrest and death.'

'Mr Kramer?' asked the judge.

'That's fine, Judge.'

'So stipulated.'

Yuki felt the tension in the air, imagined the expectation and dread of the dead woman's husband, a young man sitting only three rows ahead of her.

'Doctor Garza, how did Ms Falk die?'

'As you said, she had a heart attack.'

'That's true, Doctor. But what I mean is, can you describe her death so that we can better understand her last moments?'

Larry Kramer rose to his feet immediately. 'Objection! Your Honor, Counsel is trying to prejudice the jury. This is outrageous.'

'Your Honor, I'm merely asking *how the patient died*. That's what this case is *about*.'

'Yes, yes. Of course it is. Doctor Garza, please answer the question.'

Yuki saw surprise ripple across Garza's face. That was interesting. He cleared his throat before he spoke.

'Well, she went into ventricular tachycardia. A very fast heartbeat.'

'Would you say that would have hurt her and frightened her?'

'Probably. Yes.'

'What else, Doctor?'

'She would have tried to contact anything in her immediate environment.'

'Claw at the sheets, for instance?'

'Probably.'

'Try to call out?'

'Your Honor!' Kramer broke in. 'Out of respect for Ms Falk's family . . .'

'I'm touched, Mr Kramer,' said O'Mara. 'Be concerned for my clients now.'

'Overruled. Doctor Garza, please answer the question.'

'She may have tried to call out. I don't know. I wasn't there.'

'What else, Doctor Garza? In medical terms.'

'She went into ventricular fibrillation. As the circulation to the brain decreased, she might have developed clonic movements – like a little seizure. Her skin would've gotten clammy. She would have felt dizzy and weak before she went into shock. The entire episode would have taken only two or three minutes until she became unconscious.'

'Doctor, are you familiar with the term "psychic horror?"'

Kramer got to his feet and spoke in a tone of deep disappointment. 'Your Honor, I object. Counsel is trying to inflame the jury.'

'Overruled, Mr Kramer. Psychic horror is a legally admissible term. I'm pretty sure you know that. Doctor Garza, please answer the question.'

'Could I have the question again?'

O'Mara emphasized each word. 'Doctor, do you know the term "psychic horror?"'

'Yes.'

'Could you please tell us what it means?'

Garza shifted uncomfortably in his chair, saying finally, 'It's a term used to describe those few seconds before you die. You know that death is impending. You know there's no way to avoid it.'

O'Mara linked her hands behind her back, said, 'Doctor, an example of psychic horror is what that American journalist felt before he was beheaded by terrorists, isn't that right?'

'If you say so.'

'Wouldn't you agree that when Jessie Falk's heartbeat tripled, she was scared out of her mind? That during those two to three minutes of horrific pain and terror, she experienced psychic horror?'

'She may have.'

'Only two to three minutes of horrific pain and terror?'

O'Mara paused. A rather long, uncomfortable pause.

Yuki watched the hands of the clock move slowly, knowing what O'Mara was doing. She was making sure everyone in the room felt how long it had taken for Jessie Falk to die.

Chapter Seventy-Two

C indy was there in the courtroom's press row, her fingers scrambling over her keyboard, getting down most of O'Mara's cross-examination. It was sharp, incisive, fat-free, and merciless. One of the best interrogations she'd ever witnessed. *This girl is good, every bit as talented as Larry Kramer.*

'Doctor, you've told us that the death of Jessie Falk was a mistake. Now tell us this. *How* did this mistake happen?'

'I really don't know how the epinephrine got into her IV bag. It wasn't ordered, but look,' the doctor said, leaning forward in the witness chair, exasperation coloring his face, 'doctors and nurses are *human*. Mistakes *happen*. People die. Sometimes a bad wind blows.'

There was a gasp throughout the courtroom. Cindy's nimble fingers paused on the keys. What had he just said? *A bad wind blows?*

What the hell was that supposed to mean?

The collective gasp faded, and the room became as silent as a desert at noon. No one coughed, crossed their legs, or crumpled a candy wrapper.

O'Mara asked almost casually, 'Did you have anything to do with this "bad wind", Doctor?'

Lawrence Kramer shot to his feet. 'Objection! Counsel is badgering the witness. This has to stop.'

'Overruled. Sit down, Mr Kramer.'

'What are you accusing me of?' Garza asked.

'You don't get to ask the questions, Doctor Garza,' said O'Mara. 'Fourteen of the twenty people whose families I represent were treated by you or died on your watch—'

Garza snarled, 'How *dare* you?'

'Your Honor, please instruct the witness to answer.'

'Doctor Garza, answer the question.'

'I'll ask again,' O'Mara said, her voice level, constrained. 'Did you have anything to do with the deaths of those people?'

Garza drew himself up in the witness seat and stared hard at O'Mara. Cindy was thinking, *He would shoot her if he could.*

'I take the Fifth,' said Garza.

'I beg your pardon?'

'I said, I stand on the Fifth Amendment.'

Shock froze the faces of the jury; then the room seemed to explode with voices. Judge Bevins banged his gavel over and over.

'Thank you,' said O'Mara, a fleeting smile crossing her face. She even snuck a look at Larry Kramer. 'I have nothing further for this witness.'

'What I *meant* to say . . .'

'That's all, Doctor Garza.'

'The witness may step down. Court is in recess until nine tomorrow morning,' said the judge, slamming down the gavel one final time.

Cindy saved her file and stuffed her computer into her bag. Garza's stunning statements were still repeating in her mind as she was swept along with the crowd moving out into the hallway.

Sometimes a bad wind blows.

I stand on the Fifth Amendment.

The doc had just written his own headlines.

And they were about to go nationwide.

Yuki was waiting for Cindy at the door. Her eyes were huge. It was as if she had just won this case herself.

'Cindy, do you believe what he said?'

'I sure heard it. That fool refused to answer on the grounds that he might incriminate himself!'

'He just admitted it,' Yuki said, her voice cracking. 'That bastard is *guilty, guilty, guilty*.'

Chapter Seventy-Three

The smell of fried steak and onion and ripe plantains greeted me as I pushed open the door to Susie's. My friends were already in deep conversation when I got to the table.

I bumped Claire down the banquette and ordered a beer. 'What'd I miss?' I asked.

'I wish to God you could have been in court today, Lindsay,' Yuki said, her face animated, truly alive for the first time since her mother had died. 'Garza blew himself up,' she said. '*Spectacularly.*'

'I want to hear everything. Don't skip a word.'

Yuki had been drinking, for sure. She took me literally, impersonating both O'Mara and Garza *verbatim*.

Cindy jumped in, the two overtalking each other, until Claire and I simply cracked up.

Cindy plowed ahead. 'Thing is – no, really, you guys! All

he had to say was: "Nooooo. I had nothing to do with those patients' deaths."'

'Instead, he takes the Fifth!' said Yuki, slapping the table. She was glowering, but elated. 'What a jerk, stepping on his dick like that.'

'If you ask me, his conscience made him do it,' Cindy added. 'The more I dig into Garza's past, the more I find out what kinda bum he is.'

'More on that,' I said, holding up my empty glass. Loretta winked, returned with a refill. She also dropped laminated menus in front of us.

'For instance,' said Cindy, 'he left several of his jobs under a dark cloud. Not exactly "*You're fired*," but definitely "*Here's your hat. There's the exit.*" At least once, he ducked a sexual harassment suit.'

'Why am I not surprised that Garza's a skirt hound?' Yuki said. 'Arrogant bastard. Totally in love with himself.'

Cindy nodded vigorously. 'And more to the point, too many "accidents" happened to his patients. If I hadn't heard about other cases like his, I'd say it was unbelievable.'

'See, this is what gives me the willies,' Claire said. 'Only about one out of ten hospital mistakes ever get *reported*. Most of the time the mistakes aren't fatal – so, no problem. The patient survives and goes home.

'But even when patients *die* under totally hinky circumstances, people think doctors are so Godlike, they just accept whatever they're told. I've seen it happen.'

'Not me. I don't feel that way anymore,' said Yuki, her smile clouding over. It was like watching an eclipse of the moon. 'I don't think Dennis Garza is a god. Quite the opposite. I *know* he's e-vil!'

Chapter Seventy-Four

Yuki lay on her back in bed, watching passing headlights splash patterns on her ceiling.

She'd woken up so many times during the night, she wasn't even sure that she'd slept. Now, at a few minutes to 6:00 a.m., she was as awake as if a fire alarm had gone off under her pillow.

She threw back her blankets and went to her desk, where she booted up her computer. Three harplike notes rang out as she connected to the Internet.

She located his address on the first try. He lived less than a couple of miles away.

And he *was* e-vil.

Yuki threw her Burberry over her blue satin pajamas and took the elevator down to the parking garage, unlocked her Acura, and strapped herself in.

She felt exhilarated and reckless – as if she were about to

step out onto the ledge of a tall building in a high wind in order to see the view. Gunning her engine, she dropped the car onto the steep downhill chute of Jones Street. *Nothing ventured, right?*

She braked at Washington, watched the cable car rattle along the rails, tapped her nails against the steering wheel. She anxiously waited another long minute behind a school bus making a pickup, before turning left onto Pacific.

Then Yuki picked up speed, thinking she hadn't felt this crazed when her dad had died. She'd loved him. She'd grieved and she'd never, ever forget her love for him.

But her mother's death was different. It was a wound to her soul, a gross violation as well as a loss. She would never get over Keiko.

The fog parted as she turned onto Filbert. She frisked the house numbers on the pricy block with her eyes, finding 908 halfway down the street.

The house was very tall, three stories of pale yellow stucco frosted with a white trim.

Yuki sat parked in her car across the street watching the morning brighten in a conventional way. She stayed there a long time, hours; she was starting to feel as if she was a madwoman.

The FedEx man picked up a package. A Mexican nanny pushed twins in a stroller, a terrier on a leash trailed behind, ordinary activities that were now tinged with her own sadness.

Then the garage door of the yellow house opened. A black Mercedes Roadster backed out.

There he was. Creepy bastard.

So quickly, it felt more like an instinct than a decision, Yuki decided to follow him.

The two cars headed south in tandem, down Leavenworth, flying through twists and turns, steep climbs and drops, until the sight of Municipal Hospital filled her windshield.

Yuki signaled to follow the Roadster into the parking lot, when she saw a police cruiser in her rearview mirror. She gripped the wheel and tapped the brakes.

Had she been speeding?

She glided into an empty space at the curb, her eyes straight ahead as the cop car sailed past her. With a shaking hand, she turned off the ignition and waited for her heartbeat to slow.

Stupid girl. Stupid, stupid girl.

Her pj's were soaked with sweat, the satin collar and cuffs peeking out from her raincoat. My God. If the cop had questioned her, what would she have told him?

She'd been stalking Garza!

Pedestrians crossed at the red light in front of her. Office workers with briefcases and steaming coffee cups. Nurses and doctors, their coats buttoned over their scrubs, feet in soft-soled shoes.

Everyone going to their jobs.

Yuki reached two weeks back into her memory, remembered going to her high-rise office, being an associate in a top law firm, being a young, fast-track litigator.

She'd loved her work. Now she couldn't picture going to the office. All she was good for was obsessing about Dennis Garza. Thinking how in some way that monstrous man had killed her mother.

Chapter Seventy-Five

I saw the dusky-brown envelope lurking inside the tower of mail in my in-box. I fished it out and slit the flap with the shiv I kept in my top drawer.

I read the report. Read it again to make sure I was right. Latent had pulled fifty million smudged partials from the caduceus buttons.

There was nothing even remotely usable in the batch.

I got up from my desk, walked over to Jacobi, who was unwrapping an egg salad sandwich, piling coleslaw and garlic pickles onto a plate for his lunch.

'Join me?' he asked, holding up a sandwich half.

'Okay.'

I dragged up a chair, shifted his piles of junk, and made a space for myself.

As we ate, I downloaded my humming mind, filling Jacobi

in on Yuki's charge that her mother had been murdered at one of the city's most revered hospitals.

I told him the rest of it – my conversation with the nurse at Municipal and about the caduceus buttons I'd scored from Carl Whiteley during our executive-suite fandango.

I kept talking, and Jacobi didn't stop me. By the time I got to the malpractice suit, he'd broken out the box of Krispy Kremes. Put a chocolate glazed on a napkin in front of me.

'So, what are you thinking, Boxer? You thinking like a lieutenant, or an investigator?'

'The only autopsy report we have is Keiko's.'

'And how did Claire call it?'

'Without any evidence to the contrary? Pending, until all the facts are in.'

'So, what am I missing here? Where's the tie-in with Garza? You girls don't like the way he looks?'

'He's very handsome, actually.'

I told Jacobi that Keiko, like the patients in the malpractice case against Municipal, had entered the hospital through the ER – Garza's turf.

This was also true of thousands of patients who survived, checked out, and, for all I knew, lived happily ever after.

'I have to find something in Municipal's list of doctors, nurses, and maintenance staff that will either explain away my uneasy feelings or solidify them,' I said.

'So, what do you want from me, Boxer?' He crumpled up the rubbish from our lunch, dunked it into the trash can.

'I need you to work overtime.'

'Tonight?'

'*Unpaid* overtime.'

'Aw, Jeez, Lieutenant. I just remembered. I've got opera tickets . . .'

'Because I've used up my overtime budget for the month. Because I don't have a bona fide victim. And because I don't even know what the hell this is.'

Jacobi caved, knowing I'd do the same for him.

As the day shift stumbled out of the squad room and the graveyard shift trickled in, Jacobi and I ran the names of six hundred Municipal employees through the database.

We uncovered doctors with spotty medical histories, and rap sheets on lower-level staffers for domestic violence, assault, armed robbery, drug abuse, and DWIs aplenty.

My DeskJet spat out a summary of the 'button' victims.

I read it to Jacobi.

'All thirty-two patients came through the ER, and half were examined by Garza. They were black, white, brown, and every color in between. Ages seventeen to eighty-three and the timing of the deaths over the last three years appears to be random.'

'So, Boxer. What you're saying is, there's no victim profile.

If the thirty-two "button" patients were actually whacked – a big fat *if*, by the way . . .'

'You're right. I'm stumped, pardner. All I've got is this weird signature, and it's the only thing that ties the victims together.'

Jacobi had a coughing fit, his still-healing gunshot wound pinching his lung and giving him hell. He weighed down the stack of papers with a stapler and stood to put on his jacket.

'Just stating the obvious, but nobody is saying homicide except Yuki. What's she basing it on? She hates the guy?'

'I take your point, Warren. But buttons on the eyes of dead people means *something*. Talk me out of it if you think I'm crazy. Because I just can't put this out of my mind.'

Chapter Seventy-Six

I thought about the sick mind that had to be behind those caduceus buttons as I drove home that night. Wondering again if Yuki and I were paranoid or if we were right; a very strange killer was murdering patients at Municipal Hospital.

And no one was stopping him.

No one was even trying.

I arrived at the front door of my apartment barely remembering the drive there. I completed my pit stop in record time, and soon I was back in the Explorer, heading toward the hospital.

The crime scene – the homicide scene?

I parked near the entrance to the ER and went inside, I hung around the waiting room for a few minutes, flipping through an ancient issue of *Field and Stream*, blending in with the visitors sitting around me.

Then I took a little stroll.

The corridor was lit with a flat white fluorescence. Patients moved around carefully with their canes and IV poles. The medical staff walked purposefully, eyes straight ahead.

I kept my hands in my pockets, my baseball cap down over my eyes, hoping that the bulge of my Glock wasn't noticeable under a soft, zippered jacket.

I honestly had no idea what the hell I was looking for.

Maybe if I poked around, something would click, and the deaths and stats and tantalizing clues would add up to an honest-to-God serial crime, possibly the worst ever in San Francisco.

At the same time, I had no business surveilling the hospital. I was a homicide lieutenant, not a freakin' PI, and Tracchio would rip into me if he knew I was haunting Municipal on my own.

That's what I was thinking when I took a corner and slammed into a man in a white coat with medium-long black hair. I knocked a clipboard right out of his hand.

Christ!

'Sorry,' I said.

Then I nearly jumped out of my shoes. I'd thought of him often, but I hadn't seen Dr Garza since the day Yuki and I brought Keiko into the emergency room.

The doctor picked up his clipboard and fixed his hard black eyes on mine. It was a challenge, and I felt a nearly overwhelming impulse to throw him against the wall and cuff him.

You're under arrest for being a supercilious son of a bitch, for giving my friend nightmares, and for being a likely suspect in an unspecified number of suspicious deaths that might or might not be homicides. Do you understand your rights?

Instead, I balled my fists up inside my jacket pockets and stood my ground.

'I know who you are,' Garza said. 'Police lieutenant. Friend of Ms Castellano. She's a little overanxious, wouldn't you say? Having a hard time with her mother's death.'

'My friend is fine,' I told him. 'But I'm not so sure about you.'

His face cracked in a crazy grin that left us both in a paralytic standoff that was finally broken by his name blasting over the PA.

'Doctor Garza wanted in the ER.'

We stepped out of each other's way.

'I have work to do,' he said.

Chapter Seventy-Seven

L auren McKenna took a quick breath, then knocked on the door. She waited anxiously in the carpeted hallway of the hotel, her stomach churning, thinking she was out of her mind to do this. Absolutely nuts.

She stared down at her gold pumps, the fake croc shoes a witty touch with the silk chiffon skirt, wondering if he'd notice – and then, a split second later, going the other way again, thinking it wasn't too late to change her mind and get the hell out of there.

If she didn't like him, she was going to say, 'Sorry, I've got the wrong room.'

And then the door opened.

Her 'date' smiled. He looked Asian American, maybe thirty or so, slim, hair gelled into spikes. He was dressed okay in a blue cotton shirt and tan dress slacks, but hand-some, causing her a moment's doubt – was she pretty enough for this guy? He reached out his hand and clasped hers.

'I'm Ken,' he said warmly. 'You're gorgeous, Lauren. I love what you're wearing. You exceed all my expectations. Please come in.'

Lauren thanked him, stepped inside the plush hotel room, her heart banging in her chest.

Ken was saying, 'Let me see your face. Do you mind?'

He reached out, moved her bangs away from her eyes.

'Can you smile?' he said, then smiled himself.

Lauren clamped her jaw shut, clutched her handbag to her chest, looked around. She was trying to take in everything at once. *Fear Factor* on the TV, the bottle of champagne on ice, the man himself – a total stranger.

How had she thought she could go through with something like this?

'Come on,' he said. 'Give me a little smile.'

She did it then, baring her teeth in a clenched grin, Ken saying, 'Braces? How old *are* you, Lauren?'

'Nineteen. I'm a sophomore. In college.'

'You don't look it,' he said, smiling at her again, his teeth extremely white, that gorgeous skin, not too old, but still, this was nothing like a blind date.

She was in a hotel room with a stranger, one who wanted to pay her money for God only knew what.

Lauren started flashing back, thinking about all of the little humiliations of the past week – dodging the landlord, her bounced check taped next to the register at the campus bookstore, all the money she'd borrowed from friends.

Her roommate saying, 'Call this number. Margot can help you with an easy-breezy debt-consolidation plan.'

Easy-breezy? This was insane!

Now Ken was helping her out of her camel-hair coat. She encouraged herself: *hang in there, Lulu. Be brave. Try to have fun. Anyway, think of all that money.*

She saw Ken's eyes on her long legs, checking out her clingy, see-through blouse, her bra straps peeking out on top. So she put her hands on her hips, striking a pose like a runway model, laughing nervously when Ken looked amused.

Lauren heard herself say what she'd heard call girls say in movies. 'Mind if we get the business part out of the way?'

'Not at all.' Ken took several bills out of his back pocket. He stacked ten crisp hundreds in her open hand. 'You can count it. But it's all there. Don't worry, I'm a decent guy.'

Lauren smiled awkwardly, tucked the cash into her Kate Spade bag, and left it by the TV.

Ken offered her the wing chair near the window, and

she took it, gratefully accepting the glass of Dom. The champagne bubbled its way down her throat, damping down her anxiety.

'Do me a favor,' Ken was saying. 'Put your feet flat on the floor. Shake your head a little, like the wind is blowing through your hair. The way the beautiful models do it.'

'Like this?'

'Excellent. That's great. And you can relax, Lauren. I want you to have fun tonight.'

She *was* kind of relaxed, feeling warm in the expensive room with the velvet curtains. In the distance, the bridge was lit up and framed like a picture in the window.

Ken *was* very nice. Not rushing her or acting crude. He took the bottle from the ice bucket beside her, topped off her glass.

She said, 'I'll tell you a secret, Ken. This is my first time doing this.'

'Well, I'm honored,' he said. 'I can see that you're a real sweet girl. Hey, I'd like your opinion about something.'

He crossed the room and took some brochures out of his coat pocket. Offered them to her.

'I'm thinking of getting a new car. Which one do you like best? Porsche, BMW, Mercedes?'

Lauren was studying the glossy fliers, getting herself into the right mood, when she heard the door open from the adjoining room.

Her heart jumped as a really big guy with blondish hair came through the door as if he had every right to be there.

She shot an alarmed, questioning look at Ken.

'I was just going to tell you,' said Ken. 'This is my friend, Louis.'

Chapter Seventy-Eight

The car fliers fell from Lauren's hand, scattering around her gold shoes. Suddenly, she felt cold all over, her stomach dropping as if she were inside an elevator car and the cable had just snapped.

She gaped at Louis – broad, muscular, in khakis and a pink polo shirt. He looked like a jock, but older, maybe a coach.

He gave Lauren a look, like 'wow-ee.' Swiveled his head and looked at her again.

'Listen,' Lauren said. She felt queasy as she rose quickly out of the chair. She gauged the distance to the door. 'I didn't agree to a, a . . . threesome. That's definitely not okay with me.'

'Don't worry,' Ken said, holding up his hands, showing her his palms. 'Louis is a great guy. Look, Lauren, everything's okay. There's nothing to worry about. Your service wouldn't send you if there was.'

'I've made a mistake,' she said, crossing her arms over her chest. 'No offense, guys. I'm not like this. This really isn't *me*—'

'Louis,' Ken said, turning away from her, 'say hello, willya?'

The big man crossed the room, stuck out his large hand. His eyes were soft and shy. 'Lauren? Nice to meet you. I'm Louis.'

She kept her hand at her side, blinking into his face, imagining how she was going to paste on a smile, say she had to go to the bathroom, casually pick up her purse. Take out the thousand dollars. Put it on the TV . . . and blow the hell out of here.

'Louis, why don't you show Lauren – you know.'

It seemed to Lauren that time had slowed. She felt for the chair, steadied herself as Louis opened the closet door. *The closet door?*

'He has a heart of gold,' Ken was saying quietly, so that Louis couldn't hear. 'He hasn't been with a woman since his girlfriend dumped him last year. Such a decent person,' said Ken. 'I'd trust him with my life.'

Louis rolled a suitcase into the room, parked it next to the sofa. 'You're a seven, right?' Ken smiled at her. 'I asked your service to send a seven.'

Lauren nodded dumbly. 'It's his birthday,' Ken was saying. 'I didn't want him to be all alone.'

She was getting an idea about Louis. He was one of those teddy-bear types, maybe. A nice guy, but no game with girls. She watched him pull at the zipper on the suitcase, take out a long dress, and hold it out for her to see.

'This is for you, Lauren. Honest. It's yours to *keep*. No strings.'

Lauren stared at the navy-blue embroidered lace gown with a jewel neckline, the sheath silhouette that flared out below the knees to the floor. It was a Monique Lhuillier. Cost a ton. She could keep it?

'I have connections in the wholesale business,' Louis explained.

Could she do this? Could she?

She didn't feel so tense anymore. Two nice guys . . . let them do it to her . . . pay off her debts . . . beautiful dress . . . Suddenly she felt euphoric.

Ken was holding up a necklace, a curving chain with diamond chips, light bouncing off the facets.

'This is really your lucky night,' Ken was saying.

Lauren tried to step toward him, show him that it was okay, but her vision blurred and the room tilted. Her legs folded, and she dropped to the floor. The champagne climbed back into her throat.

I can't open my eyes! What's wrong with me?

She felt the two men jostle her onto the bed . . . their hands pulling at her clothes . . . thumbs hooked into her panties . . . her legs over someone's shoulders . . . rough bumping and . . . what was happening?

Air burst from her lungs. She felt a tremendous weight on her chest. She couldn't breathe!

'Please,' she cried out. 'Stop . . . please!'

Lauren heard someone laugh.

Something tightened around her neck. She tried to fight, but she couldn't move!

She strained for air, sucked *plastic* into her nose and mouth, stared up at Ken's contorted face through the film over her eyes, his kind brown eyes horrifically transformed.

Why?

Why are you doing this to me? I should never have come here. Oh, God, you're killing me! It's not too late, please . . . stop . . . God, give me another chance, and I'll never do anything like this again. No, nooo, I don't want to die. Please. Not like this.

Chapter Seventy-Nine

J ake Hadley glanced at his wristwatch, something he was doing about every sixty seconds now. Quarter to 9:00. He'd been standing with his boys in line outside the convention center since half past 7:00 that Saturday morning, catching their excitement as they squeezed his fingers, chased around him making car engine noises, asking, 'When, Daddy, when? Is it time?'

Today was the day his two boys had been waiting for all year – the opening of the International Car Show.

And finally, the line was moving.

'Dad! Oh boy oh boy oh boy. They're open.'

Jake smiled as he pulled the tickets out of his shirt pocket and handed them to the young man at the turnstile.

'Have fun in there,' the ticket-taker said. He was wearing a red-and-black T-shirt, the car-show logo across his chest in a speedy-looking type font with racing stripes; Jake thought he'd get a couple of those for the boys.

'Thank you. Plan to,' Hadley replied, holding his kids' hands as they jumped up and down, about to pull his arms out of their sockets.

Air-conditioning, soupy music, and the indescribably delicious smell of car wax and new leather enveloped them as they entered the glittering automobile extravaganza.

Where to look first?

Concept cars rotated on platforms. Pretty girls in tight-fitting skirt suits and prim shirts, showing a little too much leg, the ultimate blend of sex and money, performed their sales pitches.

Lights and music coming from everywhere.

Directly ahead, very attractive women with badges sat behind long tables, handing out glossy car brochures.

'If we get separated for any reason, this is Hadley Family Central,' Jake said, stooping to the height of his six-year-olds. 'Look around. Get a fix on *this* place, because this is where I'll come to find you.'

'Okay, Dad,' Stevie said. 'Byeeee!' Then he broke free, running ahead toward the European cars in the main hall.

'He wants to see the Ferraris,' Michael explained to his dad, 'and the Monstarotties, too.'

Jake laughed as he and Michael followed Stevie, the vast space filling up quickly as the crowd surged in like the tide.

Jake lost sight of Stevie for a moment; then he saw his boy on a carpeted platform as the salesman pulled the cover from the sleek, silver 2007 Ferrari coupé.

Jake called out over the noise of the crowd.'*Steven. Get down.* You're not allowed to stand up there, son.'

When Stevie turned, Jake saw a stricken look on his boy's face. A pang of fear seized Jake even though his son was in plain sight.

He gripped Michael's small hand.

'Come on, now, Stevie, get down.'

'The lady in the car, Dad. Something's wrong with the lady in the car.'

Jake Hadley started to tell his son that the model in the front seat wasn't real, but as he came closer, peered inside, his heartbeat quickened. Then it began to race.

The girl's open eyes were dulled, her pretty face tipped at an unnatural angle. He saw what appeared to be a purple shadow around her neck. She was wearing some kind of evening gown.

What the hell was this?

'Steven!' he yelled at his son, grasping the boy's arm. 'I said, come down now!'

By this time, others had seen the girl, too, her limbs frozen in a waxy parody of a mannequin – stone-dead in the two-hundred-thousand-dollar car.

The salesman in charge of the concession waved the crowd

away. His face was pale, his eyes wild, and he was shouting, 'Stand back, please. Stand back. Get the hell away from here!'

People swarmed toward the Ferrari, then away from it, a riptide eddying around Jake and his boys.

Sharp screams pierced the peppy pop music, and Jake's sons broke into tears. They pressed their faces into their father's body, fiercely hugging his waist and legs.

His heart galloping, Jake hoisted the twins onto his hips and walked quickly toward the exit.

He spoke sternly to the wide-eyed ticket-taker at the door.

'Someone's dead in there. A woman. You'd better call the police right now.'

PART FIVE

One-Stop Shopping

Chapter Eighty

The car-show visitors streamed out of the convention center looking like shell-shocked commuters who'd driven too close to the scene of a nasty, very bloody accident.

Jacobi was waiting for me just inside the big glass doors at the Howard Street entrance.

'Welcome to Groundhog Day,' Jacobi said.

'Tell me about it.'

Jacobi brought me up to date as we cut through the crowd, working our way toward the rear of the hall.

'White female, eighteen to twenty, blonde, a hundred pounds soaking wet, ligature mark around the neck, parked inside a Ferrari.'

'My God. These freaks. What *audacity*, *craziness*. What *nerve* to do this in public. Look at all these kids at the auto show!'

'They're messing with us, Boxer,' Jacobi said. 'Thumbing their noses and laughing their asses off. That's my read.'

He pointed out a couple of cops and CSU techs standing between the fast-food concessions and the European sports cars. A measly cordon of yellow crime-scene tape circled a hinged partition of fiberboard.

As if sixty square feet could contain a murder scene.

I stepped behind the partition and saw a vignette that shocked me to the bone. The victim had been dressed, coiffed, and displayed as a still life: *Blonde Woman in Slick Silver Car*. It was gallows humor, a sly inside joke, another pretty young girl killed for someone's sick pleasure.

'Get the manager over here,' I said to Jacobi. 'I'm shutting this place down.'

I got the chief on my cell, asked him to assign every available cop to the convention center and to give a heads-up to the mayor. Soon there'd be satellite vans on Howard Street and news choppers overhead, no doubt about it.

Charlie Clapper stopped shooting the scene long enough to hand me a pair of latex gloves.

'We're doing the best we can, Lindsay, but I'm going to take this car back to the lab. Give it our special detailing.'

'Any ID on the victim?'

'No wallet, no handbag, no nothing.'

I reached through the driver's-side window, touched the

girl's cheek with the back of my wrist. She was still warm. The ambient temperature was about 68 degrees and dry.

I had an idea. If we moved fast, it might work.

'Charlie? Let's Superglue her right here.'

CSU was setting up a fuming tent, when a portly man, red-faced and furious, pushed through the mob and got into my face.

His name tag identified him as 'Patrick Leroy, Show Manager,' and he was yelling, 'You can't shut us down. Are you insane?'

Spit flew as he shouted questions without answers: did I know how much revenue was going to go down the crapper? How I was turning great publicity into dog crap? How much shit was going to rain down on me *personally* because of it?

It was one long, scatological rant, and I didn't like any part of it.

'Someone's been murdered, Mr Leroy, understand? I have to preserve what's left of the crime scene and catch a killer. So while you act like a jackass, people are stampeding up and down the stairwells and spreading DNA around the bathrooms.

'The quicker your security staff help us empty this place out and submit to interviews, the sooner we'll be out of your hair.'

'And when do you think that will be?' he asked, breathing hard.

'We'll be done when we're done.'

'Give me a break! I have to tell people something.'

I almost felt sorry for him. Almost.

'Figure at least twelve hours,' I said.

'An entire day? *You're canceling out Saturday?* Millions of dollars shit-canned. *Millions,*' he said, stabbing the buttons on his cell phone. 'You have no idea.'

'There's a dead woman in that Ferrari,' I said.

Then I turned my back on him as Jacobi appeared at my side, saying that he'd collected the security tapes, including those that had been trained on the loading docks.

We paused to watch cops usher paying customers through the promotional glitz and out the door. Nobody was very happy, to put it mildly.

'If we don't nail these psychos,' Jacobi said, 'I'm taking early retirement. Without a party. And you, Boxer, you're going to be busted down to meter maid.'

'You know what I'm wondering?' I said to my old partner. 'How the hell did they get that girl in here?'

Chapter Eighty-One

I kept rubbing my arms against the chill inside the morgue as I took in the pitiful sight of our latest Jane Doe lying nude on a steel table.

She looked as innocent and as vulnerable as a sleeping child.

Claire greeted me from her stepladder, where she was shooting the victim from above, while at ground level, nonessential personnel ogled the naked, pretty woman.

'Hey!' Claire barked. 'Everyone, get out. Out! Not you, Lindsay. Bunny! Bag and tag the shoes. Give everything to Loomis and don't forget the necklace. It's right there on the table.'

Claire stepped heavily down from the ladder, adjusted the light a few degrees, revealing four faint smudges fanned out on the girl's left cheek.

Fingerprints.

I could hardly believe it. Thank God, we finally had something.

'Those are a child's prints,' Claire said, crushing my half second of elation. 'Left by the six-year-old boy who found her.'

'Nuts,' I said. 'Hey, what's that?' I moved in closer to better see the glint of something in the girl's mouth. Was it a clue? Maybe a message?

'Too sad for words, that's what it is,' Claire told me. 'Show Girl here is wearing braces.'

The air went out of me.

She was so young. Too young to die, especially like this.

Why were you working, little girl?

I watched Claire scrape under the victim's nails, clip them into an envelope. Seal it, sign it. Walk around the table and do the same to her other hand.

'I got the tox screen back, Lindsay,' she said. 'Same sorry story, girlfriend. Her blood alcohol was point one one zero and there was a ton of Rohypnol in her system. Same as the others.'

'So they liquored her up and drugged her, of course. Why take any chances she'd fight back? Cause of death?'

'Asphyxia. Like before, they probably burked, smothered, and strangled her sometime around midnight. Definitely a homicide.'

'Those pricks are consistent, aren't they? I'm guessing they gave her a bath to get rid of trace evidence. Like the other two.'

'So you think she was killed in a hotel room?'

'Yeah, and she's probably a working girl. Three girls down, and I'm still looking for one decent lead.'

Claire said, 'I think I've got something for you, honey.' She turned to her assistant. 'Bunny, help me roll Jane Doe. Can you do that?'

Claire placed Show Girl's right arm across her body and pulled her over to her side as Bunny balanced her.

'Look here,' said Claire, pointing to the smudge behind the girl's left knee.

I stooped down, saw the crisp ridges of a fingerprint that had been raised by fuming the girl's skin with Superglue.

The blue lace gown the victim had been wearing was floor-length. Her legs had been covered to her ankles.

That fingerprint hadn't been made by a bystander.

I turned my head and beamed at my best friend, Claire.

'The perp who washed her,' she said, beaming back at me. 'He missed a spot.'

Chapter Eighty-Two

Jacobi opened the double door to the morgue and announced, 'I know how they got the vic into the convention center.'

'You've got our full attention,' I said.

He walked straight through the vault to Claire's office, returned a minute later with a bottle of water.

'I've been eating hot dogs all day,' he explained.

'Help yourself,' said Claire. 'Hell, Warren, take two.'

Jacobi eased his butt onto a stool. His face was sagging from exhaustion, but sparks were going off behind his heavily lidded eyes.

'Get this, Boxer. A truck was coming from the marshaling yard to the convention center with a load of carpeting. The driver apparently stopped to take a leak against a building on Folsom. Trucks aren't supposed to stop there, but they always do.'

'So it was a hijack?'

'Yeah, but it wasn't a heist. More like a *hitchhike*. The bad guy comes up behind the driver, sticks a gunlike object into his back.'

Jacobi started to laugh.

'Oh. Tell me the joke.'

'Sorry. Imagining the guy holding his joint when he feels the gun sticking in his back. It's a guy thing, Boxer.

'Anyway. The holdup guy uses the driver to get the other guy out of the truck. Knocks them both out with a stun gun. Then he and his buddy load them into the back of the truck, tape and gag them.'

'So now they've got a truck with approved plates and the driver's ID,' I said. 'You're thinking they transferred our victim into that truck? Maybe she was inside some kind of container?'

'No flies on you, Lieutenant.'

'I try to keep up with you, Jacobi. I'm listening. Keep talking.'

Jacobi nodded. 'So they drive to the convention center loading docks, unload this young lady's container onto a hand truck, wait for the right moment. Then they decant her inside and pose her in the Ferrari.'

'Maybe the container was a suitcase,' I said. 'A big one. Leather. With wheels.'

'Could very well have been something like that.'

'Unbelievable,' Claire said. 'That they have the nerve to move a body in full sight, let alone pose her inside a car at the auto show!'

'She would've looked like a dummy if anyone had noticed her – and no one did,' Jacobi said. 'I scanned all the videos. It was pure chaos last night. Forklifts doing wheelies. Cars being unloaded. Hundreds of look-alike guys in work clothes setting up the booths.'

'Can the drivers ID their attackers?' I asked.

'It was dark. They were completely surprised. The perps wore stocking masks.'

Jacobi came closer to the victim's body. 'Smell that? There it is again. That's swamp magnolia.'

'Black Pearl.'

A thought broke through to my conscious mind like a bubble rising up from the bottom of a lake. It was so simple and obvious. Why had it taken me so long to make the connection?

'It's one-stop shopping,' I said out loud.

'What do you mean, Boxer?'

'The designer clothes and the shoes. The killers grabbed what they could off the rack, clothes for a girl they hadn't met yet. So sometimes they got the wrong size. The real jewelry, the good stuff, was under lock and key, but beads and rhinestones? No problem.'

'The perfume that they sprayed on those girls,' said Jacobi, picking up the thread. 'It's exclusive. Only sold at one place.'

'Our killers had easy access,' I said. 'They snatched it all at the same store.'

Chapter Eighty-Three

I was behind the wheel of a new Lincoln sedan at 8:00 that Monday morning. The chief was scrunched in beside me, looking about as comfortable as a pickle in a jar. He was in uniform, his hair slicked down, and he was sweating.

A dozen squad cars caravaned behind us as we took to the roller-coaster streets of San Francisco. What a ride this was going to be.

'We're pissing off a lot of important people for a dead hooker,' Tracchio said to me.

'We owe her.'

'I know, Boxer. We owe them all.'

Tracchio buzzed down the car windows, letting in the chilly 54 degrees.

I knew he was feeling the heat.

He'd taken over the job of captain without having been a

detective. And he'd inherited a police department with the most pathetic record of crime solution in the country. Right now, he was relying on me. I wanted to deliver for him.

The Sunday *Chronicle* was on the seat between us. The front page headline read CAR SHOW MURDER, and the story continued on page three with a photo of our victim, now dubbed Show Girl, along with a public plea for information on the girl, or anything else.

The victim's devastated friends had come forward, and now Show Girl had a name.

Lauren McKenna had no current boyfriend, liked pretty, trendy shoes, and while she may have been hooking, she was at Berkeley full-time.

She'd only been nineteen.

Her death was senseless and tragic. And her killers were still enjoying their freedom – and probably planning to kill again.

Tracchio drummed his fingers on the door panel as I turned right into Union Square.

I ran my theory through my mind once more. If I was wrong, the chief was going to bear the brunt of it.

Despite a nauseating flicker of doubt, it still added up for me. The Car Girl killers worked at Nordstrom.

Chapter Eighty-Four

The upscale department store, one of my own favorites, wasn't yet open to the public. But Nordstrom's employees were assembled and waiting in shifting clumps on the store's main floor.

Nordstrom's president, Peter Fox, was looking very handsome in Ralph Lauren, houndstooth plaid, and five-hundred-dollar shoes from Italy.

He had a calm demeanor, but I could see the sweat on his upper lip and worry in his eyes as he walked the chief and me through the store.

'I carefully checked the merchandise on the list you faxed me,' he said to me. 'Checked it myself. You were right that those items had been stolen, but I can't believe any of our people had anything to do with *murders*.'

The dramatic, curving escalators that connected Nordstrom's main floor to the floors above and the mall below had been shut down.

The scent of Black Pearl was in the air as I climbed a dozen steps so that I could be seen over the sparkling counters and display racks.

I introduced myself, and when the room quieted down, I explained why we were there.

'Our crime lab found prints on the victim's shoes,' I said, 'and we want to exclude anyone who may have touched those shoes in the course of doing their jobs.

'If anyone feels uncomfortable giving up fingerprints and a painless cheek swab, please give your name to Inspector Jacobi. He's the good-looking gentleman in the brown jacket standing at the information booth. Then you're free to go.'

Three long lines formed along the marble aisles. Clapper's crew took samples and directed people to a table, where their IDs were checked and their prints were taken.

Molly Pierson, the human resources director, stood beside me. She had spiky white hair and lime-green glasses framing her dark eyes. She ran a pen down the list of employees, crossing off names of those present.

'I saw him a minute ago, so I know he's here,' she muttered, nervously sweeping the room with her eyes. Her anxiety lit a match to mine.

'Who do you mean?' I asked.

'Louis Bergin. Our stockroom manager. I don't see Louis.'

Chapter Eighty-Five

'Louis was in front of me on line,' volunteered a thin man with a goatee standing a few feet away. 'He said he had to go to the can.'

The man pointed his finger toward the men's room, ten feet away from an elevator. I saw the arrow above the elevator door arc downward, the car stopping at the ground floor, three levels below us.

'What does Louis look like?' I asked urgently.

'Big guy. Over six feet. Blond.'

I turned to the chief.

'I'll cover you here,' he said. Then I shouted to McNeil and Samuels to check the bathroom. Told Lemke and Chi to block the exits to all the streets.

'*Nobody* goes out.'

Conklin and Jacobi were behind me, running down

the escalator, the three of us spilling out into the immense interior of the mall.

I pulled up short in the thickening foot traffic drifting in and out of the trendy shops – Godiva, Club Monaco, Bailey Banks & Biddle, Bandolino, and Kenneth Cole.

I didn't know where to look first, which way to turn. I didn't see anyone matching Louis Bergin's description.

My Nextel rang, and I grabbed it from its clip.

It was McNeil, saying, 'He's not in the bathroom, boss. Nobody's in here.'

'You and Samuels, take Fifth Street,' I said.

'*There he is*,' said Jacobi.

I saw him, too.

Across the mall, a coatless man in a white shirt was walking away from us, blending in with the crowd. He was about six two, 230 pounds, dirty-blond hair, smoking a cigarette.

A bruiser.

I drew my weapon, called out his name over the echoing rumble of the milling crowd.

'Louis Bergin. This is the police. Stay right where you are. Put your hands in the air.'

Chapter Eighty-Six

L ouis Bergin swung his big head toward me. We locked eyes over the crowd for a fraction of a second, and I yelled again. 'Bergin. Stop right there. Don't make me shoot you!'

He snapped his head back around – and began to run.

Adrenaline poured into my bloodstream as Conklin, Jacobi, and I dodged shoppers, followed Bergin at a run, out through the southeast exit of the mall into the morning rush on Market Street.

Bergin had to be fleeing for a reason.

Was there a warrant out for his arrest?

Or was he running from us because he'd murdered three girls?

I had another blinding moment as I tried to see through the cars whizzing by on the street, screen the pedestrians through my mind, pick a man in white shirtsleeves out of the bustling crowd.

My heart hammered as I finally saw him thirty yards ahead, loping across Market against the light, taking a right onto Powell.

'There!' I yelled out to Jacobi and Conklin. I fixed my eyes on Bergin, who was cutting a path through the shrieking crowd ahead of us.

The sidewalks flanking Powell were an obstacle course of pedestrians, street vendors, passengers lined up for the trolley.

I was already feeling the takedown as a reality, anticipating the rush of throwing Bergin to the ground – but then he knocked aside a man selling pottery on the sidewalk, mugs and bowls smashing as Bergin took to the street.

That's where he picked up speed, his long strides eating up the asphalt, expanding the distance between us.

The gangly man whose pottery stall had been overturned joined the chase, as did a group of brainless, cheering kids who'd been loitering around the newsstand.

I held up my badge, turned my fury on them all.

'Get out of the street. You could get shot!'

Jacobi was wheezing and hacking behind me. The uphill run was too much for him, and he dropped back, limping from the gunshot wounds he'd taken last May.

I shouted, 'Warren, send mobile units to Union Square.'

Up ahead, Conklin backpedaled in a circle. That's when I knew we'd lost Bergin.

I swept the doorways of dozens of shops with my eyes. If Bergin had ducked into one of the small hotels or restaurants, or God forbid, gone underground to the BART station, he was *gone*.

A blur grabbed my attention – Bergin running alongside the trolley up ahead, using it as a barrier between us.

'Conklin!'

'I see him, Lou.'

Rich Conklin's stride was a good match for Bergin's, and he was really fit. As Conklin crossed Powell behind the trolley, I heard him yelling to pedestrians, 'Outta my way. Get back.'

He couldn't close the gap.

I was close enough to see Conklin hook the trolley's grab rail with his left hand, jump onto the rear step and ride for twenty feet before executing a first-class flying tackle onto Bergin's back, pulling the big man down.

Bergin fell to the sidewalk, grunting as the air went out of his lungs.

I was heaving, my legs wobbling with fatigue. I didn't think my heart could beat any faster, but I was right there. I had my Glock in both hands, pointed at Bergin's head.

'Stay down, you son of a bitch,' I gasped. 'Stay down and keep your hands in front of you. Don't move a finger.'

Chapter Eighty-Seven

Panting, I called in our location as Conklin cuffed Louis Bergin's hands behind his back.

Bergin's palms and the right side of his face were scraped and bloody from the fall.

But he didn't say a word.

And he didn't fight.

I was thinking ahead, and I was troubled. All we had on Bergin was 'interfering with a police officer', a charge that called for minimal bail, nothing more than that.

If he could cough up a thousand bucks, he'd be back on the street in half an hour. He'd be in Vancouver by dinnertime, and we'd never see him again.

Conklin read my mind.

'Lou, you saw him. He was resisting arrest.'

My eyebrows shot up. Resisting? The man was lying on the street like a dead tuna.

'He swung at me,' Conklin insisted, rubbing his jaw. 'Got in a good one before I wrestled him down. Have to admit, Lou, this gorilla struck a police officer.'

'I wish I hadda struck you, dickhead,' Bergin muttered from the sidewalk. 'I woulda broken your jaw.'

'Shut up, please,' Conklin said to Bergin good-naturedly. 'I'll tell you when to speak.'

I understood what Conklin was doing: upping the charge so that the bail bond would rocket.

It wasn't playing fair, but we were desperate. We needed time to find out if Bergin had killed our Car Girls.

Conklin read Bergin his rights, stuffed him into the back seat of a cruiser just as Jacobi pulled up and offered me a ride to the Hall.

During the drive, I told Jacobi that I couldn't wait to inter-rogate Louis Bergin, to get answers, to get a confession, to put a name to his accomplice, to put the Car Girl killers away.

'You okay, Boxer? You sound rattled.'

'Yeah,' I admitted. 'I'm thinking, what if Louis Bergin isn't our guy? What's next? Because I don't have another idea in the world.'

Chapter Eighty-Eight

Jacobi and I waited impatiently in my office as Bergin was processed, his mug shots and fingerprints going into the system for the first time.

'You and Conklin should interrogate him,' Jacobi said.

'It's your case,' I said. 'It's your interview.'

'Let's see how Conklin handles it, Boxer. I'll be right behind the glass.'

The hulking Louis Bergin was sitting at the table inside Interview Two. Conklin and I took the seats across from him, and I reviewed the scant information we'd coaxed from the computer.

'Says here you're a solid citizen,' I said to Bergin. 'A good employment history and a nice clean sheet. This shouldn't take too long.'

'Good. Because as soon as I'm out of here, I'm gonna sue your ass for false arrest. And I'm suing *you*, for tackling me.'

'Take it easy, Louis. I think you've been watching too much *Law and Order*. Here,' Conklin said, handing Bergin a paper napkin. 'You're a mess.'

Bergin glowered at Conklin as he dabbed at his face, his palms, wadded up the napkin and held it in his hand.

Conklin said, 'So, Louis, explain to me and the lieutenant. Why'd you run?'

'I run every day. It's exercise, ya little dick.'

'I'm trying to help you, man. Give you the benefit of the doubt.'

Louis laughed. 'Yeah. My new best friend.'

'Better believe it,' said Conklin. 'Maybe you boosted some clothes and sold them. We don't care about theft, do we, Lieutenant? We're Homicide.'

'Maybe you should've asked me nice, asswipe, instead of taking me down for a bullshit "resisting arrest."'

Conklin stood, telegraphing his move, and Bergin lifted his hands to fend off the blow. As Conklin smacked the back of Bergin's head, the balled-up, bloody napkin went flying, landing softly behind his chair.

'Show some respect for your public servants,' Conklin said. 'Especially when there's a lady present.'

Conklin casually reached down, slipped the napkin into his back pocket.

'Hit me again,' Bergin said, swiveling his huge head, 'and I'm going after you for police brutality. You've got nothing on me, so either kiss my ass and let me out of here or get me a lawyer. I've got nothing to say.'

My cell phone rang – it was the worst possible time. I glanced down at the caller ID.

It was Joe.

'It's the mayor,' I said, grabbing the phone out of its holster. 'I have to take this. Sorry.'

'Yes, sir. We're interrogating him now.' I turned my back on Conklin and Bergin.

My man's voice was sweet in my ear. 'I'm on a plane to Hong Kong, blondie,' he said, not missing a beat. 'I'll be heading back next weekend. I could stop over in San Francisco . . .'

'Yes, sir. He looks good for it,' I said.

'So you think you'll be free?'

'Absolutely.'

'You won't forget.'

'You've got my word.' I glimpsed my face in the mirror, scowling even as a smile played at the corners of my mouth.

'I love you, Lindsay.'

'You bet, sir. I'll keep you posted.'

I clicked off the phone, shook off the effects of that divine twenty-second interlude, and pulled myself back to the present.

'How does it feel, Louis? You're Mayor Hefferon's number one priority.'

'It feels great.' He grinned.

Louis was right. We had nothing on him. And once he had a lawyer, we were going to be back to chasing our tails.

There was a knuckle rap on the glass. I stepped outside into the hallway, where Jacobi was waiting for me.

'Did you hear?' I said. 'Bergin lawyered up.'

'He *needs* a lawyer. A good one,' said Jacobi. 'His prints match the one behind Lauren McKenna's knee.' Jacobi smirked. 'That'll hold him for a while.'

It was like my whole body was smiling, that's how good I felt. I grinned at Jacobi, high-fived him, low-fived him, bumped hips, did everything but kiss him on the lips.

I opened the door, called Conklin outside the box.

'Louis's print is a match to the one we pulled from Show Girl's body. It's your collar, Richie. Why don't you do the honors?'

I was standing with Inspector Conklin when he said, 'Louis Bergin, we're dropping the resisting charge. You're under arrest for the murder of Lauren McKenna.'

Chapter Eighty-Nine

I touched the handle of my handgun for luck, then Conklin, Jacobi, and I entered the Keystone Apartments at the Hyde Street entrance. The seven-story all-brick building was near the cable line, a short, straight shot to Nordstrom Square.

The ancient black man who opened the front door told us that Louis's roommate was at home.

'She's an artist. She always home daytimes.'

We took the small creaking elevator, found apartment 7F at the front of the building. I pressed the doorbell, rapped on the door.

'Open up. SFPD.'

I heard scurrying inside, but no one came to the door. I knocked again, this time with the butt of my gun. The sound reverberated down the long, tiled hallway, but still, no one answered.

I tried the door, but it didn't budge.

'Break it down,' I said, standing aside.

Conklin threw his weight against the thin wooden panels until the locks splintered the door frame.

Jacobi went in first, and I was behind him, taking in the small front room, the brown leather sofa, a row of framed pencil drawings above it: pinup girls in classic cars.

I saw an envelope pinned to the drawing board by the window. It was addressed to Louis.

'Police,' I called out. 'Come out with your hands in the air.'

I pocketed our search warrant, crossed the small, dark living room, clasping my weapon in front of me. I smelled it a second before Jacobi muttered, 'Swamp magnolia.'

Behind us, Conklin switched on the lights.

The bedroom was at the end of a short hallway. I gripped the old-fashioned pressed-glass doorknob. It turned, rattling in my hand.

I opened the door, gave it a gentle shove, letting it swing slowly inside.

My eyes flicked across the clothes-strewn, rumpled bed to the open window.

I did a double take – that's how hard it was to absorb what I saw.

A beautiful Asian woman of indeterminate age was crouched inside the window frame. Her flimsy white peignoir was backlit

JAMES PATTERSON & MAXINE PAETRO

by dim sunlight. Her sleeves and the fringed layers of her short black hair fluttered in the breeze.

I was entranced by her open, childlike expression, especially given the dingy surroundings of the room.

'I'm Lieutenant Boxer,' I said softly, lowering my gun, feeling Jacobi and Conklin at my back, praying that they'd take my lead.

'What's your name?' I said. 'Come inside so we can talk.'

The woman's eyes glittered, some inner thought making her smile. I was looking at her bright, lipsticked mouth when she pursed her lips, almost as if she was blowing kisses.

'Vroom, vroom,' she said.

It happened so fast.

I sprang forward – but I was too late. She went out the window.

For a long second afterward, I still saw that glowing figure inside the window frame. Then the figure seemed to fly. Her image was burned into the back of my brain.

Jacobi and Conklin were standing beside me at the window when her body hit the street below.

Chapter Ninety

Louis Bergin hadn't weathered his twenty-four hours in jail well. His clothes were rumpled, and his scabby, unshaven face made him look like he'd slept in an alley.

But there was rage in his eyes.

And now he had a lawyer.

Oscar Montana was a sharp-faced young turk from the public defender's office. I'd met Montana before, liked him, and thought Bergin could do far worse.

'What've you got on my client?' Montana said, banging his bronze Halliburton briefcase on the table, then cracking open the locks.

'We searched Mr Bergin's apartment this morning,' Conklin said. 'There was a beautiful young woman there. Your girlfriend – right, Louis? Name of Cherry Chu.'

'She had nothing to do with anything,' Louis muttered.

Louis's voice was like the rumbling of a volcano, dangerous, barely containing his fury. Conklin only moved closer, pulling out a chair, sitting two feet from the suspect.

'No, huh?' Conklin said. 'Well, we're holding her anyway. I think she's going to flip on you. In fact, she already has.'

Louis clenched his fists and shook his head defiantly.

'She'd *never* say anything against me.'

'She didn't have to say anything. We're holding her for defenestration,' said Conklin. 'You know what that is, Louis?'

'For God's sake,' Montana said. 'What kind of sadist are you, Inspector?'

Louis looked incredulous. 'You're Homicide and you're charging her for a sex crime?'

Conklin leaned back in his chair. 'Defenestration is from the Latin meaning "out the window." Yeah, Louis. We tried to save her, but she jumped. We're holding her at the morgue. Sorry for your loss.'

Louis bellowed. *'Nooo!'*

His body seemed to inflate, the cords of his neck standing out, his muscles swelling. Then, like Samson pushing against the temple columns, Louis pressed his hands against the table and started to stand.

Conklin leaned on Bergin's shoulder with both hands, forcing him back into the chair.

'Mr Montana,' I said, 'tell your client to behave or I'll have him shackled.'

'Louis. Don't let them bait you. Just listen.'

I was listening and watching, too.

Conklin was thinking fast, moving fast. A natural interrogator. And a brave cop.

I saw why Jacobi was proud of him. I was proud of him, too.

'We found out something a little unusual at the morgue,' said Conklin. 'Tell you the truth, I was surprised when the ME told us. I mean, Cherry was such a knockout, Louis. Hard to believe.'

I was watching Louis's face as Conklin snapped first one driver's license, then another onto the table like playing cards.

The photos made a startling side-by-side comparison. Looking from one to the other, you could see it clearly. The same eyes, the same cheekbones. The same mouth.

Conklin kept going. 'I had to see these two pictures together to believe it. Kenneth Guthrie. Cherry Chu. *They're one and the same person.*

'I guess he was being Ken when you and he did the killings – right, Louis? And when he was Cherry Chu, he was your girlfriend.

'Your *girlfriend*,' Conklin said, his voice colored with wonder. 'Bro, your girlfriend *was a man.*'

Chapter Ninety-One

I watched Louis's face change from red to mottled to a blood-less, almost clammy white. He moaned, then started banging his head on the table until his attorney got up from his chair and grabbed his shoulders. Shook him until he stopped.

Montana looked up at me, his expression explosive, and it wasn't an act.

'Where the hell is your inspector going with this, Lieutenant? Do you have any *evidence* against Mr Bergin? If not, pardon me for saying drop dead, and we'll see you at his arraignment.'

'We lifted Louis's print from one of our victims,' I said, 'and his DNA is at the lab. Marked "rush" and red-flagged.'

'He gave you his DNA?'

'He abandoned it. We collected it,' I said, sitting down beside Louis, talking just to him.

'Louis, help me understand why you and Cherry killed those

young women. Inspector Conklin and I, we really want to hear your side of the story. Maybe there's some kind of mitigating circumstance—'

'Suck my dick.'

'Hunh. Well, you were right, Richie,' I said to Conklin. 'Louis really doesn't like women at all, but I do get the feeling he's drawn to them sexually. You think?'

'And that's where Kenny comes in,' Conklin said, rolling with me. 'He kinda pimped for him. Isn't that right, Louis? You did the rapes, and then the two of you snuffed the girls.

'And after you and your lover killed together, what then? You guys got your jollies? I think the jury is going to hate you for that, don't you, Lieutenant?'

'Don't answer, Louis. Don't say a word,' Montana said urgently.

'I think you're going to tell us everything,' I said to Bergin, 'because you're going to do better with us than you'll ever do with a jury. And then there's *this*.'

I placed a white number 10 envelope on the table. It was addressed to Louis in smudged blue ink. He could see it, but it was beyond his reach.

He blinked as he recognized the handwriting.

I'd been counting on that.

'The fall to the alley that Cherry took was easy compared to the one you're going to take,' I said. 'Have you thought about what it's going to be like? Twenty years or so, isolated on death row, waiting your turn for the needle?'

'That's enough, Lieutenant,' said Montana, slamming down the top of his briefcase. 'Mr Bergin hasn't even been indicted for jaywalking—'

'We're going to nail Mr Bergin on three homicides,' I snapped. 'But I can offer this much wiggle room.' I held my fingers a quarter of an inch apart.

'Really?' Montana said. 'That much?'

'A young female was found in LA two years ago, dumped alongside the freeway,' I told him. 'The DNA in her rape kit matches the DNA we found inside Louis's victims.

'If your client tells us about the Car Girl homicides and that victim in LA, we'll work with the DA. See if we can take the death penalty off the table. You have my word.'

'We'll get back to you,' said Montana. 'Louis, we're out of here.'

'This is a limited-time offer,' I said, putting my hand over the envelope.

'Can I have that letter?' Louis asked. He was almost sheepish about it.

In the last few moments, Louis's expression had melted like candle wax. His eyes were red, his face suffused with pain and loss.

'This is evidence,' I said, looking into Louis's big, wet eyes. 'But I'll read you a line or two.'

I opened the envelope that I'd taken from the drawing board in Louis's living room, took out five thin pages, inscribed from margin to margin in a neat, rounded hand.

'I think she was still writing this when we entered your apartment,' I said. 'See, the signature is smudged. The ink was still wet.'

Louis's mouth was parted. His breathing shallow. His eyes were focused on me.

'Cherry says here "Forgive me, my love, but I can't live without you. You were the one dream I ever had that came true . . ."'

'Well, this is pretty private,' I said, neatening the pages, folding them back into the envelope. 'It almost breaks my heart.'

Louis said, 'Tell me what I have to do. I'll do whatever.'

'Listen to me,' said Montana, putting a hand on Louis's arm. 'Don't say a word. Let me do my job. Their only witness against you is *dead*—'

Things got a little crazy suddenly. Louis backhanded his lawyer with a loud crack, sending Montana and his chair crashing to the floor. Blood spouted from Montana's nose.

I leaped from my seat as Louis stood, clenched his fists, and screamed down at him.

'Don't you understand, you little turd? I don't care if I live or die. My life is over. I'm never going to see her again.'

He turned his livid eyes on me. 'What do I have to say to get that fucking LETTER?'

'Just tell us what you did.'

'Okay. I said I'll do it.'

I thought my heart would explode from exhilaration.

I forced my expression to remain neutral even though I was doing jump splits and dancing under a shower of champagne inside my head.

I stepped outside the room to make damned sure that the camera was still rolling. I returned as Conklin was getting Montana back on his feet.

'I'll call the DA,' I said to Louis. 'You can have a copy of the letter. Right after we hear your confession.'

Chapter Ninety-Two

J acobi was on a high just thinking about Louis folding into a big, wet heap – feeling fantastic that he'd been on the team that had brought that psycho down. *Both* psychos.

Now, at 8:00 p.m., he was still working, trying to nail another sicko to the wall.

Maybe a worse one. Possibly the most dangerous killer ever in San Francisco.

He steered the unmarked police car north along Leavenworth, keeping track of Dennis Garza's black Roadster two cars ahead. The fog swirled up eerily from the pavement even as rain pelted down.

He braked for the red light at Clay, stared at the red-haloed taillights, thinking how Garza seemed to have a pretty damned good life for himself.

So why would he want to screw himself by playing God at the hospital?

As the oncoming traffic lit the interior of the car in front of him, Jacobi was startled to recognize Yuki Castellano driving the Acura that was between him and the Mercedes. What the hell?

Traffic rolled forward, and Jacobi accelerated, keeping both cars in view, his surprise growing into certainty as the Acura followed the Lexus through every turn. Jacobi considered his two options. Then he flicked on the siren and the grille lights, turning the gray Crown Vic into something that looked and sounded like a demon from hell.

Ahead of him, the young lawyer glanced into her rearview mirror, pulled her car over to the curb.

Jacobi slid the Vic in behind her, called Dispatch, asked for an unmarked car to pick up the surveillance. He read out the Roadster's plate number and signed off. Pulled up the collar of his tweed jacket and got out of his car.

He walked up and stooped to the height of the Acura's passenger window, flashed his light into Yuki's eyes.

'May I see your driver's license?' he said.

'Okay, okay, Officer. I have it here. What was I doing wrong?'

'Your license, please.'

'Sure,' Yuki said, shielding her eyes from the light.

She turned away, rooting in her handbag, spilling credit cards and change out of her wallet. She seemed very nervous, not herself at all. She finally located her license and handed it over.

Jacobi took the license to his car. Ran it through the computer, giving her time to think. Then he walked back through the hard, slanting rain and asked Yuki to get out of her car.

'You want me to get out of my car?'

'That's right. Get out and put your hands on the hood. Mind if I take a look inside here? Anything you want to tell me about? A weapon? Any illegal substances?'

'*Warren?* Is that you? It's *me*, Yuki. What's this about?'

'That's what I want to know.'

Yuki was getting soaked, her hair falling over her eyes, making her look like a wet Yorkie. She was wearing sweat-pants, a thin T-shirt, beaded bedroom slippers, no socks. Her teeth were chattering.

Jacobi flashed his light briefly around the interior of the Acura, then told Yuki, 'Okay, you can get back in.'

He watched her buckle up, handed her back her license, and said, 'I've been behind you for quite a while, Yuki. What the hell were you doing?'

'You were following me?'

'Please answer my question.'

'I was just going for a drive, okay?' she said, getting pissed off now.

'Don't lie to me. You were following that Roadster.'

'No – okay. But so what? I'm just – I'm just – it's nothing!'

'Think about what you're saying,' he said, raising his voice, wanting to shake her up, wanting to scare her a little. 'If that guy is the whackjob you reckon he is, don't you think he's going to get you out of his way? C'mon, Yuki, use your brain.'

He watched Yuki make fish lips, coming up with nothing.

'I'm not being a prick here because it gives me a thrill. You're a nice person and way too smart for this. You're looking for trouble, and I hope to God you don't find it.'

Yuki wiped the water off her face with her hands, nodded her head. 'Do you have to tell Lindsay?'

'That depends on you.'

'I'll go home, Warren. I won't even stop for gas. How's that sound?'

'That's fine. By the way, your inspection sticker has expired. Take care of that.'

'Thank you, Warren.'

'Okay. Drive safe. Be good.'

Jacobi walked back to his car, thinking about the job. He had a wistful thought about stopping for a hot meal at the diner near his apartment. Then home for a nightcap and the 49ers game.

He heard the radio sputtering his call numbers as he opened the car door.

Chapter Ninety-Three

Jacobi pulled up behind the blue Ford on the corner of Taylor and Washington. He climbed out into the freaking rain again, walked over, and exchanged a few words with Chi and Lemke.

As their Ford took off, Jacobi crossed Washington, ducked under the black awning with gold letters spelling 'Venticello Ristorante.'

He labored up the stairs of the cream-colored two-story building, warm air and the smell of garlic and oregano greeting him as he entered the foyer, making his stomach growl.

To his right, the hatcheck girl asked for his coat, an offer he declined.

He stood for a moment, dripping wet, taking in the L-shaped bar in the entryway, the down staircase to his left, the only public stairway to the main floor of the restaurant.

Jacobi took a barstool, ordered a Buckler's, put his coat on the stool next to him. Then he told the bartender he wanted to use the washroom.

He took the dozen carpeted steps down to the small rectangular dining room, ten occupied tables overlooking the streets through tall corner windows, a blue-tiled fireplace dominating the space.

The doctor's table was near the fire, his back to Jacobi, an attractive woman smiling into his face. Red wine glowed in the glasses in front of them.

Jacobi walked past the table, bumping the doctor's chair, enjoying the way Garza whipped his head around, his face an outraged scowl.

Jacobi apologized as if he meant it. 'Hey, I'm sorry. Sorry. Excuse me.' Then he walked across the floor, used the washroom, and returned upstairs to the bar.

He drank his near-beer and nursed another, settling the bill after each round. He dropped another five on the bar as the dark-haired doctor and his date passed him on their way to the cloakroom.

Jacobi slipped out the door just before them, and went out into the inclement night. He started up his car, turned on the windshield wipers, and called in his location.

The black Mercedes pulled out of the parking lot on Taylor, and Jacobi followed, this time keeping close, confident that the doctor wouldn't make him in this weather. Not with the pretty blond woman sitting almost on his lap, wrapping her arm around his neck, kissing him behind the ear.

The doctor turned onto Pacific for two blocks, taking a right onto Leavenworth, then four more blocks to Filbert.

Jacobi saw Garza nose the Roadster into his driveway and open the automatic garage door, then drive his SUV inside.

Jacobi drove past the pale-yellow house to the end of the block. He made a U-turn, coming back, parking on Garza's side of the street where he could watch the house.

His hip was stiffening up, and his bladder was full again. He was thinking of getting out, taking a leak against his rear tire, when the downstairs lights in Garza's house went out. A long fifteen minutes later, the upstairs lights winked out as well.

Jacobi called Lindsay on his Nextel. Told her he'd been tailing Garza since he left the hospital. Yeah, overtime. *Free* overtime.

'He didn't even run a stoplight, Boxer. The man had dinner with a babe about forty, a willowy blonde. Held her hand at the table; then she climbed all over him on the drive home.

'As far as I can tell,' Jacobi said, 'the doctor is guilty of having a girlfriend.'

Chapter Ninety-Four

I was fretting and stalking the corridors outside the ICU at Municipal when Jacobi called, saying that Garza was tucked in for the night.

I dropped into a blue plastic chair in the hospital waiting room, thinking what an idiot I was for sending my buddy out into the foul night for nothing. Still, I couldn't shake my prickling sense of wrongness about Garza.

Images flickered – Keiko's mom, her knees buckling, dropping to the sidewalk, that feisty, funny lady who should still be alive.

I thought about brass buttons on her dead eyes and on the eyes of the thirty-one others who'd been marked that way.

Those freaking buttons. Markers.

Where was the killer's fun if no one understood what he was doing or why?

I remembered the arrogance of the man who'd overseen the care of many of the deceased. The doctor who'd said, 'Sometimes a bad wind blows.'

And I wondered for the hundredth time if Dennis Garza was one of those deranged and profligate killers, like Charles Cullen and Swango, that surgeon from Ohio, medical practitioners addicted to the power of snuffing out life.

I shifted in my chair, knocked over a half-full coffee container on the floor, watched the lazy brown pool seep around my Nikes. 'Jeez, Lindsay. You expect to catch a killer.' *Can't even drink coffee.*

I sopped up the spill with a piece of newspaper, threw the cup into the trash, thinking, *The day is done.*

Garza had gone to bed, and if I had any brains, I'd do the same.

I was zipping up my jacket when my cell phone rang again.

'Lieutenant?' a woman's voice whispered. 'It's Noddie Wilkins. The nurse from Municipal? You told me to call you.' Noddie said, 'Another patient has died. There were buttons—'

A sick feeling washed through me.

'When did this happen?'

'Just now.'

'What was the patient's name?'

'Anthony Ruffio. His body's still in the ICU.'

I started running toward the stairs, wondering how many

patients had died in this hospital, how many had been found with caduceus buttons on their dead eyes.

But there was one difference this time.

I was in the hospital, and the killer was probably here, too.

Chapter Ninety-Five

I took the stairs to the ICU two fast steps at a time. A homicidal maniac might be roaming the hospital, and right now might be my best opportunity to tag him.

I badged the senior nurse at her station outside the ICU, and stayed in her face as she paged the ICU's attending physician.

Dr Daniel Wassel materialized moments later. He was a thin man in his thirties with a long, narrow nose and sleepy, red-rimmed eyes.

I identified myself, told him that I was doing an investigation and needed a list of everyone on the staff who was on the floor when a patient named Anthony Ruffio was checked into the ICU after surgery.

And I told him I wanted to see Ruffio's body right now.

The doctor became alarmed, his sleepy eyes widening as

he shook off his torpor. 'I don't understand, Lieutenant. Why is this patient's death a police matter?'

'For now, I'm calling it a suspicious death.'

'You are so off base, I can't believe it,' he said.

Dr Wassel opened the sliding door to the darkened stall, flipped on the light switch. The fluorescent light flickered.

My eyes went right to the body.

I felt a shiver of apprehension as I peeled the sheet down from the dead man's face.

Ruffio looked shocked that he'd been wrenched from life. His mouth was open, his skin pale, almost translucent. There was dried blood around his nostrils and the sticky remains of tape in the corner of his mouth where the respirator had been clamped over his face.

Pulling the sheet down farther, I saw the shocking, fresh surgical incision, a stitched line from his sternum to his navel.

I covered Mr Ruffio with the sheet right up to his hairline.

When I turned away, I saw a pair of caduceus buttons winking at me from the console beside the bed. I stood between the buttons and Dr Wassel.

'For now, this room is off-limits to hospital personnel,' I said. 'Someone from the crime lab will be here shortly, and as soon as they're done, the ME will transport Mr Ruffio to the city morgue.'

'I have to tell someone in authority here.'

'Go straight to the top, Doctor.'

I took latex gloves and a glassine envelope from my jacket pocket, scooped up the buttons before they could disappear. I phoned CSU, located a pair of night-duty criminalists who said they'd be right over. And I called Jacobi. Got him out of bed.

While I waited for support to arrive, I mounted my own investigation. It was like gunning a motorboat across the chop in a squall-tossed sea.

I flashed my badge repeatedly, questioned harried, irritated doctors, nurses, aides, and orderlies, asking, 'Where were you when Anthony Ruffio was admitted to Municipal? Where were you when he died?'

During each interview, I looked for a gesture, a tone of voice, a 'tell' that would light up the board and spell out *killer*.

I detected nothing of the kind, nothing at all.

Chapter Ninety-Six

Dr Marie Calhoun was the attending physician in the ER that night. She was in her early thirties with springy brunette curls, ragged cuticles, and an energy level I'd call manic.

We stood together behind a bank of nurses at the hub of the ER. Looking past me much of the time, speaking in a clipped, hurry-up manner, Dr Calhoun tried to explain Anthony Ruffio's death.

'Mr Ruffio had been on a flight from Geneva by way of New York,' she said tersely. 'It was a long flight, and his left leg was in a cast. He developed acute shortness of breath on the plane. As soon as it landed, he was rushed to the ER.'

'You saw him when he came in?'

'Yes. We did a lung scan. Turned out he had a big pulmonary embolus. We also did an ultrasound on the broken leg, found another big clot there.

'We gave him a blood thinner, an anticoagulant called heparin, to break up the clots; then we put him on a respirator in the ICU.

'Next thing I hear, he's vomiting blood, excreting blood, and then he goes into shock.'

'What caused this to happen?'

'I didn't know at the time. We rushed him into surgery, found out he was bleeding massively from a stomach ulcer. Because of the heparin, his blood was superthin . . .'

The doctor shook her head, her curls swinging as she described what happened next, seemingly trying to get her own mind around the patient's death.

'Bill Rosen,' she said. 'A great surgeon. Tried like crazy to tie off the major vessel to the ulcer. We gave the patient a bunch of transfusions, but he was exsanguinating and we couldn't keep up with him. He was already in severe respiratory distress, and everything just went all to hell in surgery.'

'Meaning?'

'We lost him on the table. Rosen brought him back. Stabilized him. Ruffio was in the ICU for about twenty minutes when he died.'

I was having a horrible sense of déjà vu. Keiko Castellano had received too much of a different blood thinner, streptokinase. It had caused her death.

'Forgive my ignorance, Doctor, but how often does heparin cause "superthin" blood?'

She looked at me, her dark eyes going as hard as onyx. 'What in God's name are you asking me?'

'Is it possible that Ruffio received too much heparin?'

'Anything's possible. But there's a more obvious cause of death, and that's what's going into my report,' Calhoun said emphatically. I could almost hear her teeth grinding.

'The man's blood alcohol level was point two six when he came in. In medical terms, that's blotto. He was definitely tippling on the plane. Maybe drinking is why he broke his leg on the slopes.'

'Sorry. I'm not making the connection.'

'Bleeding ulcers are common in alcoholics. He didn't tell anyone about his ulcer,' Calhoun continued. 'Maybe he was embarrassed that he was a drunk. There's a reason for patient intake forms, and this is it.'

'So you're saying it was death by omission.'

'Exactly! Now, are we finished?'

'Not quite,' I said.

A young man was brought into the ER on a gurney. I saw blood oozing from a gunshot wound to the leg, and the kid was screaming. I stepped in front of Calhoun before she could brush past me.

'Was Doctor Garza in the hospital when Ruffio was admitted?'

'I really don't remember. I have no idea. Why don't you ask him?'

'I will. Do you know about the buttons an orderly found on Ruffio's eyes postmortem?'

'Buttons? I don't know what you're talking about, Lieutenant. But Anthony Ruffio didn't die from buttons. His bleeding ulcer got him.'

Chapter Ninety-Seven

The next morning, I sat inside my battered Explorer thinking about the long hours I'd just spent with CSU and Jacobi, mulling over Ruffio's dead body.

Now I watched the light, silver rain in my headlight beams as a pale sun rose over the skyline.

I pulled out of the parking lot onto Pine, still wondering if Ruffio's death had happened as Calhoun had described it – a medical accident. Not the hospital's fault.

I remembered the despair on Calhoun's face when she said, 'superthin blood,' her expression as well as her words sticking with me.

I knew this for sure: no less than sixty hospital employees had been near Ruffio as he lay unconscious in the ICU, a respirator doing his breathing for him.

Someone could have injected Ruffio's IV bag with an overdose of heparin before or after his surgery.

Garza could have done it before he left work for the evening.

But one piece of the puzzle troubled me.

How could Garza have put buttons on the dead man's eyes?

Chapter Ninety-Eight

Cindy was at her desk in the City room at the *Chronicle*, fine-tuning her story, tweaking it again. She was on deadline, but still, she was glad when the phone rang and she saw the name on her caller ID.

She picked up the line, thinking, *Great. Maybe we'll grab a quick lunch.*

'Cindy, what the hell?' Lindsay barked, almost shouted, over the phone. 'I asked you please not to do a story on Garza and you agreed!'

'Linds, I had to do it,' Cindy said, keeping her voice low so that everyone in the world didn't tune in. 'My source at Municipal has told me that Garza is being questioned by the board—'

'That's not proof of anything, Cindy.'

'Did you read the story? I wrote, and I quote, "Suspicion has fallen on ER chief Doctor Dennis Garza." *Suspicion* means speculation with foundation. Jeez, Lindsay. Last week the guy completely melted down in court. He warrants some ink of his own!'

'What if he's guilty of more than malpractice? What if the spotlight you just threw on him drives him underground? What if he packs up and leaves San Francisco?'

'What do you mean "more than malpractice"?'

'I don't know what I mean,' Lindsay said, her voice stiff with pique. 'I'm working on it.'

'So am I,' Cindy said. 'Look, you haven't given me anything on this story. It's mine. It's been mine from the beginning. And it's not right for you to come down on me for doing my job.'

A static, gray silence followed, Cindy feeling the seconds mount up, thinking a lot of things she didn't want to say. But it all came down to this: Lindsay was leaning on her because of their friendship – and she was out of line, way out of line.

'Dozens of reporters are on this story, Lindsay! Whether I break the story or someone else does, Garza's going to get press.'

Lindsay sighed in her ear, said, 'I hoped I'd have more time.'

'Well, you were dreaming.'

Cool good-byes followed.

Cindy hung up the phone and looked down at her notepad. She read the words she'd just scribbled: *guilty of more than malpractice.*

Chapter Ninety-Nine

My all-nighter at Municipal Hospital had left me bone weary and frustrated beyond belief. I tossed the morning paper into the trash can under my desk, pretty sure that Cindy's next story would be about how people were being murdered at Muncipal – and how the SFPD was doing nothing about it.

The time had come to abandon my off-the-books investigation and make 'the brass button case' official before a very large sinkhole opened under the Hall of Justice.

I picked up the phone and called the chief, said, 'Tony, I have to see you. It's urgent.'

The Flower Market Café on Brannan and Sixth is near the onramp to 280 south and a few blocks from the Hall. Any other day I would have appreciated the cozy ambience of the eatery, its pretty tiled floor, dark wainscoting, and view of the flower-market stalls down the alley.

But not today.

Tracchio and I took one of the small, round tables and ordered sandwiches.

'Start talking, Boxer,' he said.

I found that I was relieved to tell him every bit of it – about Yuki's mom, the buttoned-up eyes of thirty-three dead patients, the rumors, the statistics, and the malpractice trial against Municipal Hospital to date.

I also told him about Garza's stinking track record at various hospitals around the country, concluding with a report of Jacobi's surveillance and our off-duty interrogations last night after a patient had died.

'Ruffio's body was in the ICU waiting to be moved to the hospital morgue,' I said, 'when someone put brass buttons on his eyes.'

'Humph,' the chief grunted.

'Garza left the hospital at six p.m. The patient died at just after eight,' I told him, 'but I can't say for sure that Garza wasn't involved.'

'If Garza wasn't there, how do you figure he had anything to do with it?'

'He has access to any place in the hospital. Maybe he overdosed the patient before he quit work for the day and it took a few hours for the medication to work.

'Maybe he has an accomplice, or maybe he's not our guy

at all,' I admitted. 'But Christ, Tony, Garza could be a world-class monster! I think he probably is. At the very least, we've got to play "beat the press." The *Chronicle* put him on page three this morning.'

The chief pushed his plate aside, ordered another round of coffee.

'Yuki filed charges?' he asked.

'Yes, but Claire's autopsy of Yuki's mom only shows that she was overmedicated. No evidence that she was murdered. I'm expecting pretty much the same report on Ruffio.'

'So, bottom line, you've got a mixed bag of nuts and bolts that don't add up to anything.'

'It adds up to a real bad feeling, Tony. The worst. And it won't go away.'

'So, what do you want to do?'

Thanks to closing the Car Girl murders, my stock had never been higher than it was today.

'I want to saturate the hospital with cops,' I said. 'Borrow some guys from Narcotics to go undercover. I'd put a detail on Garza twenty-four/seven, and I'd like to plant someone inside the hospital pharmacy.'

Tracchio drained his coffee cup, no doubt thinking how he was going to stretch our already overextended manpower based on my 'real bad feeling.'

'For how long?'

'Honestly? I don't know.'

Tracchio signaled to the waitress for the bill, said to me, 'You can have four people for a week. Then we'll reevaluate. Make sure you keep me up to speed, Lindsay. I want to know everything. No hiding the weenie.'

I reached over and shook Tracchio's pudgy hand. 'I wouldn't if I could.'

Chapter One Hundred

Jacobi was in the passenger seat of the gray car, staring up at the tall, yellow house on Filbert, thinking how Dr Garza had been home for about a half hour, probably settling down with the nightly news, when the garage door suddenly opened and the black Mercedes Roadster backed out, the tires squealing.

Rich Conklin sat up straight in the driver's seat. Jacobi called in a code 33 and stated their location.

Beside him, Conklin waited a count of five, then pointed the unmarked police car down the steep grade of Filbert, ten car-lengths behind the Mercedes.

'Take it easy,' Jacobi cautioned Conklin. 'We've got plenty of backup.'

'What the fuck?' Conklin said. 'How do we know Garza's even in that car?'

'You want to go back and watch the house?'

'Nope. I want to clone myself.'

Jacobi snorted. 'Is the world ready for two of you, Conklin?'

Then Jacobi grinned, remembering when he was as green as Conklin, when he looked forward to every stakeout, every collar, and as wiped out as he was, Jacobi was getting that feeling now.

Conklin took the hard left onto Jones, tapping the brakes at the stop sign on Greenwich, then driving past the Yick Wo Elementary School.

Jacobi called Dispatch: 'Black Mercedes sports coupé, Whiskey Delta Foxtrot Three Nine Zero, heading north on Jones,' he said as they crossed Lombard and Francisco, blowing through stop signs, braking on Columbus, calling it in again.

The radio crackled as another unmarked unit picked up the Mercedes on Columbus, calling out the cross streets, saying, 'Looks like he's headed toward the Cannery South.'

Conklin turned on the grille lights. He hooked a sharp right, then took the car on a straight shot parallel to Columbus. It was a back route to Garza's probable destination, Ghirardelli Square.

Jacobi told Conklin to park on Beach Street near the corner of Hyde. 'He should pass by here any minute.'

Traffic was sluggish at evening rush hour, and the sidewalks were still clogged with pedestrians browsing the street vendors between the street and the beach.

'That's him,' Conklin said.

Jacobi saw the sharp little Roadster pulling in to the curb up ahead, parking, the man getting out all smooth in a cashmere Armani topcoat, dark hair flowing over his collar.

He watched with dismay as Garza walked back toward their car. *Damn it.* He knocked on the passenger-side window.

Jacobi buzzed down the window, gave the doctor a bored look.

'Hang on, Inspector. I'll be right back,' Garza told him; then he crossed the street over the cable car tracks and entered the beige stucco building with the red neon sign overhead, the Buena Vista.

Jacobi could see Garza through the plate-glass windows, giving an order to the counterman.

'What was that?' Conklin asked, incredulous. 'He didn't just make us, he's calling us stupid. This is pretty bad.'

Jacobi felt a headache coming on. Garza getting over on them hadn't been in the plan. What to say to the kid?

'Well, it's a kick in the teeth, Richie,' he said. 'But it's early in the game.'

Jacobi stared grimly out the car window as Garza left the café, waited for the light, then crossed the street, coming up to the squad car. He knocked on the window again, handed Jacobi two coffee containers in a cardboard holder.

'It's black and strong,' Garza said. 'You're in for a long night.'

'Thank you. Very considerate,' Jacobi said. 'I hope to return the favor sometime soon.'

Jacobi watched Garza get back into his Mercedes, signal as he pulled back out into traffic. Jacobi called Dispatch, saying, 'We need a car to pick up a surveillance. Suspect's going south on Hyde, obeying all the traffic signals.'

Jacobi hung the mike back in its cradle.

'He'll make a mistake,' he said to Conklin with more conviction than he felt. 'These smartass pricks almost always do.'

Jacobi opened one of the coffee containers, shook in a packet of sugar, and stirred. He took a cautious sip.

Chapter One Hundred and One

It was quarter to 9:00 in the seamless, bright night of the hospital corridors. Garza had left his office many hours before, waving to me as though we were old friends, smirking as he slithered out through the pneumatic doors to the street. *He's having fun with this, isn't he?*

As I haunted the halls between the ER and the ICU, I'd expanded my view.

Maybe Garza wasn't a killer.

Maybe he just smelled like one.

But if it wasn't Garza, who could it be?

I'd been stalking this same path for so many days, I'd blown my own cover.

I sought fresh ground, took the stairs up to the third-floor oncology ward.

I'd just stepped out of the stairwell when I saw something that made the fine hairs on the back of my neck bristle.

A white male, about thirty, five eleven, 165 pounds, sandy hair under a blue baseball cap, a gray hoody, and black cargo pants, was talking to a weathered-looking white nurse in the hallway.

The man's posture felt wrong – the furtiveness as he exchanged conspiratorial looks with the nurse, an exchange that jarred me, my instincts saying, *This is wrong.*

Cappy McNeil is a seasoned homicide pro. He'd worked for years with Jacobi and was now stationed on the floor below.

I called him on my Nextel, and a minute later, we converged at the door to room 386 – just as the sandy-haired man slipped inside the patient's room.

I stiff-armed the swinging door open, calling out sharply, 'Stop right there!' I flashed my badge and, grabbing his arm, spun the suspect around. Slammed him against the wall, feeling it shudder.

Behind me, Cappy blocked the exit with his 250-pound bulk.

'What's your name?' I asked the young man.

'Alan Feirstein. *What is this*?'

'Keep your hands on the wall, Mr Feirstein. Do you have anything in your pockets I should know about? Drugs? A needle? A weapon?'

'I've got a toothbrush,' he hollered. 'I've got car keys. I've got a box of Good and Plenty!'

I patted him down, all ten pockets. 'I'm removing your wallet,' I said.

'Honey?' Feirstein half-turned his face, sending a pleading look toward the wan woman in the bed. 'Are you awake?'

Swags of tubes and electric leads ran from her arms up an IV pole, over to a cardiac monitor.

'He's my husband,' the woman said in a drugged, barely audible voice. 'Alan's my husband.'

I examined Feirstein's license, my stomach shrinking, my heart sinking.

This guy wasn't armed, had no buttons on his person. Shit, he even had the sticker for organ donation on his license.

'What are you doing here?' I asked weakly.

'I'm spending the night,' he said. 'Carol has lymphoma. End-stage.'

I swallowed hard. 'I'm so very sorry,' I said to Feirstein. 'What just happened was an awful mistake, and I can't apologize enough.'

The guy nodded, letting me off the hook, for which I was grateful. I told his wife, 'You take good care, okay?'

Then Cappy and I walked out into the hallway.

'Man,' I said, 'I feel terrible, Cappy. It sure looked like some kind of deal was going down. The guy was sneaking in to sleep on the floor! How could I have been so dumb?'

'It happens, boss,' he said, shrugging. 'Back to square one.'

Cappy returned to his post, and I returned to the waiting room outside the ER.

I was disappointed and embarrassed, but worse, I'd never had such a feeling of grabbing at smoke.

Carl Whiteley, the hospital's silky CEO, had stated repeatedly that the mortality rate at Municipal was within range for similar hospitals, and that the caduceus buttons were a joke.

I'd gotten Tracchio to go along with me based on little more than my instincts.

Risky for him. Risky for me.

The vending machines in the corner of the ER waiting room hummed, ready to dispense cheerful, colored boxes of goodies in this bleak, soul-sucking place.

I dropped a dollar in quarters into the slot, stabbed a couple of buttons, and watched the orange packet of Reese's Pieces clunk down the chute.

I was here for the night. I wanted to believe that we were going to unmask a depraved killer and save lives.

But there was an awful possibility that all I was doing was making an ass of myself. Jesus, that poor guy and his wife. What a disaster.

PART SIX

The Verdict

Chapter One Hundred and Two

*O*f all the damn days to be late.

Cindy grappled with her oversized handbag, shifted her computer bag to her left shoulder as she walked quickly up McAllister toward the Civic Center Courthouse, thinking how she hadn't missed a day of court since the trial started four weeks ago.

Now the grueling testimonies and scalding cross-examinations were over.

Today, O'Mara and Kramer would make their closing arguments whether or not she was on the courthouse steps when the doors opened.

God.

If she lost her seat to another reporter – it was a possibility too grim to consider.

Cindy sprinted across McAllister against the light, crossing to the courthouse, a pale stone block of a building cut on the diagonal, facing the intersection of McAllister and Polk.

Looking up, she was relieved to see the courthouse doors were still closed.

And she saw Yuki standing at the edge of the crowd at the top of the steps, gripping the handle of her briefcase with both hands. Her eyes were fixed on the middle distance, seeming to see nothing.

Cindy had an anxious thought about Yuki, her weight loss, her fragility. Also, the simple fact that she hadn't gone to work since her mother died.

The trial was consuming her, and it showed big time.

Cindy threaded her way through the mob standing on the courthouse steps. She called out to Yuki as she climbed.

Yuki saw her at last, saying, 'What *happened*? I was so worried about you.'

'Breakdown on BART,' Cindy told her. 'I was stuck between stations for half an hour. I almost went crazy.'

The security guards opened the heavy steel doors, and Cindy and Yuki were swept along with the buzzing crowd pouring into the courthouse.

A packed elevator took them to the fourth floor, where they got separated on their way to courtroom 4A. Cindy went directly to the last bench in the room, the one against the back wall reserved for the press.

She scanned the courtroom as it filled, then booted up her laptop.

She began to type.

Maureen O'Mara wore a tomato-red Oscar de la Renta suit, Cindy wrote. *This is her game suit, her fighting color, how she wants the jury to remember her summation.*

Chapter One Hundred and Three

Judge Carter Bevins shook his wristwatch, then turned his bespectacled eyes on Maureen O'Mara. He asked her if she was ready to proceed.

'Yes, Your Honor,' O'Mara said, standing, taking her position behind the small oak lectern.

She put her notes in front of her, but she wouldn't need them. She'd rehearsed with her partners again last night, memorized her key points, knew the tone and text of her summation inside out. She'd put everything she had into this case, and her entire future would spring from the results of this trial.

She'd done great so far, and she knew it.

Now she had to cinch it.

She took a breath, smiled at the jury, and began.

'Ladies and gentlemen, three years ago, San Francisco Municipal Hospital was privatized; it was sold to a for-profit corporation.

'Since then,' O'Mara said, 'the number of fatalities due to pharmaceutical errors has *tripled* at the hospital.

'*Why?* I submit that it's because of errors caused by incompetence and overwork.

'In the last three years, nearly three quarters of the staff have been replaced with less-experienced people who work longer hours for less pay.

'The hospital makes a profit,' O'Mara said. 'But at an unacceptably high cost.

'You've heard testimony about the twenty people who died painful, senseless deaths because they came to Municipal Hospital.

'It's sickening and it's outrageous. And the management of Municipal Hospital is fully to blame. Because they really don't give a *damn* about their patients. They care about the bottom line.'

O'Mara paced in front of the jury box, put her hands on the railing, her eyes connecting with the jurors as she spoke only to them.

'We heard from Doctor Garza last week,' O'Mara went on. 'Doctor Garza has been head of Municipal's emergency services for the past three years, and he doesn't deny that during that time, the fatality rate of patients admitted through the ER has gone through the roof.

'And Doctor Garza told us why that happened. He said, "Sometimes a bad wind blows."

'Ladies and gentlemen, there's no such thing as a "bad wind" in a hospital. *But there is bad medicine.* The legal term is "operating below the standard of practice."

'That's what malpractice is.

'When I asked Doctor Garza if he had anything to do with those patients' deaths, he said, "I take the Fifth."

'*Imagine.* He declined to answer because he didn't want to incriminate himself! Wasn't that an answer in itself? Of course it was.'

No one coughed or seemed even to breathe. O'Mara pushed on, looking at each of the jurors in turn.

'This isn't a criminal case. No one's going after Doctor Garza for a *crime*, even though he made this bizarre self-incrimination.

'But we *are* asking you to hold Municipal Hospital responsible for this "bad wind."

'We *are* asking you to punish Municipal for putting profit over the well-being of its patients.

'And we *are* asking you to award my clients fifty million dollars, a sum that will hurt the hospital, even though it can't begin to make up for the loss of those twenty precious lives.

'Ladies and gentlemen, this hospital must be stopped from practicing Russian-roulette medicine – and you *can* stop them.

'Ask yourselves, if someone you loved was ill or injured, would you want them to go to Municipal Hospital?

'Would you want to go there yourself? Would you even consider it after what you've heard?

'Please carry that thought with you into the jury room – and find in favor of my clients and those whom they have lost at Municipal. Please award them the maximum amount of damages. On their behalf, I thank you.'

Chapter One Hundred and Four

Yuki waited in the long line outside the ladies' room. Her arms folded, chin tucked down, she was thinking how powerfully she'd felt O'Mara's closing, and she was asking herself again why she hadn't dragged her mother out of Municipal before Garza, that bastard, killed her.

The line moved so slowly that by the time Yuki entered the washroom, there were only moments left before court was due to resume.

Quickly, she turned on the cold water faucet, splashed water on her face. Then she reached blindly for the paper towels.

She patted her face dry, and opened her eyes to see Maureen O'Mara in front of the mirror touching up her makeup.

Yuki was happily surprised to see O'Mara.

She congratulated her on her closing argument and introduced herself, saying, 'I'm with Duffy and Rogers, but I'm here because my mom died recently at Municipal.'

'I'm sorry to hear that,' O'Mara said, nodding; then she cut her eyes back to the mirror.

Yuki recoiled at the rebuff. A half-second later, she realized that O'Mara was probably absorbed, bracing herself for Kramer's closing.

Worrying about the jury.

Yuki wadded up her paper towel and tossed it into the trash container, taking another look at O'Mara, both in the round and in her reflected image in the glass.

Maureen O'Mara's suit was splendid. Her teeth were bleached, and her glorious hair had that seamless glow usually only seen in shampoo commercials. *The woman takes care of herself,* Yuki thought, and that observation irritated her for some reason.

She had a thought about how she hadn't had her own hair cut in months and had been alternating every other day between two dark-blue business suits. It was just easier to dress automatically.

Since her mother died, how she looked just didn't seem to matter.

Beside her, O'Mara blotted her lipstick, flicked a stray hair from her collar, and without another look at Yuki, left the bathroom.

A broad woman in a pinstriped suit asked Yuki if she minded, she had to reach across her to use the soap.

'Sure, no problem.'

Yuki stepped back from the sink, thinking, So what if Maureen O'Mara was a somewhat pampered bitch?

She still wanted her to win.

She wanted her to win *big*.

Chapter One Hundred and Five

Lawrence Kramer straightened his papers as the judge took the bench and the bailiff called the court to order.

He felt strong, and he was eager to begin, glad that he'd gone for his five-mile run that morning, using that oasis of uninterrupted time to review his closing one more time.

He was ready.

If it hadn't been for that ass, Garza, he would have no doubt about how the verdict would go. That jerk-off was going to lose his job over this. But it would be small consolation if they lost.

Kramer stood as the judge called his name. He buttoned his midnight-blue suit jacket and greeted the jury warmly, as if he'd known them for years.

'There's a big difference between human error and malpractice,' Kramer said, setting the tone for his closing.

'Think about what it's like inside an emergency room. People coming in off the street, the sick and wounded, victims of falls, car accidents, people who are traumatized and sometimes can't even speak.

'Think about the speed in which lifesaving decisions must be made even though the doctors don't know the patients, don't have their medical history in hand, and don't have time to do exhaustive tests.

'When a doctor has to move quickly to save a life, he or she often has to make a judgment call.

'This is what I mean.

'A sixty-five-year-old woman, like your mother or mine, comes into the ER with a transient ischemic attack. It's a small stroke and an arrhythmic heartbeat at the same time, and if not treated, she could die.

'One doctor decides to treat the condition with a blood thinner to break up the blood clot.

'Another doctor might decide that what's best for that patient is to put in a pacemaker right away.

'That's a judgment call.

'And either way, the decision that doctor makes carries risk; the patient could die in surgery or the patient could die from medication—'

'Kramer! I'm talking to you. You son of a bitch. You scum. Trivializing my son's death.'

A man a few rows back from the defense table was on his feet, yelling at the top of his voice. It was Stephen Friedlander, father of the boy, Josh, who died from an insulin shot meant for his discharged roommate.

Friedlander's face was gray and mottled, his muscles rigid as he stabbed his finger repeatedly at Kramer.

'Fuck you,' he said to Kramer.

Then he spun toward the defense table, jabbed his finger at each of the three attorneys on Kramer's team, two young men and a woman, their faces blank with shock. 'Fuck you! Fuck you! And fuck you!'

The judge shouted to the bailiff, 'Hold him! That man's in contempt,' even as Kramer appealed to the judge.

'Your Honor! She's using shock tactics. Plaintiffs' counsel orchestrated this stunt.'

O'Mara shot back, 'This is my doing? Are you crazy?'

'Both of you. In my chambers,' Bevins growled.

Kramer heard a woman scream! He turned in time to see Friedlander's face contort, the blood leave his face. The man was obviously in trouble, gasping in short, hard breaths, reaching out his arms. He clutched at the screaming woman beside him before falling across her lap, then spilling out onto the hard stone floor.

'Call the paramedics,' Bevins yelled to a security guard. 'Court is adjourned until two p.m. Bailiff, escort the jurors to the jury room.'

Pandemonium ensued. Kramer saw a man in glasses, a reporter for the *Chicago Tribune,* charge the fire exit, stiff-arming the lock-release bar on the door.

The high-decibel alarm on the door screamed as the EMS team clattered up the stairs and entered the courtroom.

Chapter One Hundred and Six

Cindy felt jumpy and distracted as court resumed, the whole terrifying Friedlander scene repeating through her mind on a short loop – the cursing and screaming, the poor man collapsing, the shrill shriek of the alarm as her new friend, Whit Ewing of the *Chicago Tribune*, had crashed through the emergency exit.

The judge banged his gavel, and the rustle of whispers across the public gallery quieted.

'For the record,' Bevins said, 'I've questioned each member of the jury individually, and I'm satisfied that their judgment of this case won't be affected by the incident this morning.'

He looked over to the defense table. 'Mr Kramer, are you ready to continue?'

'I am, Your Honor.' Kramer walked to the lectern, his genial smile looking forced.

Cindy leaned forward in her seat, put her hand on Yuki's thin shoulder. She whispered, 'Here we go.'

'Ladies and gentlemen,' Kramer said, 'I have a note here that Mr Friedlander has been treated and is expected to recover fully from his heart attack.

'My clients and I feel very badly for him. The man lost his son, and he's in a lot of pain right now.

'But as badly as we all feel, your charge as jurors is to decide this case based on the facts, not on emotions.

'I said earlier that it's important to distinguish between mistakes and medical malpractice.

'It's a mistake when a nurse mixes up medicine on a tray, or a doctor gets distracted by another emergency and forgets to mark up a chart, so the patient gets medicated again. Those are mistakes.

'Malpractice is gross negligence. For instance – and for your information, these are all real cases that I'm mentioning – a doctor leaves a patient on the operating table while he runs out to make a bank deposit.

'Or a surgical towel is left inside a patient's body.

'A doctor treats a patient while drunk or on drugs, or withholds treatment because of a bias against a patient or a class of patients. Or knowingly recommends treatment the patient doesn't need.

'*That's* gross negligence. *That's* malpractice.'

Kramer pushed off from the lectern and approached the jury, pacing before the railing as he spoke to them.

'It's terrible what happened to the people cited in this action. I don't have to tell you that. You know it already.

'But in every one of the situations you've heard about in this courtroom, doctors and nurses, and even the patients themselves, made the kind of errors that happen in hospitals all across this country, every day.

'Human errors. Honest mistakes.

'As much as we'd like to believe that doctors are infallible, that's an unreasonable expectation.

'Doctors and nurses are human beings who want to help other people and try their damnedest to do it.

'Last year, one hundred and fifty thousand patients came through Municipal Hospital's doors with injuries and illnesses. And they received excellent medical care, as good as they would get at any hospital in this city.

'I'm asking you to strip away my opponent's inflammatory rhetoric and focus on the difference between mistakes and malpractice and find in favor of Municipal Hospital.

'The city of San Francisco, our city, needs this hospital.'

Chapter One Hundred and Seven

Yuki stood with Cindy in the corridor outside of courtroom 4A, their backs against the cold marble wall as the courtroom emptied.

Cindy was excited, the reporter in her pumped up, asking, 'So, what did you think?'

A group of lawyers for the defense and hospital execs passed by, talking about the trial. An old fox in gray tweed was saying, 'Thank God for Kramer. Great recovery on his part. That guy's a superstar.'

Almost on their heels, O'Mara and her retinue proudly strode down the hallway. O'Mara's face was impassive as she reached the elevator, the door opening as if it had been expecting her.

'Yuki?' Cindy asked again. 'Your professional opinion. How do you think the jury's going to decide?'

Yuki heard the anxiety in Cindy's voice, saw her tracking the lawyers with her eyes, and knew that Cindy wanted to get into the action on the courthouse steps.

'Both sides did extremely well, made a hell of a case,' Yuki said. 'You know, there's no "reasonable doubt" in a civil case. They're usually decided on a "preponderance of evidence." So each juror will have their own definition of pre—'

'You can't even guess?'

'It's a coin toss, Cindy. The jury could even hang.'

Cindy thanked her, said she'd catch up with her later, then made for the stairs, running.

Yuki waited for the next elevator, got in, and watched the numbers light from four to one.

Then she exited into the lobby, passed the circular security desk, and stepped out into the brisk October air.

There were two thick scrums of reporters outside the court-house, one pack around Larry Kramer, the other around Maureen O'Mara, shoving microphones in their faces, feeding picture and sound to satellite vans parked on McAllister.

No matter what the outcome, both Kramer and O'Mara were getting a huge media boost that money couldn't buy.

As she walked past them, Yuki thought back a couple of months to the last trial she'd litigated, how good she'd been. How she'd stood on those courthouse steps, mobbed by the press.

How much she'd liked that. But how much she'd changed in the last few weeks.

Yuki's car was parked at a meter three blocks from the courthouse.

She removed the parking ticket from her windshield, put it inside her handbag, located her keys, and got behind the wheel.

She switched on the ignition, then just sat there for a while, looking out at the traffic, at the purposeful pedestrians on the sidewalk pacing past her, lost in their daily routines.

It was a world that had nothing to do with her anymore. She had no place to go.

A great torrent of sadness welled up inside her. It was so sudden, she couldn't even name it. She crossed her arms over the steering wheel, put her head down, and began to sob.

Chapter One Hundred and Eight

C laire and I were at Susie's at dinner hour, the smell of barbecued pork and fried plantains making my mouth water and my stomach grumble. As we waited for the others, Claire was telling me about a recent case that had torn her up. She'd been working on it since the small, dark hours of the morning.

'A nineteen-year-old girl, apparent suicide, was hung by an extension cord wrapped around the bathroom door—'

'Wrapped around the *door*?'

'Yeah. One end was tied to the knob, then the cord was slid under the door, up over the top, then knotted around her neck.'

'Jeez. She really did that?'

'It's really a puzzle,' Claire said, pouring us each a glass of beer from the frosted pitcher. 'Her twenty-eight-year-old dirtbag boyfriend with a history of domestic violence was the only witness, of course.

'He called it in to nine-one-one as a suicide after a dispute they had. Said he cut her down, gave her CPR. Oh, and that she's pregnant.'

'Aw, no.'

'Yeah. So the fire department responds first, and now it's about keeping her body alive to save the baby. So they try to resuscitate her.

'Then the EMTs take over, and *they* try to resuscitate her. And then the ER folks at the hospital pound away at her and do a stat C-section.

'So by the time she comes to me, she's been through the mill four times, cut up, bruised everywhere, back and neck injuries, and I don't know what the hell happened to the poor girl.

'So I'm asking myself, did the boyfriend tune her up, kill her, and then hang her to cover up the homicide? Or was it a suicide, and the trauma is all from the attempts at resuscitation?'

'What about the baby?'

'The fetus, yeah. He was too little, only twenty-six weeks old. Lived for a couple of minutes at the hospital.'

Loretta dropped off the menus and the chips. She told Claire she looked fabulous in royal blue and that I looked as though I needed a vacation.

I thanked her kindly, told her we were going to wait for Cindy and Yuki before ordering, and asked her to bring some bread. Then I turned back to Claire.

Claire sighed, saying, 'Double homicide or suicide? It's too soon to tell. I've gotta backtrack, interview all the first responders, ask what they actually *saw*—'

Claire stopped, and I turned to see Cindy come through the front door.

Her kitten-gray sweater set off her pink cheeks and her tousled blond hair. But I could read the worry lines in her forehead.

She was wondering if she and I were okay, or if we had a fight to settle.

I got up and walked toward her, gave her a big fat hug.

'I'm sorry, Cindy,' I said. 'You were right to do that story on Garza. You were doing your job, and I was off the wall.'

Chapter One Hundred and Nine

A little later at our table, Cindy's face looked electric, charged up, excited, and maybe a little scared. She was giving us a detailed update on the malpractice trial when Yuki arrived at Susie's, very late, and looking like hell, even worse than me. She slid into the booth beside Cindy, who squeezed her hand protectively.

'You got here just in time,' Cindy said.

'In time for what?'

'I'm about to drop a bomb.'

As radiant as Cindy looked, that's how totally drained Yuki looked in comparison. Her hair was dull, her eyes were shadowed, and there was a button missing from the front of her pale silk blouse.

As Cindy set up her tape recorder on the table, I mouthed to Yuki, 'Are you okay?'

'Never better,' she said with a thin smile.

'So you've got your bomb in that little thing?' Claire asked Cindy.

Cindy grinned. 'I can't reveal her name,' she said, cuing up the tape. 'But she's a nurse who works at Municipal. Wait'll you hear this.'

A bad feeling was coming over me.

I hoped to God that I was wrong.

The tape rolled, and a woman's staticky voice came from the small machine.

Noddie Wilkins had dropped another dime, this time to the *Chronicle*.

'I've seen them myself,' Cindy's source said. 'Like in the black of night. You go into the room and the patient is dead, and there are these buttons on their eyes.'

'Let me make sure I've got this right,' I heard Cindy say, her tinny voice incredulous. 'When patients die, buttons are put on their eyes?'

'No, no, not every patient. Just a few of them. I've seen it three times, and other people have seen them, too.'

'I have a million questions, but let's start with the basics. What do they look like?'

'They're metallic buttons, like coins, *embossed* with a caduceus. And nobody's ever caught anyone in the act.'

'How many patients have been found with these buttons on their eyes?'

'I don't know. But a bunch.'

'Do you see a pattern? Does anybody you've spoken to? Like a certain age or ethnic group or illness?'

'I've just seen the three, and they were all different. Listen, I have to go now—'

'One more question. Please. Have you told anyone about this?'

'My supervisor. He says they're someone's sick idea of a joke. But you tell me. It's scary, right?'

Noddie's voice became muffled, as if she was covering the receiver with her hand. She spoke to someone. Her voice was terse when she got back on the line.

'I gotta go. I'm working and we're busy. Understaffed.'

'Call me again if anything—'

Cindy shut off the tape recorder and looked into our shocked faces. Then she focused on me.

'Lindsay, tell me, please, is the hospital covering up multiple homicides?'

I closed my mouth and pushed back from the table.

My mind was spinning.

I'd just apologized to Cindy for asking her not to write a story that she had every right to report.

How could I ask her again?

'Lindsay, *you knew*,' Yuki said, picking up something in my expression that I didn't know was there. 'You already knew about those buttons, didn't you? You knew.'

'Ah, I can't talk about it.'

'Lindsay?' Cindy pressed, incredulous. 'You *knew* about the buttons? Tell me. Tell me what it means!'

'I'll tell you,' Yuki said forcefully. 'Someone is *marking* those patients. Maybe even killing them. It's arrogant. It's psychopathic. And who does that sound like, Lindsay?'

I threw a long sigh, looked around for Loretta, and ordered another pitcher. Suddenly, Yuki reached across the table and clasped my forearm.

'Please,' she said. 'Don't let Garza get away with murder.'

I looked into Yuki's dark, sad eyes. She'd saved my butt when I needed her last year, and besides, I loved her dearly.

'We're on it,' I told my friend. 'If Garza is guilty of anything, anything at all, I promise we'll get him.'

Chapter One Hundred and Ten

The pink Post-it note Brenda had stuck to my phone read, *Chief T. wants to see you PRONTO.* She'd filled in the *O*s in *PRONTO* with frowny faces.

What now?

I took the stairs up two flights, made my way through the maze of cubicles to Tracchio's wood-paneled corner office, which overlooked all the sleazy bail bondsmen's storefronts down on Bryant Street.

As soon as I stepped inside, Tracchio hung up the phone. He wagged a piece of paper in my face.

'This is a complaint, Lieutenant Boxer. Doctor Dennis Garza is accusing you of harassment. Says he's going to sue the SFPD for a shitload of money. Any reaction?'

'Well, let him. He's full of it.'

'Don't give me that, Lindsay. What's he talking about?'

As a point of law, *harassment* means words or actions directed at a specific person that annoy them or cause a lot of emotional distress for no legitimate purpose.

I had legitimate purpose to the nth degree.

Furthermore, I was running on four hours of sleep and a bowl of Special K.

My self-control broke its leash.

'We're squeezing him and he's squirming, Chief,' I shouted. 'The balls on him to threaten us! The guy's a psycho. You've got to back me up and let me follow my instincts.'

'How many millions have you got in the bank, Lieutenant? You want to take us down that road again?'

I shut up, stared into Tracchio's small brown eyes, trying to reel myself in.

'Have you got anything on him?' Tracchio asked. 'Help me out here.'

'Not a hair. Not a crumb.'

'I'm calling the guy,' he said. 'I'll try to settle him down. What's he going to say to me?'

'Jacobi and I staked-out his house most of the night. We followed him to work this morning.'

Tracchio just shook his head.

I walked to the doorway, and was almost out of there when I turned around to tell him, 'By the way, the *Chronicle* has a lead on those buttons I told you about.'

'Oh, Christ.'

'The reporter is vetting the story now, but you can bet that this bomb is about to blow up. Pronto.'

Tracchio picked up the phone.

'You're calling Garza?'

'I'm calling the mayor of La Jolla. See if that job he offered me is still open,' Tracchio snarled. 'Get out of here.'

Fine. Yes, sir. I'm gone.

As I walked away, I heard Tracchio asking his secretary to get Dr Garza on the line.

Chapter One Hundred and Eleven

Yuki was under her bedcovers when the phone rang next to her ear. It was Cindy calling, shouting into the receiver, 'The jury's coming back with their decision. Are you *sleeping*, Yuki? It's almost eleven fifteen!'

'I'm awake. I'm awake!'

'Well, get your skinny butt down to the courthouse. Hurry up.'

Twenty minutes later, Yuki entered courtroom 4A, aware of the eyes on her as she inched past bony knees and briefcases to the one empty spot.

Yuki crossed her arms and her legs, making herself into a tight little package.

She stared straight ahead as Judge Bevins said, 'I want to caution everyone. I don't want any ruckus in the courtroom when the verdict is read, or I'll have the offenders arrested.

'Anyone who might not be able to restrain their emotions, here's your chance to leave now.

'All right, then. Will the jury foreman please hand the verdict form to the bailiff.'

The bailiff took the sheet of paper from the foreman, a stocky man in his fifties, big black-rimmed glasses, sun-lined face, wearing a golfer's jacket, pressed white shirt, the cuffs of his tan Dockers touching the tops of his buff suede shoes.

Yuki thought that he looked to be a man of conservative values, the kind of person who might despise disorder and 'mistakes.' At least, she hoped that was the case.

She watched the bailiff walk the verdict back to the judge, the *click-clack* of his footsteps loud in the silent courtroom.

Judge Bevins looked at the sheets of paper for a long moment, then turned to the foreman, asking, 'Is the jury's decision unanimous?'

'It is, Your Honor.'

'In the case of Jessica Falk against San Francisco Municipal, do you find that the hospital acted negligently?'

'Yes, Your Honor,' said the foreman.

'Have you found that the plaintiff has been damaged?'

'Yes, we have.'

'In what amount has the plaintiff been damaged?' the judge asked.

'Two hundred and fifty thousand dollars, Your Honor.'

'Was the defendant's actions in this case so egregious that an award of punitive damages is warranted?'

'Yes, Your Honor.'

'And what is the amount of punitive damages?'

'Five million dollars, Your Honor.'

A collective gasp was heard throughout the courtroom.

The judge banged his gavel and glared until the room was silent again.

Then he continued reading the next nineteen plaintiffs' names individually, asking the jury foreman the same five questions and receiving the same five answers each time. Every one of the plaintiffs was awarded $250,000 in damages and another $5 million in punitive damages.

Yuki felt light-headed, almost nauseous.

The hospital was grossly negligent.

Negligent on all counts.

Despite the judge's warning, the room erupted in shrieks and cheers from the plaintiffs' side across the aisle.

Sharp cracks of Bevins's gavel rang out repeatedly, and still, O'Mara's clients swarmed out of their seats, formed a raucous ring around her, shaking her hand, hugging and kissing her, many of them simply breaking down and weeping.

Yuki felt the same explosive jubilation. As the judge thanked and dismissed the jury, she heard Cindy calling her name.

Cindy was grinning, beckoning to her from just inside the courtroom door.

'I'm supposed to be neutral,' Cindy said to Yuki as they walked together, right into the milling throng in the hallway, 'but this is a great verdict. O'Mara is over the moon. What's her share of the award? Eighteen million? Oh, Yuki.'

Yuki tried to cover her swelling emotions by coughing, but her eyes swam with tears. Then her small chest was heaving, and she was having a full-scale public meltdown.

'I'm not like this,' she said as she wept. 'This isn't me.'

Chapter One Hundred and Twelve

Jamie Sweet was crying his little eyes out, and his undulating sobs were wrenching the hearts of his parents, Melissa and Martin Sweet. They hovered over their small child's bed, doting on Jamie for the few remaining minutes before visiting hours were over for the night.

'I don't want to stay here. Please, please, no,' five-year-old Jamie wailed. His chin was scraped, his front tooth was chipped, and his lower lip was split and swollen.

And then there was the fractured arm.

'Why can't I go home? I want to go home. I have to.'

'Baby. Baby boy,' Melissa said, carefully hugging him to her chest.

'Jamie,' his father said, 'the doctors want to keep you here overnight so they can give you medicine for the pain. Tomorrow morning, we'll be here first thing to pick you up. First thing, we promise. Look what Mommy and I got for you.'

Melissa swept the tears from her face with the sides of her hands and held up a colorful shopping bag. She jounced it up and down. Something heavy was inside.

'Want to see?'

Jamie's sobs receded as his mom unwrapped the gift from the creases of tissue paper, revealing a stuffed toy monkey wearing polka-dotted pants and a striped shirt.

'His name is Hooter,' said Melissa.

'Hooter?'

'He's a hooter monkey. Just press on his tummy,' Melissa told Jamie.

The boy's curiosity immediately took over. He stretched out his left hand, the gleaming plastic cast on his right arm looking even bigger and more monstrous by comparison.

He took the toy monkey, pressed on its belly. 'Hooo-hoo-hoo,' Hooter said in a goofy voice. 'Have you hugged your monkey today?'

The little boy smiled, his eyes and mouth starting to droop as the painkiller took hold. A nurse appeared in the doorway.

'I'm sorry,' she said, her voice honeyed with a West Indian lilt. 'All the visitors must be leaving now.'

'Nooo,' Jamie cried. 'They can't leave.'

'Jamie, please. Everything's going to be okay. Just get a good night's sleep. There's the big boy I know,' his father said. 'You're the best boy in the whole world.'

Martin thought his chest was going to blow apart, that's how excruciating it was to leave his son alone. His precious, precious Jamie.

He could shoot himself now for taking the training wheels off the bike. The kid hadn't been ready, but he'd wanted to see Jamie get the thrill of that first ride as *a big boy*. He could still see Jamie's face now, looking over his shoulder to see if Dad was there, hitting the mailbox hard. Going down, breaking his arm.

It had been selfish on his part. And stupid.

'It's just for tonight, darling,' his mom told him again, leaning over and kissing her baby's damp cheek.

'I know twenty kinds of monkey business,' Hooter called out.

Jamie laughed through his tears, hugging his new toy tightly against his face.

His father leaned over and kissed his son. 'You're a real good boy,' he said.

'Hooo-hoo-hoo. Monkey see monkey do,' said Hooter.

But Jamie's smile died on his face as his parents stepped softly away, calling out, 'Good night, Jamie. See you soon,' lingering in the doorway, waggling their fingers good-bye.

Chapter One Hundred and Thirteen

The Night Walker moved quickly along the corridor, feeling a little queasy about the police in the halls and even some of the waiting rooms, feeling the need to do it anyway.

The *need* was bigger than anything.

Bigger than safety, bigger than never being caught.

The door to room 268 was closed, the child alone, sleeping deeply under the effect of his meds.

The shadowed figure pushed open the door and saw the boy in his bed. The streetlight was hitting the child, his tanned skin contrasting with the white sheets. The entire bed seemed to float in the eerie darkness.

The Night Walker picked up the stuffed monkey that had fallen onto the floor, put the toy into the hospital bed, and leaned over the side rails, thinking how nice the child smelled. Vanilla pudding and sleep.

Jamie Sweet.

The name suited him. With his long lashes and swollen cupid's-bow mouth, his arm set in a cast, the five year old looked every bit an angel with a broken wing.

Too bad.

There would be no more baseball games for this little boy. He wouldn't be falling off his bike again, either.

Nothing could change that now.

Jamie Sweet was going to die. It was the boy's destiny, his fate on this earth.

The Night Walker loaded the syringe, pocketed the empty bottle, and moved closer to the bed, quickly injecting morphine into the tube leading from the IV bag into Jamie Sweet's left arm. The prescription was meant for the 250-pound fireman in room 286 – a man with second-degree burns and a broken hand who wasn't going to get much pain relief tonight.

Minutes passed, the only sounds being the whizzing of traffic in the street below and Jamie Sweet's soft breathing.

The Night Walker used two fingers to press open the child's eyelids. His pupils were already reduced to pinpoints, the boy's breath shallow and erratic, night sweats flushing his cheeks, making his damp curls into tight ringlets against his scalp.

As if he'd heard the intruder's thoughts, the boy thrashed, arching his back, crying out wordlessly. Then his head tipped back and he exhaled, a little sputter coming from his throat.

He didn't inhale again.

The killer touched Jamie's carotid artery, felt for a pulse, then reached into a pocket for the metal buttons. Placed one on each of the child's eyes, whispering, 'Good night, sweet prince. Good night.'

Chapter One Hundred and Fourteen

Brenda paged me on the intercom.

'Lieutenant, pick up line three. The caller says it's urgent and you know her, but she won't identify herself.'

I stabbed the button on the phone and said my name. I recognized Noddie's voice even though it was cracking and she was snuffling through her tears.

'Lieutenant, he was such a young boy,' Noddie Wilkins said. 'He only had a broken bone and he *died*. He really shouldn't have died. I heard about it in the coffee room. There were caduceus buttons on his eyes.'

I called Tracchio, got him on the line, told him what I needed and what I was going to do.

Then I swallowed the load of obligatory cover-your-ass crap he dished out: was I sure I knew what I was doing?

Did I understand the dire consequences if I got this wrong?

I said, 'Yessir, yessir, I understand.'

And I did.

A blind sweep could churn up nothing more than panic: no evidence of wrongdoing, no suspects, no leads of any kind. The outraged calls would come in after that, complaints about my lack of judgment, my bad leadership instincts, and, most of all, the SFPD's inability to protect the people we serve.

But there wasn't time enough to come up with a better plan.

Another person had died.

This time it was a five-year-old kid.

Tracchio finally gave me a green light, and I called the squad together.

They gathered like a flock of large birds around the squad room: Jacobi and Conklin, Chi and Rodriguez, Lemke, Samuels, McNeil, all the other good cops I'd worked with for years, and depended on now.

I willed the anxiety out of my voice, but I felt it deep in my gut. I told them that a child had died at Municipal Hospital under suspicious circumstances. That we had to preserve the evidence while there was still time, and find the cruelest kind of killer without much to go on.

I could see the concern in their faces, and still they had faith in me.

I asked, 'Any questions?'

'No, ma'am.'

'We're on it, Lieutenant.'

The squad gave me the courage of my desperate convictions.

Chapter One Hundred and Fifteen

Within forty-five minutes of my call to Tracchio, I had warrants in hand and a caravan of inspectors and cops, some on loan from Robbery, Anticrime, and Narcotics, behind me with lights flashing and sirens screaming. We were all heading north in a broken line to Municipal Hospital.

We left the cars on Pine, and once inside the hospital, we dispersed according to plan.

Jacobi and I took an elevator to the executive floor. I badged Carl Whiteley's secretary; then we pushed past her, Jacobi in the lead, throwing open the doors to a wood-paneled conference room where a board meeting was in progress.

Whiteley was at the head of the table, looking as though he were trapped inside a very bad dream. His skin was sallow and gray. He was roughly shaven and glassy-eyed.

The other suits at the table had the same stark look of post-traumatic shock on their faces.

'There's been a report of a suspicious death on the orthopedic floor. These warrants authorize us to search the hospital,' I said, slapping the paperwork down on the large blond table.

'For God's sake,' said Whiteley, half standing, knocking over his china coffee cup. He sponged up the spill with his pocket square. 'Whatever you want, all right, Lieutenant? It's not my problem anymore.'

'If that's the case, who's in charge here?' I asked.

Whiteley looked up. 'Apparently, it's you.'

Chapter One Hundred and Sixteen

J acobi and I took a noisy, very rickety service elevator down to the basement, which turned out to be a labyrinth of unadorned concrete walls filling the city block under the hospital.

We followed the signs to the morgue, drifting behind an orderly who was wheeling a gurney in that direction, the wheels rattling and grinding ahead of us.

We stood back as the orderly and gurney preceded us into the chilly room.

A stringy, middle-aged man with a basketball-size pot belly under his scrubs looked up when we entered the room. He put his clipboard down on a nearby corpse and walked toward us.

We exchanged introductions.

Dr Raymond Paul was the chief pathologist, and he'd been expecting us.

'James Sweet's room had already been cleaned out and we had him down here by the time we got your call,' he told me.

My sigh bloomed out in front of me, a frosty plume of disappointment. I had hoped against hope that the crime scene, if that's what it was, hadn't been destroyed.

We trailed Dr Paul to the cooler, where he checked a list, then opened a stainless-steel drawer. The slab slid out with a smooth, rolling *whirr*. I drew back the sheet and saw for myself what Noddie Wilkins had described on the phone.

The boy's naked body was so small and vulnerable. The cast on his arm made him seem even more pitiful in death.

What had killed the boy?

How could a broken arm turn into this?

Jacobi asked the pathologist, 'What the hell happened here?'

'According to his chart, he had a simple fracture of his right humerus and a hairline fracture of the ulna, same arm,' said Dr Paul. 'Apparently, he fell from his bike.'

'And what else, Doctor?' said Jacobi. 'Last I heard, a broken arm isn't fatal. Or maybe it is at this hospital.'

'I was told to keep my hands off this kid,' the doctor told us. 'So, you know, I can't even guess.'

'That's fine, Doctor Paul,' I said. 'The ME is on the way. This little boy is going to the medical examiner's office.'

Chapter One Hundred and Seventeen

It was only 9:00 in the morning, roughly nine hours after Jamie Sweet had died with the side rails up on his hospital bed, presumably surrounded by people who were supposed to take excellent care of him and make him well.

I left a thoroughly exasperated Jacobi on the second floor with Charlie Clapper and his team. They were processing what was left of the scene: recovering the bed linens and the child's gown from the laundry, dusting for prints, bagging the trash and the pair of caduceus buttons that had been left inside an empty water glass when the boy's body was removed from the room.

I passed my detectives as I walked the corridors, saw that they were interviewing the doctors and nurses in the orthopedic wing, getting a timeline. Who saw the boy alive and when? What medication had he received?

Who had been on duty that night?

Who had found him dead?

I met with Jamie Sweet's parents in the cramped second-floor waiting room. They were a young couple in their early thirties, huddled together in the corner of the room, caught between anger and shock, wanting to believe anything but what I was telling them.

'This is fucked-up!' Martin Sweet shouted at me, his face bloated with grief. 'Jamie had a broken arm. A broken arm! I want to *kill* someone, Lieutenant.'

'I understand,' I said.

'Do you? I'm holding you responsible for finding out who did this to my son.'

Beside him, the child's mother rocked and moaned. Bright red streaks ran from her cheeks to her throat, where she seemed to have raked her skin with her fingernails.

'I want to die,' she cried into her husband's chest. 'Please, God, let me die.'

'The chief medical examiner is going to examine Jamie,' I said gently, tears suddenly filling my own eyes. 'I'll call you as soon as I know what happened to him.

'I'm so very sorry for your loss.'

Chapter One Hundred and Eighteen

Sometimes a bad wind blows.

A security guard accompanied me to Dr Dennis Garza's office on the ground floor, just around the corner from the ER.

An aggressively thin woman with penciled-on eyebrows and long fuchsia talons stood outside Garza's office, calmly using the fax machine at her desk.

Trying like hell to control my breathing and my nerves, I showed her my badge and asked to see the doctor.

'Doctor Garza was here earlier, but he's gone out for a while,' she said, dropping her eyes to the gun inside my shoulder holster. 'He's probably at home. Should I call him?'

I handed her papers. 'I have a warrant to search his office. I need his keys.'

The woman gave me a sidelong look as she unlocked Garza's

office and snapped on the flickering overhead light. She walked to a credenza against the back wall, opened an antique-looking silver cigarette box on its surface.

The box was empty.

'He always keeps the file keys here,' she said. 'They're gone. That's very strange.'

I told the security guard to break the locks with his crowbar, and I began to methodically trash the place.

The file cabinets held patient files and medical journals still in their glassine wrappers. I flipped through hundreds of files, graphs, and memos, looking for anything that would trigger a thought or an action, anything that would give me a clue.

Nothing did.

I jerked out the top drawer of Garza's desk, sending pens and paper clips spilling onto the carpet. I pawed through the tangle of office supplies, hoping for brass buttons, a piece of jewelry, or a hospital ID bracelet, any souvenirs or trophies a serial killer might keep of his victims.

It was all strictly Office Depot.

An overnighter hung behind the door.

I yanked the zipper down, tossed the contents: a blue sports jacket, size 42 long; gray pants; black Coach belt; two button-down shirts, one pink, one blue; underwear; a leather tie holder. I found and unzipped a small black case – a diabetes test kit complete with syringes and bottles of insulin.

Garza was a diabetic.

His toiletry kit was filled with the normal stuff – toothpaste, razor, mouthwash, some sample packets of a soporific, an acid reducer, pills for erectile dysfunction.

Why the overnighter?

Fresh clothing for his court appearance?

Stuff to wear after spending the night with his girlfriend?

Either way, this was not evidence of murder.

I was digging into the corners of the bag and inside the zipper pockets, panting with frustration when my Nextel rang.

'I'm down in the nurses' locker room,' Jacobi said, pausing to cough, then saying words that made me want to name my firstborn Warren.

'Get down here, Boxer. I've got a suspect under arrest on suspicion of murder.'

Chapter One Hundred and Nineteen

A suspect under arrest? I felt as if maybe all our hard work and risk-taking had finally paid off. Now, who was this monster?

A shifting crowd of nurses and aides were bunched against the far wall of the basement locker room. Some were squawking about their civil rights; others jeered at the cops as they used bolt cutters on the locks of unclaimed lockers.

Jacobi, bulky and scowling, looked more like muscle than he did a cop. He stood beside a dark-skinned woman in blue scrubs, sitting on a bench between the banks of lockers. Her arms were cuffed behind her back. I didn't think I'd ever seen her before.

She was in her forties, with a plain, unlined oval face and short, straightened hair. A gold charm of a praying angel dangled from a chain around her neck.

She lowered her head and whimpered softly as I approached. Did she know who I was? Was this our killer?

'I asked this lady if she'd come down to the Hall to answer a few questions. She made a break for the door,' Jacobi said.

Then he showed me a small plastic box half-filled with caduceus buttons. I took the box and stared into the glinting brass pool. How could anything so harmless-looking have such murderous implications?

I allowed myself a small but triumphant smile as I looked at Jacobi.

'These were on the top shelf of this lady's locker, Lieutenant,' he said. 'I sent Conklin and Samuels back to the Hall for a warrant to search her apartment.'

'What's your name?' I asked the woman.

'Marie Saint Germaine.' She had a hint of an accent. West Indian, I thought.

The tag hanging from the chain around her neck identified her as a CNA, a certified nurse's assistant. That meant that her job took her from floor to floor, giving her the opportunity to get into patients' rooms.

And she'd have the means to medicate them.

Had this woman killed nearly three dozen patients? Maybe even more than that?

'Did Inspector Jacobi read you your rights?'

'Yeah, I did. But now that you're here, I'll do it again,' Jacobi said, his time-roughened face a few inches from hers.

'You have the right to remain silent. If you give up that right, anything you say can be used against you in a court of law. You have the right to an attorney. If you can't afford an attorney, one will be appointed for you. You understand your rights?'

'You leave that girl alone,' someone shouted from the back of the room. 'She did nothing. Let her go.'

A group of nurses' aides picked up the chant. 'Let her go, let her go.'

'That's enough!' I yelled, slamming a locker door with the side of my fist. The chanting cooled to a low rumble.

'Do you understand your rights?' said Jacobi again.

'Yes, I do.'

'Why'd you run, Marie?'

'I was afraid.'

'Afraid of what?'

'The police,' she said.

I was already thinking how the DA's office was so over-whelmed with their ever-expanding case load; they'd tell us to kick this suspect unless we had enough on her to convict.

'Find anything besides those buttons?' I asked Jacobi.

'This is all hers,' he said, pointing to a pile of humble clothes and toiletries on the bench. The most lethal object in the pile was a Danielle Steel paperback. I emptied St Germaine's handbag, finding a worn wallet, a plastic pouch of cosmetics, a purple comb, an overdue phone bill, and a soft, wool doll the size of my thumb.

The doll was crudely made of black yarn and colored plastic beads.

'What is this?' I asked.

'It's for good luck, only.'

I sighed, dropped the doll back into St Germaine's handbag. 'Ready to go, Ms Saint Germaine?' I said.

'I'm going home?'

As Jacobi and I drove to the Hall with St Germaine in the back seat of the car, I started thinking ahead to the next forty-eight hours, wondering what Claire's autopsy of young Jamie Sweet would show, hoping the killer had made a mistake, wondering if St Germaine had a connection to Dennis Garza.

Most of all, I was hoping for a confession.

Hot damn. We'd finally gotten a break.

We had a suspect in custody.

Chapter One Hundred and Twenty

Cindy's sensational front-page story about the MYSTERIOUS MARKERS OF DEATH had already hit the newsstands by the time we escorted Marie St Germaine through the front doors of the Hall of Justice.

The chief had something to feed to the press, but as the day wore on, I started to feel the kind of nausea that comes from going around in circles. Jacobi and I had been in the box with Marie St Germaine for four hours. The room behind the mirrored glass was packed to the walls with homicide inspectors as well as the chief and the DA.

For at least an hour, the mayor of San Francisco was back there, too.

St Germaine told us she'd been born in Haiti, that she wasn't a U.S. citizen, but that she'd lived in the United States for nearly twenty years.

Beyond that, she had little to say. Hunched over in her chair, she cried repeatedly, 'I didn't kill anyone. I did nothing wrong. I am a good person.'

'Stop that damned crying,' Jacobi said, pounding the table with his fist. 'Explain these fricking death buttons so that I understand you. Or I swear to God, INS will have you in shackles on a flight to Port-au-Prince by the end of the day.' That certainly wasn't the case, but I let Warren do the interview his way.

St Germaine's shoulders started to shake. She covered her face with her hands and blubbered, 'I don't want to talk anymore. You won't believe whatever I say.'

If her next words were 'I want a lawyer,' we were screwed.

'Okay, okay, Marie,' I said. 'Inspector Jacobi didn't mean to scare you. We just need to get at the truth. You understand that? Just tell us what you know.'

The woman nodded. She reached for the box of Puffs on the table and blew her nose.

'Why did you have those buttons in your locker, Marie? Let's start there.'

She seemed to reach out to me at last, turning her back on Jacobi, fastening her attention on my face, my eyes. She didn't look or act like a killer, but I knew not to be fooled by her appearance.

'We did this in nursing school,' she told me. 'We put coins or shells on the dead people's eyes back home, to help the dead pass over to the other side. You can check this with my school. Will you call them?'

Her voice gained strength as she told me, 'I found the little boy dead this morning. It wasn't his time, so I marked him for God. For His special attention.'

I dragged my chair even closer to St Germaine. With some difficulty, I put my hand over hers.

'But did you help him pass, Marie? Did you think the little boy was suffering? Is that why you gave him something to send him to sleep?'

She ripped her hand away and pushed back from me, making me afraid that I'd lost her.

'I would kill myself before I would harm that child,' she said.

I cast my eyes toward the mirror, seeing my own haggard reflection, knowing that half the people watching this interview were thinking that if they were in this room instead of me, they'd crack this woman in half to get at the truth.

I took the list Carl Whiteley had given me out of my jacket pocket, flattened it on the table. I turned it at an angle so that she could read the thirty-two names, the terrifying death list.

'Look at this list, Marie. Did you put buttons on these people's eyes?'

403

There was a long silence as the woman ran her finger down the page, silently mouthing the names.

'I put buttons on their eyes, yes,' she said finally, sitting up straight in her chair and pinning me with an unblinking stare.

'But I swear to God Himself, I didn't hurt any of them. I think someone did. And I wanted to make sure that God knows. And that somebody knows in this life, too.'

Behind me, Jacobi kicked a chair across the room. It bounced off a wall and came to rest on its side.

'Inspector!' I admonished him, not meaning it for a second.

My eyes swept back to St Germaine. 'It's okay, Marie. Pay attention to me. Why didn't you call the police?'

'I need my job, lady,' she said indignantly. 'Anyway, what's the use? No one listens to a person like me. You don't believe me. I can see it in your eyes.'

'Make me believe you,' I said. 'I really want to.'

Marie St Germaine leaned toward me, spoke in a confiding tone of voice.

'Then you should listen to me now. Talk to the doctor in charge of the hospital pharmacy. Doctor Engstrom. You should be talking to her, not to me. I am a good person. She is not.'

Chapter One Hundred and Twenty-One

Somehow, Sonja Engstrom made an ordinary white lab coat look like haute couture. Her short platinum-blonde hair was combed back, a single diamond drop hung from a platinum chain at her throat, and she was immaculately made up with an iridescent powder and a hint of rose-colored lipstick.

Engstrom stood and shook our hands as I introduced Jacobi and myself.

As we took seats across from her desk, I noticed that her papers were in neatly squared stacks on her desk, pens and pencils all pointing in the same direction in an enamel tray, her diplomas evenly spaced on the wall.

Only the anxious darting of her light-gray eyes from me to Jacobi and back again gave me a hint that her life wasn't all hospital corners.

I was looking at Jacobi when a strange expression crossed his face. His mouth twitched, and his eyes squinted.

I'd worked with Jacobi enough years to know what that look meant.

He recognized her.

Dr Engstrom hadn't noticed. She clasped her slender hands under her chin and began to speak unprompted.

She told us that the hospital staff was in turmoil since the jury verdict yesterday, that she herself felt very shaken. 'We don't know who will have jobs,' she said. 'Or if the hospital will close. Anything's possible now.'

'You think you'll be fired?' I asked her.

'I've been worried about that for years. Those inexplicable deaths have made me a wreck,' she said, sweeping her hands through her shining hair.

'I reported my concerns to Carl Whiteley. I spoke to him more than once,' she told us. 'In fact, I prepared a report of what I thought were pharmaceutical-based errors.

'But Carl and the legal department assured me that my department wasn't at fault. He said that somebody at the hospital was playing a joke, a prank, and eventually they'd be caught.

'So on one level, I was relieved. Of course, I know that our computer system is fail-safe, so there was no way . . .'

She turned her face to the window as her voice trailed off.

'Doctor Engstrom,' Jacobi said, 'I'm an old-fashioned guy, as you can probably tell from looking at me. I'm not that familiar with computers and such.'

'It's very simple, Inspector. Our computer is programmed to dispense medication when a diagnosis is inputted into the system. It's impossible to prescribe the wrong medication because the machine simply won't dispense the order if it doesn't match the diagnosis.'

'Can't someone fool with the program?' Jacobi asked. 'I mean, don't some people have passwords?'

'Everyone on my staff can enter the diagnoses as written into the computer, but they can't change any data. I'm the only one who can do that, and I have a biometric password.'

'Beg pardon?' said Jacobi.

'My password is my fingerprint.'

'But can't a doctor enter the wrong diagnosis?' I asked. 'That's possible, isn't it?'

'Theoretically, that would be possible, but in actuality, it can't happen. The doctors themselves are the first checkpoint. My staff is the second. The computer is armed and alarmed against tampering. And you have no idea how methodical I am.

'I check and recheck prescriptions against the charts all day long. Not just my own work, but the work of all the people in my department.

'People joke that I'm half a computer myself.'

I said, 'But let me get this straight, it all hangs on the diagnosis?'

'That's correct.'

'So you personally could change any doctor's diagnosis – that's what you're saying?'

Engstrom stared numbly at me as I spoke, and then she snapped, 'That's outrageous. No, it's beyond outrageous, it's completely nuts. I'll take a polygraph test anytime. Just say the word.'

'We may take you up on that later,' I said. 'But right now, we're just talking. Do you know Marie Saint Germaine?'

'No. Who is she?'

'How well do you know Doctor Garza?' Jacobi asked.

'He's our ER director,' Engstrom said. 'We're both senior staff—'

Jacobi stood, pounded the flat of his hand on her desk. Pens and paper clips jumped.

'Cut the crap, Ms Engstrom!' he said. 'You and Garza are what we call "close", aren't you? Intimate, in fact.'

Engstrom's face blanched.

I was so startled, I thought I might swallow my tongue. What was he talking about?

I remembered Jacobi's call to me that rainy night when he tailed Garza to the Venticello Ristorante and back to Garza's house. He'd described a willowy blonde, a babe about forty.

As far as I can tell, he'd said, *the doctor is guilty of having a girl-friend.*

Across the desk, Engstrom's eyes suddenly welled up with tears.

'Oh, God,' she said. 'Oh, God.'

Chapter One Hundred and Twenty-Two

Engstrom was melting down in front of us, and loud gongs were going off inside my head. *Garza and Engstrom.* A perfect partnership for killing, everything probably as neat and efficient as her office.

I needed her to talk more – I didn't want her to shut down on us now.

'Doctor Engstrom, take it easy,' I said. 'This is your chance to get ahead of this horror show. We'll work with you if you tell us the truth, right now. Maybe Garza was using you. Does he have access to the computer software?'

I saw fear in her eyes. Slowly, reluctantly, Engstrom nodded, yes.

My skin prickled. All the hairs on my arms and the back of

my neck stood up as Engstrom said, 'I let him into the computer system a couple of times.'

'A couple of times?'

'Every now and then. But it's not what you're thinking! Dennis Garza is an excellent doctor. He's very conscientious, as am I.

'The unexpected deaths of those patients were driving us crazy. Dennis was checking for inconsistencies between the diagnoses and the prescriptions. Just as I was doing.'

'Did you ever find a correlation?' I asked.

'No. Never. We put the errors down to mistakes made on the floor. Nurses mixing things up on their trays, dispensing medication to the wrong patients after the medication left the pharmacy. That's the truth.'

'Were you with Doctor Garza every time he – what do you call it? – accessed the computer?' Jacobi asked.

'Of course. My fingerprint was needed – but I didn't stand over him, if that's what you mean.'

I saw the alarm come over Engstrom's face as she realized what Jacobi was getting at. The cords in her neck stood out. She reached out to the desktop and steadied herself.

'Dennis would never, ever harm a patient. He's a great doctor.'

Jacobi growled, 'Yeah, well, sounds like you're in love with him to me. Are you in love with Doctor Garza?'

'I *was* in love with him,' she said, a pathetic note sounding in her voice. 'But it's over, believe me. I found out that he was sleeping with somebody else. Dennis was fucking Maureen O'Mara. You know who she is?'

I nodded my head, but I was shocked. Maureen O'Mara had just put the screws to Municipal Hospital. How could it be that she and Garza were lovers?

I wanted to look at Jacobi, but I couldn't tear my eyes away from Sonja Engstrom.

'You look surprised, Lieutenant. You didn't know, did you?' Engstrom said. 'It took me a while to figure it out, too. Strange bedfellows, don't you think?

'Dennis Garza and Maureen O'Mara.' She snorted, a little self-deprecating laugh. 'Just imagine the possibilities.'

Chapter One Hundred and Twenty-Three

A s I left the hospital with Jacobi, my mind flashed back and leaped forward.

Garza and Engstrom.

Garza and O'Mara.

Imagine the possibilities.

We got into the car, Jacobi taking the wheel, starting the engine. I was feeling the charge that comes when you're *this close* to landing a big one. It's like listening to a live concert and wanting to take to the stage and sing.

Only this was better.

'Cindy was at the trial when Garza was on the stand,' I told Jacobi. 'O'Mara asked Garza if he had anything to do with the plaintiffs' deaths. And get this, Jacobi. Garza took the Fifth Amendment.'

'That makes no sense,' Jacobi said, turning the car onto Leavenworth. 'Garza wasn't on trial.'

'Right. And Cindy's reaction was "Wow. The guy was protecting himself from something." She told me that when he blurted that out, it was the turning point of the trial. He devastated the hospital's defense.'

'So did O'Mara trip him up? Let him twist in the wind? Or did he do that all by himself?'

'Interesting question, Jacobi. I wonder who is letting who twist in the wind. Both of Garza's girlfriends were involved in the case against Municipal.'

I grabbed the dash as Jacobi took a hard right onto Filbert Street.

'It's all here, but I can't quite see the whole picture. If Garza killed all of those people, where's the connection?'

Jacobi parked in front of Garza's creamy-yellow stucco house and turned off the ignition.

'Let's go ask the doctor,' said Jacobi.

Chapter One Hundred and Twenty-Four

J acobi grunted as he hauled himself out of the squad car. I joined him on the sidewalk, both of us shielding our eyes against the sun as we stared up toward Garza's spiffy three-story stucco house with a large front porch and cropped lawn on both sides of a flagstone walk.

I was thinking of Garza, wondering if he had some kind of relationship with a Haitian nurse by the name of Marie St Germaine, when Jacobi stooped along the walkway, saying, 'Lookit here, Boxer.'

He pointed out drops of blood on the path, the beginning of a trail speckling the walkway and beading up on the painted floor of the porch. A bloody smear sullied the shining brass doorknob.

'This is fresh,' Jacobi muttered.

Thoughts of interviewing Garza blew out of my mind.

What the hell had happened here?

I pressed the doorbell. At the same time, I took out my gun, so did Jacobi.

Chimes rang out, and the seconds dragged by as we waited for the answering sound of footsteps.

No one came to the door.

I banged on the door with my fist.

'Open up! This is the police.'

'I'm calling this "exigent circumstances",' I said to Jacobi. It was a borderline call. We can only enter a home without a warrant if someone's life is in danger.

There wasn't a lot of blood. Maybe someone had cut a finger, but I had an overpowering sense that something was wrong. That we had to get into the house right now.

I unhitched the Nextel from my waistband and called for backup.

Jacobi nodded, looked around the porch, then decided on a concrete planter the size of a pillow. He tipped the geraniums over the railing and, using the planter as a battering ram, smashed in a panel of the oaken front door.

I reached in through the splintered wood, flapped my hand around until I located the lock, and opened the door to Garza's house.

Chapter One Hundred and Twenty-Five

I yelled out from the doorway, 'This is the police! We're coming in!' Again, there was no answer, and the place just *felt* empty.

Jacobi and I advanced through the foyer into a living room that no longer looked like a photo feature in *Town & Country* magazine. I ran my eyes over the upended furniture and the vast amount of blood that was absolutely everywhere in the room.

'Let me be the first to say,' Jacobi said, scanning the devastation with hooded eyes, 'whatever happened here wasn't the work of a pro.'

My mouth went dry as I took it all in.

Arterial spray was splashed across the pale plaster walls and had dripped down to the baseboards. Constellations of blood spattered the ceiling. A large red-brown stain soaked into the carpet in front of the sofa. Bloody footprints crisscrossed the floor, and handprints smeared the fireplace mantel.

Bile climbed into my throat as I imagined the fury and the terror that had filled this room only a short time ago. Who was involved?

I was locked in a vacant stare until Jacobi broke the spell for me.

'Boxer. Let's do it,' he said.

We swept the downstairs rooms, covering each other. Blood smears on the dining-room walls led us to the kitchen sink, where an eight-inch Chicago Cutlery meat knife rested in the watery blood rimming the drain.

We climbed the stairs to the second and third floors, clearing the rooms, throwing open the closets and shower-stall doors, checking under the beds.

'Nobody. Nothing,' Jacobi grunted.

The master bedroom was furnished in heavy mahogany furniture, navy-blue carpet and curtains, pale-blue sheets. But the blankets had been stripped off the bed and removed from the room.

We holstered our guns and headed back downstairs to the living room.

That's when I saw the heavy crystal vase lying on its side in the niche of the fireplace.

'Jacobi. Come here and look at this.'

He stepped heavily across the room, put his hands on his knees, then bent down and examined the vase.

'It wouldn't take much to clobber someone with that thing. Take a nice chunk out of their skull,' Jacobi said.

'Look here,' I said, feeling a chill as I pointed to the hairs sticking to the bloody, sawtoothed lip of the vase. The strands were black, about five inches in length. It would take days of lab work to confirm what I already knew.

'Jacobi – this is Dennis Garza's hair.'

Chapter One Hundred and Twenty-Six

S irens screamed up Leavenworth, the swooping wail getting louder as the line of patrol cars turned onto Filbert.

'I'll be outside,' Jacobi told me.

We'd only been in the house for a few minutes, but I felt time whizzing past. I took up a position in the foyer that gave me a full view of the living room. I ran the scene through my mind again, trying to make sense of evidence that didn't want to make any sense.

It didn't look like a robbery gone bad. The doors were all locked, and the only sign of forced entry was what Jacobi had done to the front door.

I imagined someone ringing the doorbell as we had done, Garza letting in a person he knew. *But who was it?*

The overturned club chair, the broken lamp, the whatnots

scattered on the floor made me think that an argument had turned physical, had spun completely out of control.

I imagined this unknown assailant conking Garza on the head with that vase, Garza's skull splitting, the wound spewing blood as only a head wound can do.

I could see Garza falling by the fireplace, pulling himself up using the ornate wood carvings as a handhold. The attacker must've panicked that Garza was badly injured but still alive, going from a terrified 'Oh, shit, I didn't mean to go this far' to a determined 'This prick's got to die.'

There were bloody handprints on the door frame leading to the kitchen, where the killer had gotten the knife.

The castoff blood on the ceiling could only mean that Garza had been stabbed repeatedly while he was alive.

Then the attacker had taken Garza from behind and slashed his throat. That would explain the arterial spray across the walls.

The trail of blood seeping into the carpet made me think that Garza hadn't stayed down. He had tried to reach the front door, his will to survive propelling him forward, his mortal wounds slowing him down. He'd finally collapsed in front of the sofa, where he'd bled out and died.

Someone hated Garza enough to attack with such incredible violence. Someone he'd trusted enough to let inside the house. The same person who'd then removed Garza's body and locked the door.

Who?

Sirens cut out as the squad cars pulled up on the lawn. I walked out to the front steps and was calling the DA's office for a Mincy warrant to secure the scene, when Charlie Clapper, head of CSU, came up the walkway.

He greeted me with a 'Hey, Lindsay' and a flip of his hand. A second later, I heard him say, 'Bloody hell,' as Jacobi came out of the garage and crossed the lawn toward me.

'Garza's Roadster is missing,' Jacobi said. 'There's another car parked in there next to the empty space. It's a black BMW sedan, with vanity plates. Spells out R-E-D-H-E-A-D.'

Chapter One Hundred and Twenty-Seven

A dozen mobile units and the crime scene van had walled off Garza's house from the main road. Yellow tape flapped in the breeze and was tangled on the railing going up the front stairs.

I stood under glaring sunlight, blinking at Jacobi as my hypothetical reconstruction of the homicide totally blew apart. Why was O'Mara's car at Garza's house?

Had she killed Garza? Could she have maneuvered his body into that Mercedes Roadster? Or was it the other way around?

Had O'Mara clipped Garza with that crystal vase, and he'd retaliated with killing force?

Either way, we had no body, a missing car, O'Mara's car in the garage, and one of the bloodiest crime scenes I'd ever seen.

'Okay,' I said to Jacobi, 'so where is O'Mara? Where is Redhead?'

While inspectors and uniforms canvassed Garza's neighbors, Jacobi and I used our squad car as an office. He got out a BOLO on Garza's Mercedes while I called O'Mara's office and got her assistant, Kathy, on the line.

I imagined her sharp blade of a face, her big hair, as O'Mara's assistant talked and ate her lunch in my ear.

'Maureen's taking a week off. She needed a vacation,' Kathy said. 'She's earned it.'

'I'm sure. Where'd she go?' I asked, hearing the edge in my voice. Repressed panic.

'What's the problem, Lieutenant?'

'It's police business, Kathy.'

'Maureen didn't say where she was going, but I can give you all her numbers.'

'That would be a big help.'

I dialed O'Mara's cell phone, got her mailbox. I left my number on her pager. Called her house and got a busy signal, again and again.

Jacobi punched out O'Mara's name on the console computer, and got data from the DMV.

He read it out loud. 'Maureen Siobhan O'Mara; Caucasian; single; date of birth eight, fifteen, seventy-three; height, five nine; weight one fifty-two. She's a big girl,' Jacobi mused.

He turned the screen so I could see O'Mara's photo and her address.

'We can be there in fifteen minutes,' he said.

'Let's try for ten.'

Jacobi backed the car away from the curb and, with tires scraping the concrete, cut around the scene-mobile and into the traffic lane.

I flipped on the grille lights and the siren as we shot up Leavenworth toward O'Mara's house in the tiny enclave of Sea Cliff.

Chapter One Hundred and Twenty-Eight

Number 68 Seaview Terrace was a mango-colored Mediterranean-style villa with an unobstructed view of the bay, the bridge, Sausalito, and maybe Honolulu, for all I knew.

Birds chirped in the shrubbery.

Jacobi and I mounted the porch, my mind seething with vivid images of the carnage at Garza's house and the cyclone of questions whirling in my mind.

Come on, Maureen. Please be home.

I pressed the doorbell, and a no-nonsense buzzer blatted loudly at my touch. I heard no answering voice, though, no footfalls coming toward the door.

I shouted, 'Police!' pressed the buzzer again, stood back as Jacobi stepped in and banged the door with his fist.

No answer. Nothing at all. *C'mon, Redhead.*

That creepy feeling came over me again – the horrors of death playing my vertebrae like a xylophone.

O'Mara was missing, and her assistant didn't know where she was. We'd already played fast and loose with exigent circumstances once today. I was going to chance it again.

'I smell gas,' I lied.

'Take it easy, Boxer. I'm too old to walk a beat.'

'Garza's place looks like a slaughterhouse, Warren, and O'Mara's car is there. It's my ass if we screw up.'

I wrenched the doorknob, and it turned in my hand. I let the door swing open slowly, as if a breeze had given it a tap.

We took out our guns. Again.

'This is the police! We're coming in!'

The entranceway opened into a bright, many-windowed living room with tropical printed furnishings and large, brilliant oil paintings. I was looking for trouble inside O'Mara's house, but as far as I could see, nothing had been disturbed.

We swept the ground floor, calling out to each other.

'Clear!'

'Clear!'

'Clear!'

We found one bright room after another, empty and spot-lessly clean.

As we climbed the stairs, a scent I'd thought was potpourri got stronger, leading us to the master bedroom.

The bedroom was painted peach. A life-size oil-on-canvas painting of an entwined couple doing the deed faced the king-size bed. I don't get this kind of 'art' in bedrooms, but obviously some people must like it. Apparently, Maureen O'Mara was one of them.

To the left of the bed was a wall of windows with a view to die for.

The opposite wall was made up entirely of closets. The mirrored bifold doors were open, all eight of them, and O'Mara's clothes were strewn everywhere. What happened here? How long ago?

Shoes were scattered against the baseboards under black scuff marks where they'd been hurled at the walls.

Cosmetics had been swept off the dresser, and a perfume bottle was lying broken on the hardwood floor.

Inside the bathroom, a cordless phone had been hammered against the green marble counter, splintered into plastic shards and colored wire.

That explained the busy signal.

Had Maureen gotten a phone call she didn't like?

My radio sputtered at my hip, Dispatch with a report from a squad car.

The patrol unit had been going north on the 101 when it

spotted Garza's Mercedes heading in the opposite direction. The cruiser had crossed the nearest break in the divider, tried to follow, but had lost him.

This much we knew: only minutes ago, Garza's Mercedes was pointed toward the airport.

Chapter One Hundred and Twenty-Nine

Dennis Garza gripped the steering wheel, stared at the center line as the dull highway scenery blew past his windshield.

His mouth was hanging half open, and his reflexes were dull. He knew he was in some kind of shock, but the outrage was tangible, just below the feelings of vertigo and disbelief.

What had happened today still made no sense to him.

He'd woken up feeling fantastic. Then the day had taken a one-hundred-eighty-degree header straight to hell.

Fucking Maureen.

She'd known from the start that after the trial, he was going to take his share and leave the country.

She was supposed to stay in San Francisco, bank her millions, become the hottest litigator in town.

That was her dream, wasn't it?

When had she gone off track? Why had she changed her mind?

It had been a memorable affair and an elegant heist. No doubt about that. They'd both come out huge winners. Wasn't that enough?

Why couldn't she leave perfect alone?

'I didn't do it for the money,' she'd told him this morning, her voice swimming in tears. 'The money is *nothing*. I did it for *you*, Dennis. I did it because I loved doing this with *you*.'

He would have shaken his head in disgust, but he was feeling queasy again.

He clenched the steering wheel. Then he touched the loose teeth in his lower jaw with his tongue, felt his whole head throbbing.

A wave of images flooded back. Unbelievable. Unthinkable.

First, the shouting match with Maureen. Then the sickening events that followed. He could still hear the terrible screams. See the torrents of blood all over fucking everything, until finally the screaming had stopped.

Garza wrenched himself back into the present. He had to keep a grip on himself. Forget what had just happened and get the hell away from San Francisco.

Staying within the speed limit, Garza took the exit at South Airport Road. He followed the green overhead signs to the Park 'n' Fly long-term lot.

His hand was shaking as he collected his ticket from the

machine and parked the car along the Cyclone fence on the west side of the ugly, dust-blown lot between two dirty American cars.

Good-bye to all this. Good-bye USA.

He could already see the approach to Rio from the air. The magnificent South American city planted in the green-sheathed mountains, rising up from the sea. The stunning statue of Christ presiding over everything.

He could sort out everything once he got to Brazil.

Garza turned off the car engine; then he shook her awake. Not wasting any charm on her now.

'Hey, let's go,' he said. 'C'mon. You're going to have to handle your own bags.'

Garza got out of the car, opened the rear door of the Roadster, pulled his luggage out of the back seat.

Called out to her again.

'Did you hear me, Maureen? The bus to the terminal is loading now. If we miss this flight, we're fucked.'

Chapter One Hundred and Thirty

I insisted on driving us to the airport, and Jacobi reluctantly let me take the wheel.

'Whatsa matter, Boxer? What's your problem?'

'I want to drive, okay? Rank has its privileges.'

'Suit yourself, *Lieutenant.*'

I sped throughout that twenty-minute drive, cars parting left and right in front of our wailing siren. I turned up the volume on the crackling two-way radio, hoping for another update, worried, because after that single reported sighting of Garza's car, it hadn't been seen again.

As I drove, two questions chased around inside my head.

Who had been driving Garza's Mercedes?

Who had been stabbed to death on Garza's floor?

I veered right into the departure lanes, Jacobi calling out

the side window as he saw Sergeant Wayne Murray from the Airport Bureau waving us down outside Terminal A.

Sergeant Murray climbed into the back seat and directed us through a service entrance to the core of the terminal. From there, we followed on foot through unmarked doors and up back stairways to the squad room and the office of Lieutenant Frank Mendez.

Mendez was wiry, five foot nine, about my age, polite but busy. He stood to shake our hands, offered us chairs across from his desk.

Then he briefed us on the American Airlines 777 jet that had been grounded a hundred yards south of gate 12 for the past hour, doors sealed, takeoff denied.

'Doctor Garza's name is on the passenger manifest,' he told us. 'So is Ms O'Mara's. They're on a flight to Miami, connecting to Rio. I don't know how much longer we can keep that bird on the ground, though.'

Mendez pointed out the Mr Coffee machine on top of his file cabinet; then he disappeared out of the office.

The phones on the lieutenant's desk rang without pause. Just outside the office, banks of flickering video monitors showed grainy black-and-white images of passengers going through ticket checkpoints, scenes of luggage-loading docks and carousels.

Uniforms and military units bustled around the room while

Jacobi and I babysat the lieutenant's fax machine, waiting for it to cough up the paperwork we needed.

I wondered if Garza and O'Mara believed that a maintenance crew was working on a small mechanical problem.

Were they sipping mimosas and reading the *Financial Times*?

I slugged down the dregs of my coffee, sunk the empty container into the trash can.

Jacobi coughed, buried his face in his hands, said, 'Damn,' and coughed again.

At 6:05 p.m., the fax machine burped, and the DA's letterhead chugged out of its works followed by the warrant we'd been waiting for.

As the last sheet ended its halting journey, Mendez returned. He took the pages out of the tray, read them.

'Okay,' he said with a smile. 'Let's rock and roll. We're legal.'

Chapter One Hundred
and Thirty-One

M y pulse raced as sixteen of us put on oversized black
Windbreakers with POLICE stenciled front and back.
We all checked our weapons, then jogged down four steep
flights of stairs to the garage.

I joined Mendez in the lead cruiser, thinking ahead as we
sped across the tarmac. Mendez contacted the control tower.
Barked into his radio, 'Shut down this runway. *Forthwith.*'

I was anxious, but more than that, I was exhilarated to be
leading this command. And I was anticipating bringing Garza
down. I wanted him so badly it hurt just to think about it.

Striplights blazed on the airfield, and a United jumbo jet
roared overhead, its impossible weight lifting into the wind-
whipped gloaming.

I peered up at the grounded American 777, then

watched as the rolling staircase was locked to the side of the aircraft.

Patrol-car doors opened and closed all around the plane.

Cloaked in twilight, we trotted toward the aircraft.

My adrenaline flowed as Mendez, Jacobi, and a sharp team of young cops followed me up the stairs, the soles of our shoes ringing on metal as we climbed skyward.

I tapped on the aft door with my gun butt, and it slid open.

I signaled to the flight attendant to be quiet and to step aside. We entered the first-class cabin from the rear.

I saw the back of Dennis Garza's head right away. He was in the third row, right side, aisle seat, an ugly red gash blazing through his hair.

A redheaded woman sat beside him at the window.

Maureen O'Mara.

And I saw a problem. A big one.

Two hundred pounds of beverage cart filled the aisle from one side to the other. That cart and two flight attendants stood between us and Garza.

Garza heard us approach, turned his head, and squinted at me.

'*You,*' he said.

O'Mara patted his hand, said, 'Be cool, Dennis. Everything's okay.'

'Dennis Garza. Maureen O'Mara,' I called out. 'I have warrants to take you both into custody as material witnesses.'

'Like hell!' Garza shouted. He fumbled in his jacket pocket. Then he rose out of his seat, stepped into the aisle.

O'Mara yelled out, 'Dennis! No!'

Moving with the sudden-strike swiftness of a snake, Garza grabbed the flight attendant closest to him, wrapping her streaked hair around his hand, pulling her head back hard so that it was only inches from his face.

I saw something glint in his hand. It was a syringe!

He had his thumb on the plunger, the needle already piercing the taut skin of the flight attendant's neck.

The young woman screamed, the sound of her terror filling the cabin, reverberating off the walls.

'I want safe passage out of here, or I'll shoot her full of insulin. She'll be dead before she hits the floor,' Garza threatened.

The doctor's once-handsome face was almost unrecognizable. His features were bruised and twisted, his lips curled back, eyes huge, pupils darting.

He looked every bit the maniac I believed him to be.

'It's up to you,' he said. 'I don't care if she lives or dies.'

I finally spoke back to Garza. 'That much I already knew.'

Chapter One Hundred and Thirty-Two

I went cold inside, staring into Garza's dark, thoroughly crazy eyes. Maureen O'Mara was kneeling on her seat, also staring at Garza in horror, as if she didn't know who he was, either.

Sweat beaded on my upper lip as panic drove shrieking passengers to push past the cops and clear the rear half of the cabin.

In front of me, the remaining first-class passengers hunched forward, covering their heads as sharpshooters formed a wall behind me, using the seat backs as gun rests.

Garza's back was to the cockpit. He couldn't move forward or back, but he could endanger everyone on the aircraft.

And he could kill the flight attendant on his way down.

Garza tightened his painful grip on the attendant's hair. A

drop of blood at the girl's neck fell, spotting the collar of her starched white blouse. She whimpered, stretched up onto her toes.

I read her name stamped into the gold wings pinned to her vest. 'It's going to be okay, Krista,' I said, making eye contact, watching the tears slide out of her eyes.

'Let her go, Dennis. No one is putting away their guns,' I said in a steady voice. 'And you're not going to kill anyone. We're all getting out of here alive.'

Just then, the cockpit door opened behind Garza with a sound like a vacuum seal breaking. A young flight officer stepped into the cabin, a baton cocked like a baseball bat over his shoulder.

Garza turned his head, only slightly loosening his hold on the flight attendant. She wriggled and tried to wrench herself free.

The split second I needed was there, in the grip of my hand. I aimed and squeezed the Taser gun trigger, sending fifty thousand volts into Garza's shoulder. It was enough juice to stun a rhino.

Garza choked out a scream and dropped to the cabin floor, curling into a fetal position. I stood over him, Taser pointed at his head as Jacobi cuffed him.

'You're under arrest for reckless endangerment,' I said as Garza groaned and writhed at my feet. 'You have the right to remain silent, you son of a bitch. Anything you say can be used against you in a court of law.' *And it most certainly will be.*

Chapter One Hundred
and Thirty-Three

It was after 9:00 p.m. when Jacobi and I brought Dennis Garza and Maureen O'Mara into the squad room, both of them in handcuffs.

'How the mighty have fallen,' cracked Jacobi.

I was bone tired, scraping the bottom of my energy reserves, but elation kept me going. Dennis Garza was in custody, charged with reckless endangerment, possession of a deadly weapon, obstruction, and suspicion of murder.

He wasn't killing people at Municipal Hospital.

And he wasn't sunning himself on a beach in Rio.

O'Mara had been charged as an accessory after the fact, but we were bluffing and she knew it.

We had no evidence whatsoever that O'Mara had witnessed a crime or had even seen the blood in Garza's house.

Twenty minutes after we brought them in, O'Mara was calmly reading a book in her cell, keeping her mouth shut, waiting for one of her law partners to bail her out of jail.

But we weren't finished with her yet.

I still felt a little shaky and weak in the knees. I went to the bathroom, washed my hands and face in the old porcelain sink. Ran my damp hands through my hair.

I remembered the last time I'd eaten, the granola bar I'd bolted down after Noddie Wilkins called to tell me that Jamie Sweet had died.

All of that seemed like a week ago.

I rejoined Jacobi in my office and had just ordered a meatball pizza, extra large, when Sonja Engstrom returned my call.

She, too, was pulling a late night at her office in the hospital.

'We're going through the dispensary computer's history, byte by byte,' she said in her crisp, self-assured tone. 'The hospital is completely invested in getting to the truth.'

'Glad to hear it.'

'If Dennis was screwing with the computer system, he's a killer and he was acting alone. The police can have him,' she said. 'We're happy to help.'

We still had no proof that Garza had killed anyone at Municipal. I wished we could subpoena the hospital's computer records ourselves, but I knew what the DA would tell me.

You want us to scrutinize three years of Municipal's computer records? With what staff, Lieutenant? We don't have the time, the money, or the manpower to go fishing.

But with the hospital backing her up, maybe Engstrom could pin a tail on our killer.

I said, 'Sonja, for God's sake don't burn, shred, alter, or delete anything. Call me if you detect a pattern or find *anything* I can take to the DA. Please.'

I'd just wished her good luck when the next call came in. It was Conklin. His voice was triumphant, almost giddy.

'Lieutenant,' he said. 'I'm looking at Garza's car.'

Chapter One Hundred and Thirty-Four

I leaned forward in my seat, slapped the desk to get Jacobi's attention. I put Conklin on the speakerphone.

'Garza's Mercedes is in the Park 'n' Fly lot,' Conklin told me. 'We haven't touched it.'

'Excellent. What do you see?'

'Car's clean and empty, Lieutenant, except for a newspaper on the floor of the passenger side. The doors and trunk are locked.'

'Stay where you are. Don't touch anything,' I said to Conklin. 'We're doing this a hundred percent by the book.'

I still had friends in the DA's office, and I found one who was young, persuasive, and not afraid to call a judge after the dinner hour. Forty-five minutes later, I had a search warrant in my hand.

I called Conklin.

'Open up the trunk,' I told him. 'I'll hold while you do it.'

I heard Conklin talking to McNeil in the background, the metallic crack of a crowbar snapping the trunk lock, McNeil barking, 'Oh, shit. Goddamn it.'

'Conklin? *Conklin?*' I was gripping the edge of my desk, white-knuckled by the time Rich got back on the line. He was breathing hard.

'There's a frickin' body in the trunk, Lou. Wrapped up in a quilt.'

I stared at Jacobi, not having to say what I was thinking because I knew he was thinking it, too. The missing body had turned up. But whose body was it?

'You checked for a pulse?'

'Yes, Lieutenant. He's dead. White male. Brown hair. Looks to be in his thirties. He's covered with blood, Lieutenant. Soaked with it.'

'Lock-down the scene. Stay with that car until the ME and CSU arrive,' I said. 'I want that car brought back to the lab. And, Richie, make sure it's handled like a newborn baby.'

Chapter One Hundred and Thirty-Five

It was after 11:00 p.m. on what was turning out to be one of the longest days of my life. Jacobi and I were in the box with Garza, the three of us stinking of sweat. The flat overhead light was making shadows dance dizzyingly against the gray tile walls.

I figured that I felt like Garza looked.

And he looked like a gargoyle, a monstrous, murdering gargoyle. And, like a gargoyle, he wasn't talking.

I was this close to squeezing his purpled jaw between my fingers to make him scream, I hated the sight of him so much.

Instead, I gave him a Tylenol, a cup of water, and a bunch of ice cubes in a paper towel for his swollen jaw.

And he'd given me nothing back.

His arrogance was remarkable, stonewalling us even though we'd found a dead man inside his car.

'You should help yourself, you know, Dennis?' I was on a first-name basis with him because I knew he resented it.

'I should have an X-ray.'

'Uh-huh.'

'I'm pretty sure my jaw is fractured. I might have a concussion, too.'

'How'd that happen?' Jacobi asked, tapping the point of a pencil on the table. It was a faint, brittle sound. Irritating. And menacing. I thought if I left Jacobi alone with Garza he'd bounce him off the walls. Might even kill him. I pulled out a chair and sat down.

'I'm guessing this fellow came over to have a few words with you,' Jacobi went on. 'What did he say? "You killed my *son*? My little boy is *dead* because of you?" Maybe he clocked you with that vase. Is that what set you off?'

'I want a doctor,' Garza said thickly. 'I'm in a lot of pain, and I demand to see a doctor right now.'

'Sure,' I said. 'No problem. But you ought to know that we found blood on the soles of Maureen's shoes.' I was lying my face off. 'As soon as the DA gets here, Maureen is going to talk about what went down at your house this morning. She's going to say how she walked in on you doing a murder. She'll plead to accessory after the fact and testify for the prosecution, Dennis.

'She'll get a year or two in minimum security, and you'll get the needle. Is that what you want?

'Or do you want to tell us now how you acted in self-defense. Because if you talk to us now, you're cooperating. And that's your best chance to save your sorry life.'

'Is that right?' Garza croaked.

'Yeah. That's right, asshole.'

I thought about Martin Sweet, that bereaved father crying out to me in agony, *This is fucked-up! I want to kill someone, Lieutenant!*

Dennis Garza had beaten him to it.

''Scuse me,' Garza gurgled. He stood up and looked around.

I was about to grab him by his collar and drag him back to his chair, when he went down on his knees and barfed into the trash can.

Long, retching moments later, he lifted his gigantic head.

'I want my lawyer,' Garza said.

Jacobi and I exchanged disgusted looks.

The interrogation was over.

I stood up, shoving my chair away from the table. It snagged on the table leg, so I pulled at the chair, wrestling with it noisily, banging it until all four legs were on the ground.

I knew my anger was running away with me, because I didn't care who was watching from behind the glass.

I leaned forward, hands on my knees, stuck my face right

up to Garza's stinking snout and gave him everything I had left.

'I *knew* that man you stabbed and slashed to death, you murdering piece of shit. We talked right after his little boy died of a broken arm.

'Did you see that child when he checked into the ER? A cute little guy. Weighed about fifty pounds. He was found dead with a pair of buttons on his eyes.'

'I don't know what you're talking about,' Garza said.

'He doesn't know anything,' I said to Jacobi as Garza stood up, walked weakly to the chair, hands cuffed in front of him.

'He doesn't know anything about the button murders. He doesn't know anything about Martin Sweet's body in his trunk. He certainly doesn't know how tenacious we are.

'He doesn't know us at all.'

'I'll call an ambulance,' Jacobi said wearily.

I slapped my cell phone down on the table under Garza's nose.

'Here. Phone your lawyer. Tell him that you're under arrest for the murder of Martin Sweet. Tell him he can find you at Municipal Hospital's emergency room, cuffed to a gurney under police guard. Tell him that we've got enough evidence to convict you a hundred times over.

'Tell him we're taking you down.'

I was putting on my jacket as Garza fiddled with the tiny buttons on my Nextel, getting it wrong, trying again. I left him in the box with Jacobi.

But before the door swung shut, I heard Garza crying.

Chapter One Hundred and Thirty-Six

Garza's beat-up face was still large in my mind as I drove home from the Hall, thinking it was too bad Yuki hadn't been behind the mirror, watching Garza barf his guts out and cry like a baby.

Was he afraid?

Feeling sorry for himself?

I didn't care.

I hoped he was in excruciating pain. The bastard was a proven flight risk charged with a homicide. Bail would be set in the millions, but chances were, he'd still be out by Monday morning.

He was going to have a long, humiliating weekend cuffed to a hospital bed, his former colleagues getting a close-up look at Dr Garza's dark side.

His weekend would drag by very slowly.

Mine would fly way too fast.

I cruised up Sixteenth Street, turned onto Missouri. I passed the pretty moon-washed Victorian homes on Potrero Hill, thinking about the long shower I would take to rinse the stink off me, and the six blessed hours of sleep, resting up for my weekend with Joe.

I smiled, thinking about the pure pleasure of being with Joe, lying next to him with my head in the crook between his neck and shoulder, our hands clasped, the small, frequent kisses and the deep ones that would leave us dying for more.

I thought about the hours and hours of talking with Joe. I could hardly wait to tell him about this day, for instance, the eighteen hours of non-stop adrenaline rush that had ended with taking the bad guy out of the game.

I parked the Explorer four doors down from my front door, climbed heavily up the hill, and made my way upstairs to my home-sweet-home with its sliver view of the Bay.

I talked to Martha through the shower doors, telling her how sorry I was that I didn't have a life. She talked back, a yappy dialogue between the two of us. If pressed, I'd have to guess she was complaining that her dog-sitter loved her more than I did.

I told her it wasn't so.

Maybe twenty minutes later, I was naked under the sheets, about to switch off the bedside lamp, when I noticed the flashing light on my answering machine.

I wanted to let it go, but instead I pressed the Play button, knowing that if I didn't, my sleep would be colored by that damned thing blinking next to my head all night.

'Lindsay, it's me,' said Joe's recorded voice. I sighed, calling his face to mind, hearing his disappointment, sensing that mine was only nanoseconds away.

'Honey, I'm sorry. It's bad news. I caught an earlier flight. I was going to get in early and surprise you, but there was a major flap at the airport, and the runways were closed down for a couple of hours.

'We got detoured, Linds, and now I've been reassigned. I'm on a plane to Hong Kong.'

I heard the voice of the pilot in the background telling the passengers to turn off their electronic equipment.

Joe's voice came back.

'I'll call you as soon as the wheels touch down. We'll make a new plan. A bigger one. A better one. Hang with me, Lindsay. I love you.'

There was a click, and then the dial tone cut in.

I pressed Rewind, listened to the message once more, listened to Joe's voice. The flap at the airport – it would be funny if it wasn't so damned sad – was me arresting Garza.

Chapter One Hundred and Thirty-Seven

Claire, Cindy, and I were at Bix that Saturday night, an outrageously wonderful restaurant hidden away on Gold Street, known for its fantastic food and also Art Deco trappings calling to mind the glory days of speakeasies and the glamorous steamships of the thirties and forties. We were draped around the booth we love best on the mezzanine, with its view of the action at the mahogany bar on the floor below.

I'd shut off my cell phone and was drinking a perfect martini. Twenty hours after the arrests of Garza and O'Mara, I was still tired to the bone.

And I was worried about Yuki, who should have been here a half hour ago.

I was leaning against Claire's shoulder, and she was kidding me.

'How long since you had some vitamin *L*, girlfriend?'

'I don't remember. So that must mean it's been way too long.'

'When's that man of yours coming to throw you onto the bed?'

I laughed. 'We've made an unbreakable date for this coming weekend. Nothing short of a terrorist attack can stop us. Are you clairvoyant, Butterfly?'

'Yeah, pretty much,' said Claire. 'But I can't read your mind on what happened with Doctor Garza. We both want to know. Please don't make us wait for Yuki.'

I saw that I wasn't going to get out of this.

Cindy and Claire had fixed their eyes on mine, so I took a sip of my martini, put down my glass, and then told the girls about the scary takedown at SFO, and that we'd booked Garza, charged him with everything we had.

'O'Mara went for a deal,' I told them. 'Get this. She and Garza were working together on that lawsuit against Municipal. It was all planned out. A scheme. When he took the Fifth—'

'That was planned?' Cindy asked.

'Sure was. Garza did a superfine job of turning the jury against Municipal. O'Mara raked in her cut of the millions and shared it with Garza. Also, she was in love with the guy.'

'Defies logic and reason,' Claire said.

'Doesn't it, though? But in her deluded mind, they were going to run away together and live happily ever after.'

'But he dumped her?' Cindy guessed.

'Tried to,' I said. 'He was packed and ready to fly when Martin Sweet showed up at his house. Mad as hell. We think he took a swing at Garza with a lead-crystal vase to the back of the head.'

'Ouch,' said Cindy.

'Yeah. So then Garza went nuts and wound up killing poor Martin Sweet. How many stab wounds, Butterfly?' I asked Claire.

'Forty-two. Sliced his neck through to the spinal column.'

I nodded, kept talking.

'Maureen says when Garza told her to "have a good life," she drove over to his house, wanted to change his mind. Instead she caught him stuffing Martin Sweet into the trunk of his car. And that earned her a ticket to Brazil with Garza.'

'He would have killed her down there, I'll bet,' said Cindy.

'I think so, too. We probably saved her life by getting those two off that plane.'

'What about the button murders?' Cindy asked. 'Are you still working on that case?'

'Not officially,' I said. 'I have a couple of ideas about the button murders. Maybe even a solid lead.'

I explained that Sonja Engstrom was pulling out the stops. 'She's hired a staff of data-security experts, and they're turning the computer system inside out.

'It's only going to get worse for Garza. As for O'Mara, she'll be disbarred for fraud. Conspiracy. Witness tampering, you name it.'

'You nailed him, honey. You did a spectacular job,' said Claire.

'Unbelievable,' said Cindy, shaking her head, blond curls bobbing around her face. 'We're so proud of you, Lindsay.'

'Come on, guys, I had an awful lot of help. I sure didn't do this alone.'

'Shut up. You're a superstar,' said Claire, she and Cindy lifting their glasses to toast me. I was still squirming under their lavish praise when Yuki suddenly appeared and slipped into the booth beside me.

I almost didn't recognize her.

Chapter One Hundred and Thirty-Eight

Yuki looked gorgeous.

Her hair was glossy, her skin was radiant, and she was wearing an off-the-shoulder black dress, giving her a girlish sexiness I hadn't seen before.

She apologized for being late, said something had come up and she hadn't been able to call.

By the time our dinner plates were cleared away, and coffee and dessert were served, my fatigue had been burnished with pleasure; I was feeling warm and safe in the company of my closest friends.

I'd just sunk my fork to the hilt in chocolate brioche bread pudding when Yuki said almost shyly, 'I have *big* news.'

'Do tell,' Cindy said. 'Enquiring minds and all that.'

Yuki's smile blazed. She paused, holding onto her news

for a last few moments before she finally told all.

'I've quit my job at Duffy and Rogers – and I have a new job.'

A barrage of overlapping questions came at her, and Yuki laughed her rolling chortle, a lovely sound I hadn't heard in a very long time.

'I'm switching sides. I want to prosecute criminals,' she said. 'Put the bad guys away. I'm going to work on Monday in the district attorney's office. It's official. I'm an ADA. Want to see my card?'

We clapped and whistled, took turns hugging Yuki and congratulating her.

I was so happy for my friend. This was a great life change for Yuki, and I knew she wouldn't regret working for less money and more satisfaction. She'd be a terrific addition to the office of the DA. An instant star, I'd bet.

'To Yuki,' I said, raising my coffee cup, the others doing the same. 'And to putting bad guys away.'

Music floated up from the piano, and a lovely young chanteuse began singing 'Sentimental Journey.'

As I sat back in the banquette, basking in so many good feelings, my thoughts skipped a couple of grooves. And I found myself thinking again about Dennis Garza.

I wondered at the complex nature of the man.

Could his personality be so divided that he could kill as

savagely as he'd done to Martin Sweet? And on the other hand, kill so stealthily we weren't even sure that those patients at Municipal *had* been murdered?

I wondered if I'd ever know? But I did have one good lead. Maybe it would work out.

'Where are you, Lindsay?' Claire asked me.

'Right here, Butterfly.'

She pressed my hand. 'No, really,' she said.

'I was thinking about Garza and his dark, crazy eyes,' I said. 'He's forty-five years old. He'll die in prison. He'll never hurt anyone ever again.'

Yuki put her arms around me and hugged me really hard.

'I can't thank you enough,' she said. 'Thank you for taking my mom's death to heart, Lindsay. Thank you for chasing Garza down.'

Yuki took a breath, then slowly let it out. 'When my dad came home from the war, he was changed in many ways. He told my mom about the Four Horsemen of the Apocalypse – Death, Famine, Pestilence and War – you know. But he said the Fifth Horseman was Man, and that Man was the most dangerous of all. You got Garza, Lindsay. You got the Fifth Horseman.'

EPILOGUE

Unfinished Business

Chapter One Hundred and Thirty-Nine

It was the start of the midnight-to-8:00 a.m. shift at Peachtree General, the largest hospital in the metropolitan Atlanta area.

The nurse stepped into a single room in the crowded cardiac wing and approached a patient who was lying restless and awake in the dark. She turned on the lamp at her bedside.

'How're you doing tonight, sweetheart?'

'Just like I told you yesterday. I'm depressed as hell,' said Mrs Melinda Cane. She was a middle-aged white woman with gold hair extensions, looking at Botox or a facelift pretty soon. 'With Frankie dead and gone, and my kids living God knows where, I might as well be dead myself.'

She twisted her heavy gold wedding band as if that might bring her husband back.

'Look around,' she continued. 'See any flowers in the room? Any happy helium balloons? No one cares about me.'

'Now, I don't want you to be so worried,' said the nurse. 'I've brought you something to help you sleep through the night.'

'Luz, keep me company while I drift off,' said Mrs Cane.

'Tell you what,' Luz said. 'Take your meds. I'll see to my other patients and come back.'

Melinda Cane smiled, took the cup of pills, the glass of water, and, being a good girl for Luz, swallowed all her medicine.

The Night Walker tucked the blankets up to the woman's chin, thinking how much she liked her new identity. Wondering at how easy it had been to get all that new ID for only $175. Not that anyone ever did much of a background check on a nurse.

She walked down the hall with her rolling cart, stopping in every room, checking beds, dispensing medication, saying good night. Then she returned to Melinda Cane's room.

She closed the door behind her and walked out of the shadows to the bed just as the patient began to gasp for breath.

Melinda Cane reached out to her, patting the air frantically with her hands.

'Something's wrong, Luz,' she wheezed. 'Help me. I can't breathe. Please help me!'

The Night Walker took the woman's hand and squeezed it gently. 'It's all right, lovey. Luz is right here with you.'

Melinda Cane strained desperately for air, the cords of her neck standing out, her hands clutching at the blue flannel blankets as the opiate paralyzed her central nervous system.

She looked up at the nurse with disbelief, tried to pull her hand away, to reach for the call button beside the bed.

The Night Walker moved the call button to the nightstand, but she stayed with Mrs Cane the whole time, winding the lady's blond ringlets around her fingers.

She steeled herself for the spasms when they came, and in just a few moments, Melinda Cane was still.

Luz Santiago had also been Marie St Germaine, and before that, Yamilde Ruiz, and way before that, she'd been born and raised LaRaine Johnson of Pensacola, Florida.

It was truly a gift to have this power over life and death, and also to be invisible to everyone.

In a few minutes, the Night Walker straightened the woman's body in her bed, arranged the bedding.

Then she reached into her pocket and took out a small black doll. She'd hidden the buttons there, inside the rough woolen strands.

She took the buttons out from between the threads of the doll, put one on each of the dead woman's eyes. The caduceus, serpents around the winged staff, symbol of the medical profession.

'Good night, princess,' she said. 'Good night.'

The Night Walker stepped out into the hallway – and saw the police waiting there for her. A half dozen officers, at least.

She even recognized one of them, the lieutenant from California.

The tap on her shoulder from behind surprised her even more than the police waiting in the hallway. She turned to see Melinda Cane. Melinda was very much alive, and she was holding a gun.

'Put your hands in the air, Luz. Or whatever your name is. You're under arrest for attempted murder. I'm Detective Cane.' Then the Atlanta Homicide detective smiled. 'You probably remember Lieutenant Lindsay Boxer from San Francisco. She's the one who nailed you to the wall.'

Turn the page for a preview of the next compelling thriller in the Women's Murder Club series.

THE
6th
TARGET

JAMES
PATTERSON
AND MAXINE PAETRO

PROLOGUE

The Midnight Hour

Chapter One

A killer in waiting, Fred Brinkley slumps in the blue-upholstered banquette on the top deck of the ferry. The November sun glares down like a big white eye as the catamaran plows the San Francisco Bay, and Fred Brinkley glares right back at the sun.

A shadow falls across him, a kid's voice asking, 'Mister, could you take our picture?'

Fred shakes his head – no, no, no – anger winding him up like a watch spring, like a wire tightening around his head.

He wants to smash the kid like a bug.

Fred averts his eyes, sings inside his head, *Ay, ay, ay, ay, Sau-sa-lito-lindo,* trying to shut down the voices. He puts his hand on Bucky to comfort himself, feeling him through his blue nylon Windbreaker, but still the voices pound in his brain like a jackhammer.

Loser. Dog shit.

Gulls call out, screaming like children. Overhead, the sun burns through the overcast sky and turns him as transparent as glass. *They know what he's done.*

Passengers in shorts and visors line the rails, taking pictures of Angel Island, of Alcatraz, of the Golden Gate Bridge.

A sailboat flies by, mainsail double-reefed, foam flecking the rails, and Fred doubles over as the bad thing whips into his mind. He sees the boom swing. Hears the loud crack. *Oh, God! The sailboat!*

Someone has to pay for this!

Startling him, the ferry's engines grind into reverse and the deck vibrates as the ferry comes into dock.

Fred stands, works his way through the crowd, passing eight white tables, lines of scuffed blue chairs, his fellow ferry riders giving him the eye.

He enters the open compartment at the bow, sees a mother berating her son, a boy of nine or ten with light-brown hair. 'You're driving me *crazy*!' the woman shouts.

Fred feels the wire snap. *Someone has to pay.*

His right hand slips into his jacket pocket – finds Bucky.

He slips his finger into the trigger loop.

The ferry lurches as it bumps the mooring. People grab on to one another, laughing. Lines snake out from the boat, bow and aft.

Fred's eyes shoot to the woman, who is still belittling her son. She's small, wearing tan clam-diggers, her breasts outlined in the soft skin of her white blouse, nipples pointing straight out.

'What's wrong with you anyway?' she yells over the engines' roar. 'You really piss me off, buster.'

Bucky is in Fred's hand, the Smith & Wesson Model 10 pulsing with a life of its own.

The voice booms, *Kill her. Kill her. She's out of control!*

Bucky points between the woman's breasts.

BLAM.

Fred feels the jolt of the gun's recoil, sees the woman jump back with a little hurt yelp, a red stain blooming on her white blouse.

Good!

The little boy follows his mother's fall to the deck with his big round eyes, strawberry ice cream plopping out of his cone, pee spreading across the front of his pants.

The boy did a bad thing, too.

BLAM.

Chapter Two

B linding white sails fill Fred's mind as blood spills on to the deck. Trusty Bucky is hot in his hand. Fred's eyes pan across the deck.

The voice in his head roars, *Run. Get away. You didn't mean to do it.*

Out of the corner of his eye, Fred sees a big man charge him, rage on his face, hell in his eyes. Fred straightens his arm.

BLAM.

Another man, Asian, hard black eyes, a white line for a mouth, makes a grab for Bucky.

BLAM.

A black woman stands nearby, locked in place by the crowd. She turns toward him, round-cheeked, wide-eyed. Stares into his face and . . . *reads his mind.*

'Okay, son,' she says, reaching out a trembling hand, 'that's enough now. Give me the gun.'

She knows what he did. How does she know?

BLAM.

Fred feels relief flood through him as the mind-reading woman goes down. People in the small forward compartment move in waves, cowering, shifting left, then right as Fred swings his head.

They are afraid of him. Afraid of *him.*

At his feet, the black woman holds a cell phone in her bloody hands. Breath rasping, she presses numbers with her thumb. *No, you don't!* Fred steps on the woman's wrist. Then he bends low to look into her eyes.

'You should have *stopped me,*' he says through clenched teeth. 'That was your *job.*' Bucky screws his muzzle into her temple.

'Don't!' she begs. *'Please.'*

Someone yells, *'Mom!'*

A skinny black kid, maybe seventeen, eighteen, comes toward him with a length of pipe over his shoulder. He's holding it like a bat.

Fred pulls the trigger as the ship lurches – BLAM.

The shot goes wide. The metal pipe falls, skitters across the deck, and the kid runs to the woman, throws himself down. *Protecting her?*

People dive under the benches, and their screams rise up around him like licks of fire.

The noise of the engines is joined by the metallic clanking of the gangway locking into place. Bucky stays trained on the crowd as Fred looks over the railing.

He judges the distance.

It's a drop of four feet to the gangway substructure, then a pretty long leap to the dock.

Fred pockets Bucky and puts both hands on the rail. He vaults over and lands on the flats of his Nikes. A cloud crosses the sun, cloaking him, making him invisible.

Move quickly, sailor. Go.

And he does it – makes the leap to the dock and runs toward the farmers' market, where he dissolves into the throng filling the parking lot.

He walks, almost casually, a half-block to Embarcadero.

He's humming when he jogs down the steps to the BART station, still humming as he catches the train home.

You did it, sailor.

PART ONE

Do You Know This Man?

Chapter Three

I was off duty that Saturday morning in early November, called to the scene of a homicide because my business card had been found in the victim's pocket.

I stood inside the darkened living room of a two-family house on Seventeenth Street, looking down at a wretched little scuzzball named Jose Alonzo. He was shirtless, paunchy, slumped on a sagging couch of indeterminate color, his wrists cuffed behind him. His head hung to his chest, and tears ran down his chin.

I had no pity for him.

'Was he Mirandized?' I asked Inspector Warren Jacobi, my former partner, who now reported to me. Jacobi had just turned fifty-one and had seen more homicide victims in his twenty-five years on the job than any ten cops should see in a lifetime.

'Yeah, I did it, Lieutenant. Before he confessed.' Jacobi's fists twitched at his sides. Disgust crossed his timeworn face.

'Do you understand your rights?' I asked Alonzo.

He nodded and began sobbing again. 'I shouldn'ta done it, but she made me so *mad*.'

A toddler with a dirty white bow in her hair, wet diapers sagging to her dimpled knees, clung to her father's leg. Her wailing just about broke my heart.

'What did Rosa do to make you *mad*?' I asked Alonzo. 'I really want to know.'

Rosa Alonzo was on the floor, her pretty face turned toward the flaking caramel-colored wall, her head split open by the iron her husband had used to knock her down, then take her life.

The ironing board had collapsed around her like a dead horse, and the smell of burned spray starch was in the air.

The last time I'd seen Rosa, she'd told me how she couldn't leave her husband because he'd said he'd hunt her down and kill her.

I wished with all my heart she'd taken the baby and run.

Inspector Richard Conklin, Jacobi's partner, the newest and youngest member of my squad, walked into the kitchen. Rich poured cat food into a bowl for an old orange tabby cat that was mewing on the red Formica table. *Interesting*.

'He could be alone here for a long time,' Conklin said over his shoulder.

'Call animal control.'

'Said they were busy, Lieutenant.' Conklin turned on the taps, filled a water bowl.

Alonzo spoke up.

'You know what she said, Officer? She said, "Get a job." I just *snapped,* you understand?'

I stared at him until he turned away from me, cried out to his dead wife, 'I didn't mean to do it, Rosa. *Please. Give me another chance.'*

Jacobi reached for the man's arm, brought him to his feet, saying, 'Yeah, she forgives you, pal. Let's take a ride.'

The baby launched a new round of howls as Patty Whelk from Child Welfare came through the open door.

'Hey, Lindsay,' she said, stepping around the victim, 'who's Little Miss Precious?'

I picked up the child, took the dirty ribbon out of her curls, and handed her over to Patty.

'Anita Alonzo,' I said sadly, 'meet the system.'

Patty and I exchanged helpless looks as she jostled the little girl into a comfortable position on her hip.

I left Patty rummaging in the bedroom for a clean diaper. While Conklin stayed behind to wait for the ME, I followed Jacobi and Alonzo out to the street.

I said, 'See ya,' to Jacobi and climbed into my three-year-old Explorer parked next to six yards of garbage out by the street. I'd just turned the key when my Nextel bleeped on my belt. *It's Saturday. Leave me the hell alone.*

I caught the call on the second ring.

It was my boss, Chief Anthony Tracchio. An unusual tightness strained his voice as he raised it over the keening sound of sirens.

'Boxer,' he said, 'there's been a shooting on one of the ferries. The *Del Norte*. Three people are dead. A couple more wounded. I need you here. Pronto.'

Double Cross

James Patterson

A PSYCHOTIC KILLER WHO CRAVES
AN AUDIENCE

Just when Alex Cross's life is calming down, he's drawn back into the game to confront the Audience Killer – a terrifying genius who stages his killings as public spectacles in Washington DC and broadcasts them live on the net.

AND A MURDERING MASTERMIND
WHO WORKS ALONE

In Colorado, another criminal mastermind is planning a triumphant return. From his maximum-security prison cell, Kyle Craig has spent years plotting his escape and revenge. Craig prefers to work alone, but if joining forces with DC's Audience Killer helps him to get the man who put him away – Alex Cross – then so be it.

BOTH ARE AFTER THE SAME DETECTIVE
– ALEX CROSS

From the man the *Sunday Telegraph* called 'the master of the suspense genre', *Double Cross* has the pulse-racing momentum and electrifying thrills that have made James Patterson a No. 1 bestselling storyteller all over the world.

Praise for James Patterson's bestselling novels:

'James Patterson does everything but stick our finger in a light socket to give us a buzz' *New York Times*

'A novel which makes for sleepless nights' *Daily Express*

'Pacy, sexy, high-octane stuff' *Guardian*

978 0 7553 4941 8

headline